# Reckless Liar

## A Ridgewood Novel

### Linnea March

# Contents

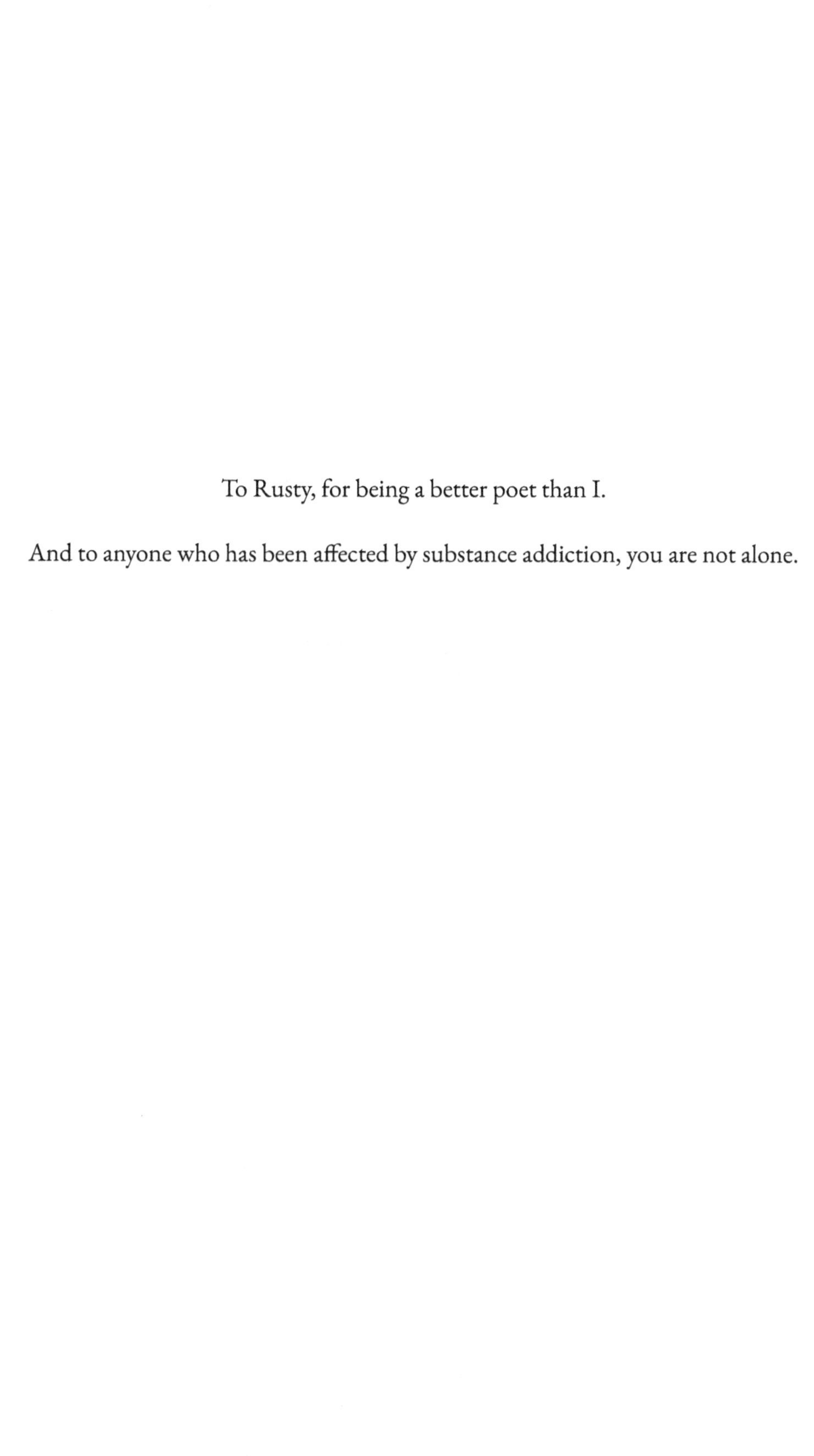

To Rusty, for being a better poet than I.

And to anyone who has been affected by substance addiction, you are not alone.

# Foreword

This book contains allusions to drug and alcohol abuse, infidelity, death, and child abuse.

# Prologue



Worrying about my boyfriend was the last thing I wanted to do after a grueling twelve-hour nursing shift in the emergency room.

At the hospital, I got cussed out by a patient after I refused him more painkillers on top of the pills he'd taken an hour before, had a patient throw up on my scrubs, and almost peed my pants from a lack of bathroom breaks.

Driving home, I sucked my bottom lip into my mouth, my teeth snagging against a scab. With the acrid taste of blood against my tongue, I grabbed my phone off the charger to toss it in my purse. The screen lit up with a picture of my boyfriend, Max and I—taken a few months before. We're standing on top of the bunkers in nearby Fort Townsend. He looked handsome, all dark stubble and bright blue eyes. His skin was tan and healthy, while I was slightly sunburnt, my nose pink between the brown spots of my freckles. My red hair was in a constructed bun that took me thirty minutes to perfect. Light is shining through my copper strands as they lie against the darkness of his hair. Fire and Night. My upper lip was a too thin to balance out my bottom lip. My eyelashes were their natural reddish-blonde because I'd forgotten mascara that day. In the picture our cheeks were smashed together, my smile was big, with my gums showing in a way that always made me self-conscious.

Max had a way of making me forget myself. Whether it was the way his calloused hand fit in mine or his breath in my ear as he teased me about sneaking into the dark and dirty bunkers to do equally dirty things.

In the eight years we'd been together, he had an indelible charm over me. When he told me I looked beautiful, I believed him. Even as teenagers, when he chose me, I was awed. Max Constantine was the handsome baseball player in high school. He was a charismatic joker. He was voted homecoming king. And he wanted me.

Ever since I met him, I was smitten. I was new to town, moving to my mother's hometown of Ridgewood a month before. A shy, red-headed eleven-year-old, whose father was hired as the new doctor at Ridgewood Community Hospital.

I was riding my bike wearing a floral print dress and frilly ankle socks my mother insisted were 'adorable.' I came upon two boys my age being chased by a large man. A fury such I'd never experienced before came over my body in a rush. Without a thought, I picked up a rock and chucked it at the man. As the two boys escaped into the woods, the man ran toward me, screaming, the scent of liquor and sweat clinging to his clothes. He quickly realized that he couldn't lay a hand on a girl without repercussions. He left me on the street with a few choice words, and shaky knees. I later learned the man was Max's stepfather.

A few minutes later, the boys returned from the woods. Without thinking, I threw my arms around the shorter of the two and he held me tight. That was the first day I met Max Constantine and Alexander Eberhardt. It was the beginning of our friendship that spanned more than a decade. From that day forward, I trusted Max implicitly and he vowed to protect me. The three of us were inseparable.

It was our sophomore year of high school when Max and I started dating. We were seniors the first time we broke up. I caught him kissing another girl at a party. By then, he'd dropped out, with nothing to keep him in town. He moved away for almost a year to live with his uncle in Boise, leaving me and Xander behind.

He returned the day after prom. Max vowed he made a mistake leaving me. That it was a mistake to kiss another girl. That he would do whatever it took to get me back.

All I had known was Max, and I wanted to believe in him. I allowed myself to give in to his charm and his sweet words. Again, I let myself fall.

Now here we were, almost twenty-five. After I graduated from nursing school, when I got a job at Ridgewood Community Hospital, Xander asked us if we wanted to move into the duplex he'd been renting. The three of us all under one roof worked out well. It was nice to have a break on rent costs, and Xander was the most dependable roommate a person could ask for. We had many nights, the three of us, eating dinner and drinking beer on the patio overlooking Freedom Bay. Max would grill and Xander would prep the food. I would be in charge of cleanup. Those were good days.

Pulling into our driveway, I threw my phone into my purse and leaned back against the headrest. Those good days were fading. The same warning signs were there as before.

I was older now and had a good job as a nurse at the hospital. I didn't deserve to be mistreated. I wanted to think he didn't realize how much his erratic behavior was affecting me, but sometimes, late at night, my mind would go into the dark space of suspicion.

The Max of these days was a different man than the one I fell in love with so many years ago. As worrying as his recent behavior was, the idea of being without him was terrifying. My best friend, Scarlett, had been telling me to stand up for myself and set better boundaries. But how do I do that with someone I've trusted since I was eleven?

I rubbed my lips together, finding a stray piece of skin. Tugging on it, there was the familiar sting. Holding my hand away from my lip, I looked at the little dot of blood. I needed to stop picking at my skin.

When I left the night before, Max was sitting on the couch watching TV, a bottle of beer between his knees. I kissed him goodbye, and he swatted my butt, eliciting a yelp. It was a familiar gesture, and one that I hoped was a good sign. I wondered if he'd be home when I got there.

Normally I wouldn't question it, but in the past few months he had been taking off at odd times, not coming home for hours. He was cagey with his phone. They were all signs something was going on.

I hoped he'd hold my hand the way he used to, squeezing each fingertip in his fist before grasping my palm. Maybe today would be the day he looked deep into my green eyes the way he used to. Maybe today would be better.

Making my way to the door, my arms were full of groceries. I tried the door of our duplex and found it locked. I swore under my breath. Even after years of living on my own, I wasn't used to locking the door. My parents never locked theirs. Of course, they lived across town in the gated community of Avonwood Pond. The duplex we lived in was closer to the projects of Queenie Hill, where Max and Xander grew up.

I couldn't count how many times I'd get a frantic message from Xander, berating me for not locking the door.

*Our stuff could get stolen. If someone broke in and took all our shit, and we had to tell the cops you didn't lock the door? It would be our fault.*

Alexander Eberhardt, the king of the fretful.

As I fumbled with my purse, fishing to the bottom to find my keys, the sour cream rolled out of the plastic bag, bouncing off my black Danskos and down the porch, stopping a few inches from the stairs. I narrowed my eyes at the vagrant dairy as I untangled my keys from my headphone cord. Shoving the door with my shoulder, I pushed into the house. Balancing the shopping bags in each arm, I hefted them into the kitchen and onto the counter. I hung my keys and the keys Max had left on the counter, on the ugly wine-bottle-shaped key hook that Xander's ex-girlfriend left behind. The clock on the stove let me know it was nearly nine a.m.

Grabbing a step stool from the corner, I put my groceries away. Because of the small size of our kitchen, we had to get creative in our storage. Cereal was relegated to above the fridge, far above my short stature. Standing on the stool, I took the time to line up my *Life* cereal next to Xander's *Honey Bunches of Oats,* so they were straight, and the nutrition labels were facing out. I separated the banana's so they wouldn't ripen too quickly and arranged them in a circle around the apples in the bamboo bowl.

Once I had everything put away where I liked it, I brought out the ingredients for pancakes. Putting on music as I mixed the flour and milk together, the whisk beat against the side of the bowl in rhythm to the music. When I mixed the blueberries, I realized I hadn't heard Max moving around. He was a light sleeper and typically would get up when I walked in the door.

He mentioned the day before that he had to stop in and check on his younger sister, Eloise. Eloise was his half-sister, but it never mattered to them. They shared everything, including how their biological fathers left them with little more than different last names. He was a Constantine, and she was a Dunning.

Eloise meant the world to Max; she was the one person he would do anything for. I considered if he would've gone over to his mother, Dana's, place, but I shook that idea off quickly. Max didn't get along well with his mother's boyfriend, Greg. As far as I could tell, Greg was a lot better than her previous boyfriends. At least Greg had a job, liked Eloise, and even took her to school in the mornings. Greg drank a lot, but he was a happy drunk, telling the same off-color stories about his time in the Army and cracking misogynist jokes. He was the best boyfriend Dana had had in a long while.

I wiped my hands on the Christmas towel I'd forgot to pack away a few weeks before. I made my way to the stairs that lead to our bedroom, pausing in front of Xander's room. The door was open, his comforter strewn in a heap on the floor. A dirty water cup sat on his bedside table. His favorite beanie was sitting on his dresser. He must've been in a rush that morning if he forgot it. In the Pacific Northwest, it can be chilly at four in the morning, especially in January.

I shut the door; I didn't want to look at his mess every time I walked by on my way to the stairs. Climbing the stairs, to our second story, I listened for the sounds of Max snoring. The door to our room was slightly ajar, cold winter sunlight trickling through the small window above the bed.

Walking into our room, it looked empty at first glance. The duvet still had my tight corners and the feather throw pillows that molted if you hit them too hard. I almost missed his feet sticking out from the end of the bed. I rounded the corner and saw him sitting on the floor between the bed and the wall. He was slumped against the wall, his head resting back.

"Max. Wake up," I said, trying to keep the annoyance out of my voice. I'd seen an empty bottle of Jack in the recycling bin. He drank too much last night. It wouldn't be the first time he didn't make it to bed. Most nights, he crashed on our living room couch downstairs.

When he didn't stir, I bent down, patting his leg a few times. With no response, my chest became tighter, a low whistle forming in my ears. "Max, this isn't funny," I said again, harsher.

I grabbed his foot, pulling him down flat on his back. His head hit the floor with a loud whack and then rolled to the side. Falling to my knees at his side, I tipped his head back to check for breathing. When I couldn't feel anything, my hand began shaking as I grabbed at his wrist, searching for a pulse. His skin was cold against my fevered fingers. I tipped his head back and gave a rescue breath. Acrid vomit clung to the corner of his mouth.

Pumping against his chest, I felt his ribs crack beneath my hands. His color was all wrong, his tan skin pale. I watched my hands pushing down against Max, my breaths bursting out of me into his mouth. I looked for the rise and fall of his chest from my breaths. For oxygen that wouldn't reach his brain. His skin chilled more and more. The stiffness in his neck got worse.

I think I knew the truth the moment I sank down beside him; he was gone long before I walked up those stairs.

I had no concept of time. At one point I collapsed on top of him. It must've been early afternoon when I heard the door open downstairs and, after a few minutes, Xander calling out for me and Max. I listened as he climbed the stairs. Xander's heavy footsteps came closer until I could feel him standing over us, seeing me slumped over Max's body. I registered the cursing and the yelling. But I didn't move my head off Max.

Xander's lanky arm wrapped around my waist, pulling me up. I wanted to fight him—to bite, to scratch, and claw to stay with Max. I wanted to wound Xander with my resistance. But all I could do was lie slack against him, bisected over his arm in my fatigue. All my energy had been spent trying to bring back a man who was already gone.

With Xander's arm around my waist, he half carried me downstairs, settling me on our couch. The tan micro suede thing the three of us had saved for months to buy—a hopeful domestic purchase. Pressing my palms into the overstuffed material, my hands were numb against the slick fabric. It was there we waited for the officials to arrive. I stared at their shoes, black industrial no-nonsense things that could only be the police. Xander must've called at some point. Was it when

I was still lying over Max's body? How long did I stay there, covering his prone form, my head against his rib cage? My ear pressed against the flames tattooed along his sides. My hair had matted to Max's arm crease where he was ticklish.

Did Xander call after he pulled me off, my body pendulous against him? My knees were too weak to hold me up on my own. Fervently, I rubbed my hands on the couch. The red and blue flashing lights splashed our white walls like a Kandinsky painting. I watched the paramedics walk up the stairs into the bedroom.

Our bedroom,

*My* bedroom.

They came down minutes later. I knew what that meant. It didn't take long to pronounce someone beyond rescue measures.

At some point, Xander sat next to me, pulling me into his side. I fit into the nook of his armpit; I felt so small and alone. The woman officer crouched down in front of me to ask questions. I couldn't tell you what they were. I kept staring at the stairwell. After a minute of questioning, Xander said we'd come to the station later. The officer nodded her head, looking from my dirty scrubs to Xander's hand on my shoulder to the floor.

"I'm sorry for your loss," she said.

Behind the officer, the coroner brought a stretcher down the stairs, a black bulk in the middle. I watched them wheel it out the door before realizing that was Max. Jumping up, I tried to follow them out, with Xander pulling on my arm. We got down to the ambulance, and I watched as they loaded his body into the back. I stepped forward to climb in with him, but Xander placed a hand on my shoulder, holding me in place.

"You can't go, Ana." He pulled me tighter against him. "You just can't."

I watched as the door swung shut in front of me. Sinking down onto the front yard, I plunged my fingertips into the grass, digging out clumps of dirt. Slowly, the ambulance drove away on our little dirt road, maneuvering through the potholes. I watched until the lights turned away onto the main road. I watched until there was nothing to see, and then I watched the clouds in the sky dissipate into another perfect winter day. A day not unlike our trip to Fort Townsend. All those sun-soaked days were gone. At some point, I let Xander pull me to my feet; I grabbed a hold of his arm, steadying myself. With the back of my other hand, I wiped my mouth, Max's dried vomit and blood mixing bitterly with the dirt against my tongue.

Licking my lips, I could almost feel Max on our last good day. The way his lips had been so firm against mine, his tongue tasting of weed and cinnamon gum. How stupidly happy I was at that moment.

How stupidly happy I thought I could be.

# CHAPTER ONE

THE FUNERAL WAS A shoddy affair in the smallest room of the funeral home. Xander and I could only afford was the cheapest plan they had; cremation and a small urn to hold his ashes. Max's mother's only contribution to the funeral was to shout at the director. Xander and I pooled our savings to pay for a small plot in Apple Tree Grove Memorial Park, the run-down cemetery behind the hardware store.

A handful of family members came. Girls from high school who I'd never really talked to kept approaching, their mascara-streaked faces stark, offering hugs and future coffee dates when I was ready. Guys Max worked construction with over the years came, hugging me too close, whispering in my ear that if I needed, *"anything, anything at all, to call me,"* slipping me their phone numbers scrawled on greasy gas station receipts. Every touch felt like a betrayal to Max, that I should have these sensations against my skin. That I had the right to experience disgust for his old boss's chewing tobacco breath against my ear. The way I could endure the pressure of Mrs. Bishop, our old algebra teacher's shoes, as she stepped on my toe. When Max would never again feel a thing.

I wasn't asked to speak. What Max and I had was mine alone. How could I explain that I'd give anything to have one more day with Max, even if it was our worst day? That when I saw him, I knew he was gone? That my chest was a deep lacuna. Every breath I took was a whistle against the edge.

Weeks after Max died, we got the official ruling on his cause of death. Accidental death brought on by a lethal mix of alcohol and opioids.

Case closed. No more follow-up questions about what the troubled boy did to himself.

I tried to work, but when a patient threw up, my mind took me back to the bedroom. I could feel his cold mouth against mine, his stiff skin under my hands. Blood throbbed in my ears and my clipboard clattered against the linoleum floor. A pounding sensation took over my head, my ribs constricting in my chest. My breath came out in short bursts and tiny dots swam in my vision. My shoulder struck the wall, and I slid down until I was crumpled on the ground with my head between my knees. Behind my eyelids I could see Max's body on the ground, hear the crunch of his ribs under my hands, feel the slip of my knees next to him. I rocked back and forth, dulling the buzz of chatter above me.

My mother picked me up that day and drove me to their home, depositing me in my childhood bedroom and shutting the door. I spent days sleeping under the sunflower comforter of my youth, the walls around me adorned with posters of boy bands and Audrey Hepburn. I wish I could say I dreamed of Max, but I don't remember my dreams. Only that upon waking I had a moment where I forgot what had happened. Then I'd lose him all over again.

For the first few weeks there, I hardly left my parent's house except when my mother forced me to walk with her and her two border collies—Nancy Drew and Trixie Belden. We'd walk from their house up the long dirt road, taking the wooded path that cut right into the baseball fields bordering the high school. My parents lived close enough to the school that I was never offered bus service growing up. But we were far enough I'd have to slosh through the muck, arriving at school with mud splattered jeans and the faint stench of earth clinging to me all day, despite the *Love Spell* body spray I doused myself in before leaving the house. I wasn't the only one suffering through the weather. October to April is notoriously soggy in the pacific northwest.

Despite my mother trying to distract me from my grief, everything reminded me of Max. The opening of the trailhead across the street from St. Olaf's, nicknamed 'The Hole' where we would sneak out to smoke cigarettes and take turns having tiny sips of the brandy Peter Jorgensen swiped from the Ridgewood Yacht Club where his father was the general manager. I'd think of how Max and I would slip away together, sit on fallen logs, talking, kissing, laughing, and sometimes fighting. What I wouldn't give to fight with him one more time.

Without him, the air was heavy with absence. When I closed my eyes, I felt the phantom of his touch on me—the whisper of his hand against my back—then the force of nothing at all.

After six months of fog at my parents, I knew I needed to face reality. If I didn't go back, I could pretend his coat would no longer be hung wrong on the back of the chair, that his toothpaste was tucked between the back of the faucet and the wall. I needed to face the absence of these little things that reminded me of him. Then I needed to figure out how to put my fractured pieces back together and act as if my world wasn't falling into rain around my feet.

Pulling into the gravel driveway, the tires made the familiar crunch as I slowed. Six months after Max died and everything looked the same. Gripping the steering wheel, I glanced up at the duplex. Next door, Mrs. Holland peeked out her window, her eyes glaring at me. She never liked us living next door and would complain each time we made the slightest noise after nine p.m.

Before, when I'd catch Mrs. Holland spying on us, I'd give her an exaggerated wave and smile at her, yelling, "Good morning, Mrs. Holland. Lovely day, isn't it?"

There would be a lot of "befores" now.

The spot where Max's car should be parked sat empty. He abandoned his car at his friend's house months before he passed. He'd talked about getting the parts to fix it, but that costs money, and without a steady job, he was broke. There was little left of his paychecks when most of the money went to all the things that he chose over me.

Seeing the empty spot on the side of the house made my chest burn. I knew what I'd find inside, and I knew what I wouldn't.

As I parked in front of the house, coming back seemed like a horrific idea. I couldn't do it. I couldn't walk in there. I turned the key in the ignition, then killed it. Turned the key, killed it, turned the key, and killed it. My heart beat fast in my chest as I performed the ritual over and over. I could see Max's face, feel the scrape of his stubble against my mouth. My hands shaking, I laid my head on the steering wheel and squeezed my eyes shut.

A knock on my window startled me out of my stupor. I looked out my window to see Xander peering down at me, his brow furrowed. We stared at each other as I tried to figure out what I was going to do. He had a smudge of dirt in his eyebrow, a single fleck of grass in the middle. I brought my hand down, gripping the key in the ignition. I pulled it out and then stuck it back in, pulled it out and stuck it back in, and pulled it out, then stuck it back in, and then pulled it out. Holding the keys in my hand, the teeth from my house key dug into the soft flesh of my palm.

Opening my car door, Xander crouched down in the space between the door and my seat. His legs were so long he was practically sitting on the ground in his squat position. His hazel eyes soft, he assessed me. "Hey, Ana-Sweet."

"Hey," my voice cracked at his use of the nickname Xander began using for me in junior high.

"I didn't know you were coming home today."

I glanced at the house. At my parents, it was easier to forget about what happened. I knew the keening affliction that was waiting for me at our house would be so much worse. "I still don't know if I can."

He placed his hand on my arm, rubbing it softly. Instinctively, I leaned into him. Tears leaked out of my eyes, ruining my mother's yellow silk tunic she shoved at me earlier that morning.

"I'll wait here with you until you're ready."

I considered telling him I didn't need him to help me, that I was okay, that I could do this alone. When I said nothing, he reached down and took my hand. His palm was calloused from long hours of landscaping. I looked down at our hands clasped together. Squeezing his hand once before pulling away, warmth flooded through me. I hadn't been warm since that day; the contrast was amazing.

"Thanks, Xan."

I wiped the tears off my face, smearing my makeup worse than ever. I pushed the button for my seatbelt, then shoved the buckle back in. Xander stepped aside so I could climb out, watching as I unbuckled my seatbelt three times. Once I was out, he reached inside, grabbing my bag sitting on the passenger seat.

On the porch, the Adirondack chair where I'd sit when Max called me to pick him up in those last few days was still angled the same, overlooking a small sliver of Freedom Bay through the trees. The house was in a state of stagnation. In the July heat, it was hotter than it'd been since I'd been there in January. I glanced around the living room. Several dirty coffee mugs littered the side table. The stereo was left on, the radio played softly in the kitchen.

"Like I said earlier, I didn't know you were coming home. I would have picked up better if I'd known..." he trailed off, dragging his hand through his blond curls.

"It's okay, Xander," I said as I took in the rooms. "It doesn't matter. Not anymore."

Sitting on the couch, I looked across the room at the stairwell. It was all too real. The vision of Max's body was being wheeled away. The dull clack of the wheels against the carpet, the spot where the stretcher hit the wall, leaving behind a black smudge. My heart sped up, the blood rushing to my face as I struggled for breath. I could feel it again—the chill in the air as the door kept opening for medical personnel. The smell of antiseptic and rubber in the air. The loud stomp of their boots as they climbed the stairs.

I rubbed my chest as I struggled to catch my breath. Pinching my outer thigh, my thumbnail dug into my soft flesh. I let go, then pinched again, let go, then pinched, let go.

Xander sat next to me, his arm going around my shoulders. "Hey, hey. Breathe, one deep breath. Through your nose, take in one good breath."

The weight of his arm on my shoulders pulled me into him. Looking into his hazel eyes, I listened to his words as I strained to breathe, following his instructions.

"Good. Breathe in through your nose, now blow out through your mouth." He held my arm tight, my body fitting under his arm. I tried to replicate the way he was breathing. "Great. Out goes the bad air, in goes the good. Over and over, you can do this, Liliana. We can do this. I'm here, I've got you."

Taking in his words, I kept breathing, letting them wash over me.

I knew what I'd find up there. His cologne would still be on the dresser, tipped against my favorite lotion. The room would be cleaner than Max left it. His clothes hung neatly in the closet, arranged by style and color the way mine were.

I couldn't handle seeing it like that. Once I regained my composure, I turned to Xander. "I can't go up there. I can't walk up those stairs today."

He rubbed my arm. "That's okay. I knew you'd have a hard time. I moved your stuff into my room for now. You can stay down there if you want. I can sleep upstairs. You can take my room down here."

"Are you sure? The last thing I want is to inconvenience you." I was relieved he was sparing me what was likely going to be the hardest thing to face today.

"I already did it. Actually, I did it a few weeks ago. It was only after I moved everything it occurred to me you might not like it."

"I did, I mean, I do. I mean, ugh." Frustrated, I wiped my hand over my face. "Thank you."

"I didn't do a great job packing your stuff. You have a system for how things should be and I kind of dumped your drawers into different boxes and then dumped them into my dresser. Knowing you, you'll be busy the next few days tidying up my mess."

"I'm sure it's fine, Xander. I appreciate the effort." A fresh spill of grateful tears threatened me, as I imagined Xander going into our room, painstakingly going through all my clothes so I wouldn't have to.

He said nothing, squeezing my arm one last time before getting up from the couch.

I knew Max was gone. Every moment at my parent's house over the last six months reminded me of the fact. I felt his absence in every breath I took. But he was in this house. His favorite mug was on the coffee table, the spot where he got mad and kicked a dent in the closet door, the shelf of his old CD cases he insisted on keeping from high school.

I could tell Xander cleaned his room. The bed was made with my Grandma Pryce's threadbare afghan, a choice I never would've made. The pillowcases were the tan and red ones that went with the mod daisy set Max and I bought from a Swedish furniture store when I began nursing school.

There were boxes stacked in front of the closet. My jewelry box sat on top of Xander's dresser. I felt the crush in my lungs, my breath hitching. I gripped the knobs and pulled the drawer out slightly, then pushed it back in. Pulled it out, pushed it in, pulled, pushed, pulled. My shirts were in disarray in the top drawer where my underwear was supposed to be. I repeated the pull and push routine with the other drawers, three times each. My pants were in the pajama drawer, the pajamas in the shirt drawer.

"Like I said, it's a bit of a mess." Xander said behind me. I didn't realize he was watching me, but I was too exhausted to be ashamed that he saw me checking out the job he did.

"It's okay, it doesn't matter."

"That's not true. I know how you like things. If I'd known you were coming back today, I would've done a better job."

"You didn't need to do this for me. You don't need to take care of me."

"I don't mind, Ana." His eyes swept over the room as if he couldn't quite look at me.

"Was it hard going through…" I let the words die in my throat as I avoided looking at him, instead pulling a shirt out of the dresser and refolding it in the way I liked. I ran my hand over the creases three times. This could calm me. Order, gentle creases on shirts, and the tidiness of creating space in a dresser.

He paused before clearing his throat. "Yeah, it was. But I knew it'd be harder for you."

"I could've handled it." I muttered as I pulled another shirt out.

"No, you couldn't."

I rubbed the fabric between my fingers. The shirt was old, Max's from his high school baseball days. It'd shrunk after years and years of being washed and eventually relegated to its rightful place in my pajama drawer. I dropped the shirt back in the drawer, deciding to leave the mess for later. He was right. If I couldn't walk up the stairs to see our room, how could I have gone through Max's things?

"You're right." I sank onto the edge of the bed, looking around. "I couldn't."

Xander hesitated before sitting next to me, the old bed creaking under his lanky frame. "There's nothing wrong with that. I don't think anyone could handle it so soon."

"Why couldn't I save him, Xander?" Glancing up at him, I felt my tears struggle to the surface. Our arms brushed as we sat side by side.

Xander's arm was a steady pressure against mine. The same steady pressure Xander always gave me. The same support. Xander reached up to tuck a strand of wayward red hair behind my ear. "I've been asking myself that same question. We'll never know what was going on in Max's head."

"I knew him, or I thought—I knew he did—I never thought he'd..." my voice broke. Xander's arm came up to rest lightly over my shoulders. I closed my eyes, counting to ten. Tears ran undeterred down my face.

"It was an accident." Xander hugged me closer to him, my shoulder sliding right under his armpit, fitting me to his side. "You can't blame yourself, Ana."

"Then who can I blame?" I rested my head against his chest. His work tee smelled like grass clippings and sunscreen. A familiar scent that always lingered in the air when Xander would move. A heady essence that calmed me. Everything could fall apart around us, and yet Xander still smelled the same.

I turned my face to look at him. "You say it was an accident, that it's senseless. But this? There were warning signs. I should've seen it coming, stopped it. Stopped him." If I'd only said something, if I'd told him to stop, then maybe he'd still be here.

Xander shook his head against me. "It wasn't your fault."

I pulled away slightly. Xander's arm dropped between us. I stared at the carpet. It was the same shade of mottled cream as the upstairs carpet. I pictured how right above my head was the spot where Max lay dying. It was easy for Xander to say that. So easy to recuse himself from this mess. This was my burden that I carried every day.

# Chapter Two



*"I'm fine." –Ana after getting a C on her pharmacology midterm.*

WHEN MAX WAS GONE our senior year, I asked the only safe choice—Xander—to prom. We had a great time as friends, dancing all night. I'd felt safe in Xander's arms; it was nice to feel so comfortable with someone.

Around Xander I could forget about Max for a single night. I wasn't sure how long it'd been since I'd felt that way. Xander was a perfect gentleman that night, insisting on paying for everything, even though I knew he had to work for months at his father's landscaping company to afford it. He bought a corsage the exact shade of purple as my dress. His rented black tux with silver accents offset my gown beautifully. He opened the car door for me.

For the first time since the day I met Max, I considered that I'd need to move on from him. I let myself lean into Xander as he held me on the dance floor. Xander placed his hand on the small of my back and I didn't move away. Xander told me I looked beautiful, and my chest expanded from the compliment.

At the end of the night, I leaned in to kiss Xander's cheek and he turned his head the wrong way. My lips landed on his. I quickly pulled away, putting my fingers to my lips.

It took me a long time to fall asleep that night, my mind racing with questions about that kiss. The feeling of Xander's lips on mine was different from Max's. Xander's lips were soft and warm. With Xander I felt safe and cared for. It was a new and scary feeling after years of fiery kisses with Max. Everything with Max felt a little dangerous. Being with Xander felt calm, and for the first time since the day I met both those boys, I'd wondered if feeling safe and cared for would be better. Falling asleep to the memory of Xander's lips on mine and the way his hand felt against my back as we danced, I'd allowed myself to wonder as I never had before.

That next morning, Max showed up on my front porch with a bouquet of lilies. For a moment, I wondered if he somehow knew that Xander had kissed me.

It didn't matter. With Max home, the kiss between Xander and I had felt like an accident—ill-timed head placement—nothing more. I told myself that any confusing thoughts that swirled in my head the night before were a side effect of missing Max. I couldn't let them be anything else with Max around.

I tried to be strong when Max just showed back up in my life, letting him know how much his leaving hurt me. But I couldn't stay firm with Max. He knew exactly how to make me crumble. I wanted to say it took him begging and pleading for me to take him back. But I never made Max work hard. I was always his, and he knew it.

Nine months after Max died, I felt like things might be better. After using up all my leave, I returned to work part-time, phasing slowly back into the duties I'd studied so diligently to do.

I'd wake every morning in Xander's bedroom with the sunlight coming through the wrong window. I'd see the wooden chair his dad found in an alley and took the time to polish for him. We used to tease him over that chair with the big roses carved into the headrest and cascading down the arms.

I'd get up and make myself a cup of coffee and show up to work on time. I talked with patients, followed directions, moved my feet until they ached. After work, I'd venture out to the store to get a gallon of milk. I'd stop by the racks of glossy magazines and thick paperback books with shirtless men in cowboy hats. For a moment, I'd forget him, and there'd be a fleeting breath of silence in my head.

Then I'd see his favorite cereal on the shelf, or hear his favorite song on the radio. I'd get a piece of junk mail; an envelope with a small metal key glued onto bright pink paper advertising in big comic lettering. *'This key could open your new car!'*

The simple act of reading his name on the mailer could ruin my day.

Death makes heroes out of men.

In the grocery store I had the eighty-year-old owner, Giselle Keller, come up and take my hands in hers, squeezing my fingers with her paper-thin skin scratching against mine.

"Ve are so sorry about your Maximilian. He vas a good boy." Her German accented speech was as harsh as her grip. "A good boy. Such sad news."

I fought my retort back, smiling a little at her before excusing myself to the frozen foods aisle. I opened the door to the frozen pizzas, closed the door, opened, closed, opened, closed, opened, and removed a pizza to put in the cart. My breathing felt haggard in my chest.

What was I supposed to say? Mrs. Keller was the one who fired Max in high school after he egged the store after hours.

And yet, here she was singing his praises after he'd passed.

It made his death harder to bear. Because if they could lie about who Max was with these whitewashed stories, then he really was gone.

And I had no one to share my pain with. No one who understood how I loved Max—that I loved *all* of Max—the awful dirty things inside him, as much as the charismatic man who the world saw.

Back at the duplex, I set the groceries on the counter. Above my head, I could hear Xander walking around in our old room. I still thought of it that way, although I hadn't set a foot on the stairs in nine months. I had to do deep breathing every time I passed the stairwell, digging my nails into my palm. then flexing my hand three times before I could draw a steady breath.

Xander never said a word about it, but I could tell he noticed. Our linen closet was upstairs. At the first early October chill I bundled up under the covers instead of getting more blankets. Xander must have noticed, because when I returned from work the next day, there was a pile of heavy blankets on the foot of my bed.

With half the groceries put away, Xander came up behind me. Grabbing the cereal from the bag, he opened it, poured himself a bowl from the cabinet above my head. I looked up at him, his arm above me. He was so close I could smell the soap he used and the clean earth he worked with. Acutely aware of his warm body above me, I poured the whole coffee beans into their airtight canister beside the coffee machine.

"Thanks for getting my favorite," he remarked, smiling down at me.

"Sure thing. It's a habit by now, I guess."

He stuck a spoon in the bowl and ate as I put the groceries away. Even with my back turned to him, I could feel the heat of his gaze on me.

"You really don't need to get my groceries too, you know."

I slid the cans into the cabinet, all their labels facing out the way I liked. "I know. I was already at the store, and I knew what you liked."

"You're too good to me."

"Nah, you're the one who's too good, Xan," I replied, shooting him a quick smile. "Nicer than most people have been."

He sat his bowl down on the counter, a little milk splashed over the side. I eyed the spot, frowning.

"Trouble in town?"

I grabbed a paper towel and handed it to Xander. He smirked as he wiped up the spill.

"Not really. Just Giselle Keller trying to chat about how great Max was."

Xander laughed. "No way!"

"Yeah! Honestly, I almost wished she would've talked to me about how much she detested Max. At least then her condolences would've been more honest. Instead, I had to stand there in front of the hot case hearing about how sad she was to hear about his death. As if she cared. He wasn't even allowed in that store!"

"Oh, I remember. Who do you think drove the car that night?"

My eyes widened. "You didn't!"

He waved a hand at me dismissively. "You knew I did. I was the only one with a license back then."

"But Max..."

He nodded at me. "I know. I wanted to confess, but Max told me not to. He didn't see the point of both of us getting into trouble. They had him on tape, but not me."

"You guys never told me that."

"I think Max was embarrassed about getting caught. He was impulsive, you know. Hot-headed. He was going to ride his bike there. He was planning on smashing in the front windows, but I talked him into egging it instead."

With security footage in hand, that incident earned Max his first stint in the criminal justice system. Along with the community service and lofty fines he had to pay, he was banned from Town and Country Market for the next five years. While it was a fairly small sentence, it put his name on the list of kids to watch out for.

"You still should've told me."

Max could be heedless to rules when he was worked up about something. I could see him riding his bike to the store in the middle of the night, smashing things up, laughing, setting off alarms. The punishment would've been much more serious than a minor count of vandalism.

Max getting arrested was the beginning of a string of bad things for him, some of his own volition. We broke up for the first time a month later, and he moved away soon after.

Xander laughed at me. "Yeah, okay."

"Hey," I looked at him, shocked. "I'm serious. I never liked him doing that stuff. I should've been told."

"What would you have done? Are you really telling me that part of Max's appeal wasn't his bad boy ways?"

"Not at all."

"I don't believe you." Xander picked up his bowl off the counter and shoveled a big scoop of cereal into his mouth.

"I didn't like him getting in trouble. I worried about him constantly."

He held the spoon up as he talked, milk dripping onto the floor. "But it was exciting for you, wasn't it? Someone your parents didn't really like. So different from your wonder-boy brother, or from your dad."

"Not in the slightest." I threw a dish towel at him. "Wipe that up. You're making a mess of my kitchen."

He smirked at me, throwing the towel on the floor, moving his foot around to mop up the spill. "It's my kitchen, too."

"It won't be if you keep making a mess like you do. I'm about ready to kick you out of here. You need some lessons on basic eating habits. Ever heard of a table?"

He shrugged before tipping the bowl back to drink the last of the milk.

I rolled my eyes. "So childish."

He put his bowl in the sink, rinsing it and putting it in the dishwasher the wrong way. I'd need to fix it once he left.

"Have you thought about moving?"

"Moving," I snorted. "Moving where? My job is here. My parents are here. You and Scarlett are here. We still have a few months on our lease."

"Ana, you know I could find someone to take over your share if I really needed to."

"Where would I go? This is my home."

"You could start over somewhere else. Move to Salt Lake City, take up rock climbing. Move to Vermont and own an apple farm."

"I could never do that. I love this place."

"Even if it doesn't always love you?"

His words felt a little too close to something I didn't want to face. Trying to keep my tone light, I shrugged. "Ridgewood loves me fine. It'd miss me if I left."

"You're too good for this place. You always have been." Xander's face became more serious.

I shook my head. "No way. This is where I belong. This is where Max is buried. I couldn't leave him. I belong here, near him."

The smile on his face faded as he looked at me. "You belong to something so much more than this. You deserve so much better than you've gotten, more than all of us."

"Don't be silly, Xan." I tried to laugh. Something about his demeanor had changed during our exchange. I wasn't sure what it was. "I don't know what you're talking about."

He studied me for a moment, his warm hazel eyes soft. "I know you don't. I know." He walked to the kitchen table, grabbing his wallet. "I'm heading out. You need anything at the store?"

I shook my head, confused. "I just went."

He paused in the doorway. "Right, okay." He knocked on the doorframe three times as if to dispel some energy he had. As I watched the doorway, Xander gathered his things up and walked out the front door with nary a backward glance.

After he left, I tried to decipher his words. I felt like there was so much more Xander wasn't telling me.

It wouldn't have been the first time I'd read a double meaning in Xander's words. There were times when I thought I caught him watching me. Times when I could feel him in the room before I saw him. It meant nothing. We were friends, that was the way friends were.

It had to be.

# Chapter Three

*"Yeah. I can totally taste the note of currant." –Ana during her first wine tasting.*

AFTER MONTHS OF ONLY being able to work a part time, I'd worked myself up to full time at the hospital. By then I knew the warning signs of the panic attacks—the heart palpitations, the sweating, the constriction of my chest making it hard to breathe. Most days I could quell the panic by doing my little patterns—clicking my pen three times before writing, turning the knob three times before entering a room, scrubbing my hands three times. Triple checking everything I'm doing, convinced that if I didn't do the ritual, I'd give the wrong medication. I'd use the patient's name three times in my conversations with them before I feel comfortable treating them. These patterns calm me enough to get through the day.

I wasn't about to tell anyone about the patterns I created. They'd likely talk to my mom, and then where would I be?

I was twenty minutes late for my wine date with my friend, Scarlett. I was on edge. While at work, I had to treat a patient who seemed to know Max. While the woman said nothing too suspicious, the conversation jarred me.

"I hope you don't mind. I ordered for you," Scarlett said as I sat down at a high table. We'd decided on The Cabin, a dockside restaurant in Ridgewood's touristy waterfront area.

"No worries, I have shit taste, so I'd probably order the same as you."

I picked up the glass in front of me and took a deep swallow of the red wine, draining nearly half the glass.

"Bad day?" She chuckled as she watched me set the wine down.

"You'd never believe the day I had today," I said.

She ran a finger over the rim of her oversized glass of Malbec. "I think you're going to overexert yourself."

"I swear, Scar. If I say I'm fine, I am," I assured her. I'd already been given a lecture by both my parents, Xander. I even had my older brother talk to me, granted it was only a five-minute conversation on Father's Day before he left early to head back to Seattle to hang out with his friends. Some compassion he had.

The worst of the guilt trips was from my best friend, though. Scarlett was worse than my mother some days, hovering over me, making sure I was eating, bringing me clothes from the boutique she owned with her mother. As much as I appreciated her help, it could be stifling.

"You know I'm worried, is all. I feel like you've been avoiding me."

"I've been surviving, Scar."

"Avoiding your BFF, who can be there for you, isn't surviving."

"Scar, you can't tell me how to grieve."

"It's been ten months. I'm not telling you how to grieve, I want to see you trying to." Scarlett wiped at the corner of her lip, the blood red lipstick accenting her jet-black, chin-length hair and copper skin wonderfully. If I tried to wear lipstick that shade, it would look garish.

"Have you seen Dana?" I asked, changing the subject. The hotel Max's mom worked at was down the street from Scarlett's boutique.

She shook her head absentmindedly. "No, but I heard through the grapevine she got kicked out of the Skol House the other day. She started a fight with a bartender after they cut her off. She had to get picked up by Eloise, I guess."

Dana was well known around town for her antics at the local bar, the Skol House. I'd picked her and Max up there several times over the years.

"Eloise doesn't even have her license yet." The guilt of leaving Eloise behind thrummed through me. With Max gone, who was making sure Eloise was eating? Did she have enough clothes? Was she going to school when she was supposed to? "I should go see her. I can't believe she didn't mention that her mom was making her drive around."

"She probably didn't want to worry you." She raised her hands over the top of her head, her arms a V-ing out. "You don't need to be there for them, you know."

"I should've been there to support his family," I whispered.

She scoffed loudly and rolled her eyes. "Fuck, Ana." Her hands came down at her sides with a whack. "You're killing me here. You need to forget Dana."

"What about Eloise?"

Scarlett frowned as she considered me. "Eloise is tougher than you think, and you were not her mother, Ana. Max was not her father. It's not your responsibility to take care of her."

"She's the only family Max had," I reminded her.

Scarlett grabbed her clutch from under her arm, snapping it open and then snapping it shut several times. "I don't want to fight with you, Ana." She opened her clutch one more time, pulling out her red lip gloss. "I'm saying you did more for Max than his mother. You and Xander both. You're the ones who should be grieving, not paying for the funeral in the background."

In my fist, I dug my nails into the flesh center of my palm, alternating which nail to press hardest until I could feel the half-moon indents on my skin.

She grabbed the bottom of her dark chin-length bob. "I need you to take care of yourself. And if you can't, let me know so I can take care of you."

My body felt heavy as I nodded at her. "I understand."

"Do you want to have a sleepover at my place? You know you can stay with me as long as you need to."

"I thought you were going out with Aspen later? I'd be in the way."

She rolled her eyes. "Ana, you are more important than some random I'm dating. If you want to stay with me, you can."

"I..." I closed my eyes and focused on my shaking hands, the tremors running through my fingers. "I can't, Scarlett."

She stared at me for a few moments. Then she seemed to decide it was a conversation that wasn't going anywhere.

I could tell she disagreed, but thankfully, she let it go. "Tell me about your bad day."

"Bizarre is more like it." I wrinkled my nose, thankful for the change of subject. "I had a really odd patient. She knew Max. I guess she worked with Dana at the hotel." I took a drink of my wine. "She kept making these weird comments about Max. She obviously had a thing for him. I guess I shouldn't be surprised."

"Yeah," Scarlett replied softly, as if she was thinking about something she couldn't quite say yet.

"But the way she was talking about him, like she knew him, *like* really knew him. It put me on edge. I've never heard her name before today, but the way she was talking about him..." I hesitated, looking away from her. Out the window, I could see all the boats tied up on the dock. I twirled the stem of the wineglass in my hand, making three twists before taking my hands off the table and setting them in my lap. "You don't think he might've..."

I expected Scarlett to refute my comment. When she was silent, I looked back, her fingers playing with the stem of her wineglass as she bit her bottom lip. Looking up at me with pained eyes, she sighed heavily. "I don't know her. I haven't heard about Max cheating recently."

"Recently?"

"Oh, come on, Ana. Would it have been that surprising? If he did cheat, it wouldn't have been the first time, right?"

I didn't like to think about the first time we broke up. I caught him kissing another girl at a party. "But that was back when we were kids. Things were different then."

She cringed at me. "Not that long ago."

I knew how Scarlett felt about Max. She was with me through everything. Aside from Max and Xander, Scarlett had been my first friend when I moved to town. She saw the first inklings of a crush, was the first to hear about our first kiss. The first time we broke up and all the times after. She was the one who helped me box up all his things and send them to Boise when he left town in high school.

I knew her reservations weren't baseless, but after what happened, it would hurt too much to go down that path.

Opting instead to change the subject, I picked up the happy hour menu between us. "Should we get some edamame too?"

# CHAPTER FOUR

I WAS REMINDED DAILY that the world was moving on without Max. Despite my ability to keep a firm grasp on his memory, the world had other ideas. I was getting better at acting like I was working on getting better.

After locking my car with the key fob three times, I walked into the house, carefully hanging up my jacket on the coat rack. Xander's work boots were lying haphazardly on their sides in the walkway and I nudged them back flush with the wall. Through the kitchen, I noticed two empty beer bottles on the counter. The screen door was open, and I could see Xander sitting in a chair on the back porch. While it wasn't especially early to be drinking, Xander rarely drank on nights when he had to get up the next morning. I bit my lip as I considered his back. He hadn't heard me come in yet. It was possible he was having a hard day and would likely want his space as he quietly sulked. I considered going into my room and getting ready for bed. Like Xander, I needed to be up before the sun rose the next day for my six a.m. shift at the hospital.

I walked to my room but seeing the bottles on the counter irked me. I could at least put them in the recycling bin and out of sight. As quietly as I could, I grabbed them off the counter, placing them in the bin under the sink softly.

"Sorry about that."

I jumped, startled by Xander's voice at the door. He leaned against the doorjamb, one hand on the sliding glass door and another beer in his other hand. He nodded his head at the recycling bin. "I meant to do that before you got back, but I didn't expect you to until after ten. I thought I had to time to hide the evidence."

I laughed awkwardly. "Princess shift today. Only eight hours at the hospital, I got off at six."

He nodded his head quickly at me. "How was work?"

I grabbed a cleaning wipe from under the sink to scrub a spot where it looked like Xander had dripped either peanut butter or brown mustard. "Fine. Short, which was nice. I think I'm going to take on another shift next week."

He furrowed his brow. "Are you ready for that? You shouldn't overload yourself."

I rolled my eyes at Xander. "I'm fine, Xan. Honestly, another shift at the hospital would do me good. I've already blown through all my savings with the time I took off. I can handle work  now."

A pained look stuck on his face, and he looked away from me, taking a large slug of his beer.

"What?"

He avoided my eyes, looking into the living room. He tapped his thumb over the top of his beer bottle, making a low popping noise.

"What is it, Xander?" When he didn't respond, my heart sped up in my chest, my breathing got weak. When he didn't say anything, I threw the wipe on the counter. I was hoping for a dramatic noise, but only got a soft wet splat. "Goddamn, Xander. Are you okay? Something's wrong, isn't it? Is someone hurt? A friend of ours? Is it Scarlett? Is she sick? Are you sick? You are, aren't you? Fuck, I can't lose you, too."

He glanced at me, a tick in his jaw. He shook his head at me. "No, nothing like that. God, is that the first place your mind goes?"

I slapped my hand down on the counter and narrowed my eyes. "You'll excuse me if I don't have the reaction you want. But you're acting like you have some terrible news, and I'm rightfully freaking out here."

"No one is sick, I promise." He walked into the kitchen, setting his beer down next to our mail pile. He picked up an envelope and handed it to me. "But on the subject of money..."

The envelope was addressed to Alexander Eberhardt from Peninsula Rental Management. I read the enclosed letter three times before looking back at Xander. "They're raising our rent by two hundred dollars? Can they do that?"

He leaned against the counter with his ankles crossed. "I guess so. I asked a client who's a real estate lawyer, and he said that all they have to give you is a thirty-day notice."

"But we could barely afford this place before..." I scanned the letter again, hoping for a line I missed. Shouldn't there be a grace period for us?

"That's not the worst part," he said. He grimaced as he ran a hand over his face, his calloused hand scratching against his unshaven cheek. "I guess Max didn't pay a few months, but he talked Mrs. Jarett into letting us stack it onto the new lease when it came around. He made her promise not to tell us."

Max could be so damn charming when he wanted to be. We were constantly getting up-sized drinks, extra portions at restaurants, better service at stores. He knew exactly how to play a woman to get what he wanted. I wasn't the least bit surprised he could get the owner's wife to do that for him. I'm sure he thought he'd deal with it when this came around. Not having any idea that he'd...

"So how much would that be?" I asked, grimacing.

"With the rent increase and the back rent, it'd be almost three grand."

Sighing with exasperation, I scrubbed my face with a hand. "I don't have that kind of money. You know, I had to ask my parents for money to pay my portion of the rent."

He frowned at me. "You didn't tell me that."

Shrugging my shoulders, I screwed up my mouth, pouting to the side. "I didn't want you to know. I was embarrassed."

"But if you would've told me I would have…"

I chuckled, "What, Xander? You're broke all the time, too. You bought all that new equipment for the business. I know all your money is tied up right now. There's no way you could've covered both our rent by yourself."

"But you should have told me," he urged on.

I put my hand up to stop him. "I'm not your responsibility. As embarrassed as I was asking my mom for money, it was fine. I think she feels guilty since she never really liked Max, and I always knew that. Oh, God." My eyes widened at him. "Oh, shit."

"What?"

"She's finally going to get her wish. I'll have to move back home now. Shit! I so did not want to have to do that."

"You don't think we could try to swing it? Stay here? I mean, it'd be tight, but we could try to make it work."

"No way. There's no way," I sighed. "But you knew that already, didn't you?"

"Yeah." He scratched his nose. "You couldn't move into your own place?" he asked.

Shaking my head, I answered. "Maybe, but it'd be tight. God, I was feeling like such an adult. I was almost back on track here."

"Well, we could always..." He glanced away from me as he spoke. "I'd totally get it if you don't want to be my roommate anymore. But I know a guy. He's moving away and needs someone to take over his lease. It's not as nice as this place, but it's cheaper. No water view, no yard. It's a little condo. Way smaller. But it's two bedrooms. Not that much farther from your work than this place."

I sighed, relief flooding through me. Xander had already made a plan. "Do you think you could ask him about it?"

He nodded, smiling a little. "Yeah, I'll be working at his building on Friday. He likes to come up and ask for tips for his mother's hydrangeas."

"Are you sure you want to move in with me? It's a little different from when we all moved in together before."

"It has two bedrooms, right? All the annoying things you do, I already know about. I can handle you. I'm not sure about anyone else." This was absolutely true. Xander was always a respectful roommate. If he was messy, he quickly tried to clean up. He was quiet like me, paid his bills, he didn't eat my food. He didn't steal my shampoo.

I had an awful roommate in college who used my tweezers to pluck out her nose hairs. When I found out by walking in on her in the bathroom, I threw the tweezers away. I knew Xander would never do something like that. Xander, I could trust. Xander, I knew.

"I was thinking you'd be happy to leave."

I looked away, embarrassed at how obvious I must have been. "I wouldn't say happy, but it might be good for me."

"Ana, you won't walk up the stairs. You know that's not normal, right?" I knew that. But I couldn't discuss whatever these little panicked episodes were with him. "A clean break from this place might be a good move for both of us."

Excusing myself, I went to my room, changing into sweatpants and my '*I like drugs and I've got the grades to prove it*' T-shirt from when I finished pharmacology.

Despite the weather cooling into fall, I opted to join Xander on the back deck, drinking beer and sitting silently. That was something I always appreciated about Xander. Silence was peaceful for us. We could sit comfortably quiet for long stretches of time. I didn't need to entertain him, and he didn't need to entertain me. We got each other in that way.

Xander tipped his beer back, finishing the dregs. Before he could put it down, I took it from his hand, walking into the kitchen to get two more beers.

When I returned, his eyes were focused on the low tide end of Freedom Bay. I set his beer on the table between us and sat down next to him.

He kept his eyes on the half-buried kayak someone abandoned in the bay a few weeks prior. Reaching up, he scratched his head, his fingers disappearing into his blond curls. For anyone else, they would assume he didn't want to say anything. But I knew him better than that. He had something weighing on his mind. Scratching his head a few more times, he glanced over at me, his eyes soft. "You're so good to me. Isn't it exhausting sometimes?"

"I enjoy helping people, you know that. I always have."

He stared at me for a moment, opening his mouth, and then closed it. "I don't think it's healthy, that's all. Not that I'm complaining. It's nice to have someone do the grocery shopping, tell me exactly how much to pay in bills, someone who washes all the towels. But you know I can do that stuff too, right? You don't have to do things for me."

"I'm already doing that stuff. Might as well throw in a few things for you, too."

"I'm talking about more than all that." He waved his hand around in the air as if that clarified his statement.

"You need to be more specific, Xander."

"Fuck, An. You know I'm bad at talking about this kind of stuff."

Ordinarily, I would've messed with him, but something about his face stopped me. There was an openness in his eyes I hadn't seen in a long time. He was never much for eye contact with people, but this time he stared at me, his hazel eyes locking me into his gaze. He sighed heavily and shook his head, slowly looking away. "I really should probably stop talking about this, but it's built up for so long. I think about telling you this and when I think about how you'll react—but I've had it with trying to keep this in."

I set my beer down on the table between us. "Dude, you're freaking me out here."

"Listen, I'm going to say this once: you can love someone too much."

I scoffed at him, ready to stand up. His words felt too dangerous to something I didn't want to admit. "This is a bullshit conversation."

He grabbed my wrist and tugged it down softly. I considered turning away, but I let him sink me into the chair next to him. His hand was hot on my wrist, burning a path up my arm. "Look, I've been building up the courage to say this for months, okay?"

His hand was still on my wrist, gripping me hard enough to have my pulse quicken against his palm. A tingle traveled up my arm at the contact. His touch always did that to me. My voice was a forced roughness. "Okay. So, say it."

"You can love some too much in the wrong way. Max never loved you the right way."

"Why are you talking about him like this? He was *your* best friend. He loved you like a brother."

Xander leaned forward toward me. "I can talk about him however I want, Ana. You're right, he was my best friend. He was my first friend. He was the closest thing I had to a brother. But you know what," He gritted his teeth. "Max was a shitty best friend. He took advantage of every opportunity. He did things..." He shook his head. "Just things you don't need to know about. How much work did you put into your relationship, Ana? How much should you have been expected to take?"

"What do you know about relationships, Xander? The last girlfriend you had only lasted six months. Max and I were together for eight years."

"Yeah, and how were those years? Happy? Fulfilling?"

I narrowed my eyes at him. "You have no right to talk to me about what Max and I had. Despite you *always being* around, you were not a member of our relationship."

He raised an eyebrow at me. "Wasn't I, Ana?"

We glared at each other for longer than I thought possible. He was the first to look away, grimacing at the floor. "I was there for you through all his shit. Each time you two broke up. Every time he didn't come home. When the phone rang, and it was Max needing to be picked up from the side of the road. Who came with you? Who drove the car, who called the towing company to get his car out of impound?"

Xander looked at me. "He was my best friend, Ana. But that doesn't mean he was a good friend."

"No, that's not true. I know he had his issues, but…" My throat felt thicker as the words came out. The lies I wanted to tell about Max dying in my throat.

Xander shook his head at me. "No, Ana. You think that because *you're* good, because you choose to see the good in others. But sometimes there is none. He did so much to you, to me. And then he leaves. He's gone. I don't understand, how can you still have faith in a man who failed you?"

The tears brimmed over, soaking my cheeks. I took hungry gulps of air. He looked grief-stricken, watching me as his words sunk in. Standing up, he pulled me to my feet, wrapping his sturdy arms around me. I sobbed into his shirt, greedy breaths escaping me. Xander rubbed my back as I cried, murmuring for me to stop crying, that it was okay. But I continued. A well bursting inside that had no valve.

He pulled me away from his chest and looked down at me. "Hey now. I got caught up. Please don't cry. I'm really sorry. I'm tired, okay."

"No, Xander I get it." I whispered. "Max could be a hard person to care about sometimes. I'm tired too."

He studied me with his hazel eyes, appraising me. I wiped my tears with the back of my hand.

"I don't want to think about the bad stuff, you know? I don't want to be angry at him," I said, sniffling.

Xander picked up my hand, still wet with my tears, never taking his eyes off mine, and pressed his lips to my palm. His mouth against my skin seared hot. My fingers moved to cup his face. His stubble was rough against my fingertips and my pinky grazed his jaw, skimming his skin. His eyes darkened and my heart beat hard in my chest.

Pulling away, he gazed at my face, his look serious. "I know you don't." He curled my hand into a fist and dropped it between us. He stepped around me and into the kitchen, leaving me on the back porch.

That space in my chest was cracking slowly. Taking a shaky breath, I dug my nails into my palm, scoring the skin where his lips had been. Whether it was to hold on to the feeling or make it go away, I didn't know.

# Chapter Five

WE REALIZED HALFWAY THROUGH loading that we should've gotten a bigger truck. What looked like it would take two trips to transport was going to be more like five.

Through the years we lived in the duplex, we'd accrued a plethora of what could only be called junk. We filled garbage bags full of cords that had no electronics to charge, screws, nails, and bolts of various sizes. We tossed out half-burned candles, flavored syrups given as a Christmas gift we never opened, decorative pillows I hated but never had the heart to tell my mother.

There was only one exception to our purge. When we came across some of Max's stuff, I would set it aside, telling myself I'd go through it later.

Without a word from me, Xander had taken over the Max collection, boxing everything that was Max's, sight unseen. Into the boxes went old car magazines, beer signs, the ceramic 'vase' he made in pottery class, and books of baseball cards.

I wasn't sure I'd be ready to go through his stuff. I knew I'd have to, eventually. Xander had kept the boxes in the upstairs room. With my move downstairs, I never had to see Max's shirts hanging in the closet or his shoes haphazardly resting against the wall.

The place was certainly smaller than the duplex. The kitchen was so narrow, if we opened the oven no one could pass through the space unimpeded. Through the window in the living room there was a partial view of the Olympic Mountains, but our bedrooms looked out on the parking lot. Definitely a downgrade from Freedom Bay.

Most of our furniture was in a clump in the middle of the living room. While it drove me crazy to see all our things in such disarray, I was covered in a thick layer of dust and sweat. My legs felt like lead and my arms were jelly. I had a bruise on my hip from where the coffee table had slipped from my arms and the corner jabbed me. There was a gash on my leg from a wayward dining room chair, countless scratches on my hands from the boxes, three broken nails, and what I suspected was a bald patch from where my ponytail got caught on a nail while trying to pull a bookshelf from the wall. As much as I wanted to organize things, I was dead on my feet and desperately needed a shower.

I'd packed away my bathroom things in one of many countless boxes that were piled in the middle of the room. So, I used the travel toiletry kit I kept in my gym bag which got about as much use as my idealistic gym membership. The full bottle was screwed on tight and as I used my teeth to get the lid open, I squirted shampoo into my mouth. Rinsing my mouth out twice, I knew I'd be tasting soap for a week. The water pressure was lighter than the duplex, but I figured that was the price of living in a building with ten connected homes.

When I got out of the shower, I took the travel-sized toothpaste and my electric toothbrush, the only thing I had on the counter. I brushed my teeth, rinsed, brushed again, rinsed, brushed again, rinsed.

When I came out of the bathroom, Xander was sitting at the breakfast bar, a line of Styrofoam boxes in front of him. "I got us some Los Cazadores. I hope that's okay?"

"Obviously," I sat down next to him, reaching across to grab a tortilla out of the box, "God, I'm so hungry. Who knew moving would take so much out of me?"

"I did. Remember, we did this not that long ago. We didn't really live in the duplex that long." He handed me the Verde sauce and I took it.

"Yeah, but I don't remember it being this bad." I stuffed a chip in my mouth, chewing as I put my taco together.

"Maybe it wasn't quite this hard." He walked to the fridge and took out two beers, handing one to me. "Of course, you didn't really help with all the moving stuff the last time. You left that for me and Max."

I slapped a hand to my heart in feigned shock. "Hey, I had college. I was starting nursing school. I had a lot going on."

He put his hands up in a defensive pose. "I'm just saying. We did the heavy lifting. You came behind us organizing and color coding everything."

"Remember how when we moved in, we only had three plates? We had to hand wash them for each meal." I grinned at the memory.

He laughed. "That's right. And we used a toolbox as our TV stand." He leaned back on the stool, pushing the front legs off the ground so he was balancing on the back legs.

"Max and I slept on an air mattress for months, before we bought that mattress for a hundred bucks at that discount store." I laughed as I brought the beer up to my mouth.

"That was shady."

"Right? Looking back, we could've gotten bed bugs or something. That mattress had to be used. Why would we get it so cheap?" I laid my head on my arms on the countertop. "Ugh, I don't want to drive back to the duplex tonight. Would it be bad if I crashed on the couch here? I'm sure I can track down a spare blanket somewhere."

"You think I'm going to judge you for sleeping on the couch?"

"No, I know. It's not how I pictured my first night in our new place, but I didn't plan on the actual moving to take so much time. I thought I'd have time to move my bedroom set here, not leave it at the duplex with half the boxes."

"And you don't want to sleep in the duplex alone?" he finished for me.

I paused, licking my lips, salt from the food clinging to them. He was right, of course. Since I'd returned from my parents, there wasn't a single night that Xander wasn't in the apartment with me, upstairs if I needed him. The idea of sleeping alone in the half-empty house scared me more than I wanted to admit. "It wasn't part of my plan, no."

"Well, I found a few camping things in a box when I was looking for a towel. The sleeping bags were in there." He leaned forward, the legs of his stool hitting the linoleum with a thud. "I'll go grab them."

While he was gone, I fished the last piece of Chile Colorado out of its sauce, eating it off my fork. He walked back into the room, an oversized army green sack under his arm.

I hopped down from the stool, taking the bag from him. The gigantic green bag bulged as I tried to pull the sleeping bag out. Xander took it from my hands and loosened the drawstring top, opening the hole. I had to tug it hard to get it, but eventually I wrestled it out. I laid it on the ground, looking it over for a moment before laughing. "Where's the opening? How am I supposed to sleep in this thing?"

He took it out of my arms and found the zipper, unzipping it. "It's a mummy bag; it was my dad's when he was in the Marines. He said it can stand up to twenty-degree weather."

"I don't need anything like that. I need a blanket."

"Yeah, it gets a little hot inside, so don't zip it up all the way. Most times I use it, I end up with half my body laying outside of it by morning." He set it on the couch, leaving for a moment before returning with a pillow from his bed. I stood back as he made my bed for me, struck with how nice he was being. A warm feeling came over me as I watched him try to take care of me. It was bewildering how foreign the sensation was. After he had the sleeping bag all set up, he straightened, looking over at me with his warm hazel eyes. I realized I'd been staring at him as he worked. "What?" He looked from the bed and back to me. "Does it look okay? I know it's not what you're used to, but..."

"No, it's great, Xan. Thank you."

I tossed and turned on the couch, the moonlight coming in full force through the curtainless window. The sounds of the highway were loud compared to the quiet seclusion of our duplex. Even after unzipping the mummy bag, I was swelteringly hot. Staring up at the ceiling, going over happy moments in my life, remembering the first time I rode my bike to school by myself, my first kiss, the first time I took Max's hand and I felt that jolt of something I couldn't really identify. I only knew that my chest felt like it was filling up like a balloon and I had to look away, I was so overcome with emotion. I counted the shadows on the ceiling, grouping them in threes. After I had twenty-seven groups of three and one stray shadow, I sat up, frustrated. I wasn't going to fall asleep. Getting up from the couch, I grabbed the pillow, making my way to Xander's room. When we first looked at the apartment, he'd offered me the bigger room with the attached bathroom at the end of the hallway. His room was smaller. His door was ajar, and I stepped into the room. Xander lay on his back, a single fleece blanket crumpled up around him. No sheet on the mattress—a bare box spring and mattress resting on the floor. I walked over to his side and sunk down close to him.

He stirred and opened one eye to look at me. "What are you doing, An?" his voice was husky and low with sleep.

"I can't sleep on the couch. It's uncomfortable," I said, my voice whinier than I intended it to be.

"No, it's not. That couch is great," he mumbled, his eyes closing again.

"Then you sleep on it," I told him.

He opened one eye to glance at me. "I have a bed. I have my bedroom all set up."

"A mattress on the floor is set up?" I snapped, annoyed.

"You were the one who planned the order we'd be bringing things here. You made a chart and everything," he reminded me, fatigued.

I sighed, "I know."

I waited him out and sure enough, after a minute, he rolled to the side away from me, patting the space next to him. "Come on, then."

No discussion, no cajoling. He made room for me on his bed. Carefully, I laid my pillow on the bare mattress. "Thank you, Xan," I whispered.

We climbed into bed, Xander pausing at the single blanket covering him, trying to decide whether he wanted to lie under it with me or not.

From this angle, I could see he'd nicked himself shaving. There was a slight cut below his chin. I studied him in the soft light of the parking lot. He looked so mature in the darkness. Had his face always been so striking? When did that happen? I held up my hand and softly touched the scab. "Did you put antibiotic ointment on this?" I asked quietly.

His eyes still closed; his jaw tightened. "No, it's a little scratch."

I held my finger to the spot, his pulse thrumming against my finger. A tingle from the contact of his skin traveled down my arm and into my chest. The moment to pull away from him was long gone. Slowly I slid my hand up to cup his jaw, the bristle of his unshaven face rough against my palm. My hand fit his face. How could I have known that?

Beside me, I could feel Xander take in a ragged breath, as if to say something.

I shouldn't have touched him like that. It was inappropriate. Pulling my hand away, I tucked it under my cheek, trying to ignore the sensations touching him had created. After a moment, he sighed loudly. I felt his arm reach over me. For a moment, I thought he might try to hold me. Instead of placing his hand over me, he pulled the lightweight blanket up to my elbow, covering me.

"Goodnight, Liliana."

I could feel the tears coming up. I kept my eyes shut. He was silent next to me. I listened as his breathing slowed. Outside, the wind whistled through the trees, the branches scraping against the window in a rhythmic tapping that seemed all too familiar.

Rolling away from Xander, I tucked my traitorous hands under my cheek. Across from me was Xander's bookshelf, full of graphic novels, landscaping books, and business textbooks. Tucked between a copy of *Garden Ponds of the Northwest* and *The Tipping Point* was a framed picture of Xander, Max, and me. I bought the frame at a two for one sale at Pier One years ago. Max and I had the same one in our room.

My room.

Even in the dark, I knew everything about the photo. How I'm tucked under Max's arm, looking up with a small smile playing on my lips. Xander to the side, looking over the photographer's shoulder, a big smile on his face. Between us is Max, his head thrown back, laughing at some joke he'd made. We were at Scarlett's for a barbeque. The weather acted up halfway through, so we had to rush under the large awning that jutted off the side of the O'Keefe house. My hair is plastered to my head, raindrops hanging off the flat curls that hours before I'd spent so much time twisting around a hot iron. I didn't have the chance to wipe the mascara from under my eyes. Xander and Max's T-shirts have darkened shoulders from the rain. I couldn't tell you the joke Max had cracked. Only that we'd barely made it out of the rain before Max said it, throwing his arms around us both. Scarlett snapped the picture as Max got to the punchline. No one was laughing harder than Max.

The day that picture was taken, Max was recently released from jail on an assault charge. He got into a fight with a classmate of mine he thought was hitting on me. The guy pressed charges and Max was gone for three months. I ended things between us and tried to move on without Max. I'd tried to distance myself from him, but weeks after he got out, he found me again.

Until hours before that party, I told myself that it was better for me to be apart from Max. Then he showed up at my parents' house with a bouquet of stargazer lilies. He begged me to take him back, promised he'd never hurt another person again, that he was going to stop drinking so much, and he would trust me when I said I was just friends with someone. He swore I was the only one he's ever wanted to be with, that I was the only one who could understand him. He talked about how he wanted to take care of me, how he was going to make it all better.

That was the last time we broke up.

Staring at the picture, I thought about Xander's face when we walked into the party, hand in hand. Xander was standing beside his girlfriend Tianna, waving his hands in the air, telling his story about when a customer's mini pinscher had attacked him while he was trying to weed their rose garden. He told me the story weeks prior. The dog bit into his arm and Xander had to shake his arm up and down until the dog released his jaw.

Xander's arm was frozen halfway up as he caught sight of us. His brow furrowed, and his arm slowly fell to his side. Beside me, Max was surveying the party. Xander bent down to whisper in his girlfriend's ear and before she could respond, he jogged toward us.

"So, you guys are back together?" he asked with no preamble, pointing at our clasped hands.

Max smiled big at Xander. "Yeah, well, you can't keep a good man down, can you?" He smacked Xander on the shoulder hard enough Xander took a step back. Max didn't seem to notice as he looked across the lawn. "Now, where's the keg at?"

Xander hooked his thumb behind him on the lawn. Max nodded, "Thanks man, you want to play beer pong later?"

Xander took one last look at our hands together before nodding. "Sure bro, find me later."

Max pulled me away. Wordlessly, I followed him as he led me through the party. I spared one glance back at Xander as we walked away. He had thrown his arm over Tianna's shoulder but was watching us, a frown on his face.

I hadn't thought about that moment for so long. I was so caught up in starting over with Max. Soon after that party, Max and I moved in together, despite my parent's vehement objections that they weren't paying for my boyfriend to crash at what was effectively their place since I was currently without an income.

After that moment, I don't think I gave Xander's reaction another thought. He never brought it up. It was even Xander who asked us if we wanted to move into the duplex with him.

After tonight I couldn't help but see those moments a little different. Was there something else in Xander's reaction?

With his breaths evened out, I leaned closer and pressed a small kiss to his cheek, his blond stubble was coarse against my lips. He smelled the way he always did—of sunshine and grass. Of calm. Breathing him in deep, I settled beside him, closing my eyes.

"Goodnight, Alexander," I spoke, my whisper filling up the darkened room.

I awoke before the sun came up. At some point, we'd turned to each other. His arm was slung over my hip, his feet wedged between mine. Xander's face was inches from mine in the light of the moon. As delicately as he'd touched me, I traced the shape of his lips with my finger. They were inexplicably soft. In his sleep, his lips curved into a small smile, and I let my hand rest on the pillow between us. The silk of his lips scored into my skin.

# Chapter Six

AFTER MUCH CAJOLING FROM Scarlett, I agreed to a haircut. Scared I'd change my mind, Scarlett got me an emergency appointment at Bei Cappelli, an upscale salon facing Freedom Bay. While we waited, the receptionist brought me a glass of champagne, that I drank faster than I meant to. By the time I had my shampoo, the tension in my shoulders was fading. Scarlett sat in the chair next to mine, not bothering to ask for permission. She chatted with my stylist, Beth, telling her all about her new crush, Emma. A name I'd never heard her say before. Or did Scarlett tell me, and I didn't remember?

A pit formed in my stomach as I thought about how neglectful I'd been with our friendship over the past eleven months. Before, I was always the first one to know about Scarlett's new relationships. Now, I'm hearing about it by eavesdropping on a conversation she had with her hairstylist.

Beth ran her fingers through the bottom of my hair. "Gorgeous. Could use a deep conditioning at the ends, but it's such a lovely shade. Do you color it?"

"No, not for years. That's all my natural color," I answered. Through the years my hair had lightened but kept its copper tones. Max loved running his hand through my hair, flipping bits around in the sunlight, watching how the light reflected off it. He loved when I wore my hair up in a high ponytail. Grabbing the bottom of my hair, he'd twist it around his hand to pull me closer, tugging enough to get my attention. He loved my long hair.

She held up pieces in the light coming through the window. "People would kill for this thickness and color. This is the type of hair those companies use for wigs."

I caught her eye in the mirror. "Like for kids with cancer?"

She continued to comb through my hair. "That, or there's one for kids with severe alopecia."

"Do you know how to send them hair?" She stopped combing through, her hand stilled mid-brush stroke.

"I do."

Without looking at Scarlett, I squared my jaw. "Then cut it off. I don't want it."

She balked for a moment. "How short?"

I laid a hand on my shoulder. "Here. I want it here."

Next to me, Scarlett laughed. "Live fast, cut your hair!"

I gave her a smile, and she winked at me. For the first time in a long while, I felt light. Even if it was only for a moment.

The entire ride home, I kept looking at my reflection in my rear-view mirror. It was a drastic change, much shorter than I'd ever had it. I felt like I was a different person, stronger, coquettish even. Scarlett walked me to my car with a pair of earrings she said would complement my new hairstyle perfectly. She hugged me at my car, her oversized bag stuck between us.

"I love it. You look like a new person. So bold."

"I didn't want to be bold. But I needed a change." I paused, grabbing her hand to squeeze it. "Thanks for forcing me out. I know I need a push more often these days."

Squeezing my hand back, she smiled. "I'm glad you came out. It looks great." She tilted her head to the side as she tucked a tendril behind my ear. "I bet Xander will like it, too."

"You think?" I touched the ends, my thumb touching my chin.

She looked as if she was suppressing a laugh. "Yeah, you look amazing. I don't know why you let all that hair bog you down for so long. Not many people can pull off a shorter style like this. You were made for it."

My smile faded. Thinking back to Max, how he'd run his fingers through my hair, braiding the ends while we lay on the bed. I remembered the scent of his hair as he buried his face in my neck. I gripped my key and pulled away from Scarlett. "Thank you, again."

Back home, I walked through the door, setting my keys in the small bowl next to Xander's. I hung my jacket up on the coat rack before placing my purse over my coat. I picked up Xander's sweatshirt, rehanging it from the hood and not the tag. Noticing several coats hung sloppily on the rack, I grabbed them all, draping them over my arm, and hung them back up, one by one.

"What are you doing?"

I jumped at Xander's sudden question, dropping the jackets on the floor. I clapped a hand to my chest and whirled around to see Xander standing there, his eyebrows raised. "Holy Hell, you scared me."

He leaned against the wall between the kitchen and the living room, a glass of water in his hand. He gave me a sheepish grin. "Sorry."

I crouched down, picking up the coats off the floor. I turned back to the coat rack, placing the coats on there, one by one, smoothing them down so they hung straighter.

Once I was happy with how the coat rack looked, I turned back to Xander who watched me from his spot on the wall.

I walked past him into the kitchen. He turned to follow me. He reached up and touched the bottom of my hair directly above my shoulder. "You cut your hair."

I brought my hand up to touch where my hair stopped, and my neck began. "Yeah, Scarlett talked me into it." I heard the lie pass so quickly that it didn't sound like me. Looking away, I worried I'd betrayed myself. "I know it's drastic."

He toyed with the end of a curl I'd never be able to recreate. He was looking at his hand in my hair. "No, I like it."

My face went hot at the compliment. "Do you? I wasn't so sure. I haven't had it this short since…"

"Since we were in eighth grade," he finished softly. His fingers were close to my neck. I could feel the warmth of his skin so close to mine as he played with the end of my hair. "I liked that haircut."

His finger barely brushed against my throat and I felt my breath hitch. A shiver went down my spine, my body betraying me. Turning away, I pulled my hair out of his grasp. "I know Max liked it long. I'll probably regret it tomorrow morning."

Behind me, I sensed Xander tensing up, as if he wanted to say something. With a shaky hand, I grabbed a glass from the cabinet, filling it with water from the tap. I finished a whole glass in one long gulp, trying to calm my nerves. He set his glass down on the counter, then put his hand down, so his arm was under mine.

"It looks nice, Ana. You look nice."

"Thanks," I whispered. I could feel his body behind me. The heat of him radiating through me. I had the sense that if I leaned back, his body would support me. That maybe his hand would move to cover mine.

He was silent for a moment, and I thought he was going to leave, but he leaned closer to me, his words a breath against my ear. "Cutting your hair doesn't mean you didn't care about him, Ana. You're allowed to be your own person. You're allowed to live your life."

"I *am*," I replied, my voice more forceful than I meant to be.

"I don't think you are." He leaned in closer to me. "And it's been longer than you think."

I furrowed my brow in confusion. He leaned in closer to me. "It's been a year."

"I know how long it's been, Xander."

"Do you? Time passes a little differently when you're stuck."

"I am *not* stuck," I insisted. Xander stared at me silently, waiting me out. I looked away first. "And who cares if I am a little?"

"I care. You know I care. It's not healthy. It's not right."

"Who's to say what's healthy, or right?" I whispered. I closed my eyes, trying to get on stable footing. With him standing so close to me, I could smell the earthy scent of his skin.

He tensed up next to me and his arm slid away. Without a thought, I grabbed his forearm with my hand, holding him closer. I looked up at him. Energy thrummed down my arm at the connection. "I miss him, is all. Don't you ever miss him, Xan?"

"Of course. I miss him every day." He relaxed slightly under my touch. I kept my eyes down, looking at his arm undermine. His sleeve was pushed up, revealing the white downy hairs on his arms, the smattering of freckles above his wrist. His skin was warm under my palm. "But that doesn't mean my whole life needs to be about him. And neither should yours. Not anymore. He wouldn't have wanted that."

"I don't know what he would've wanted," I murmured. "I'm not sure if I really knew him."

"He was complicated. And it's okay to feel complicated about him."

Our eyes locked together, the space between us seeming to be too close, and yet I leaned in closer. "Is that how you feel? Complicated?"

He looked down at me, his hazel eyes boring into mine. "More than you'll ever understand."

We stood there, looking at each other, the air grew thick with something between us. My skin felt tight, and I could hear my heartbeat in my ears. I licked my lips and his gaze flickered to my lips. I thought about my first kiss—our first kiss. How he'd tasted like bubblegum. He didn't know where to put his hands, so he'd held them straight at his side like a soldier. I'd felt a dip in my stomach and thought, *so this is what a kiss is.*

Had Xander always been this comfortable standing so close to me? Why was I reacting this way to him? I'd known him forever—he was my family. He'd been my rock for the past year. That's all it was, right? Security and familiarity. I looked away. I felt his eyes staring through me, but when I didn't look back, he pulled his arm out from under my hand. The absence of his skin beneath mine burned my palm.

Waiting until the door closed with an audible click, I let out a deep breath. I grabbed the glass off the counter and set it in the sink to wash it. Filling the glass up to the brim, I dumped it out, filled and dumped, filled and dumped, filled halfway and scrubbed the side with a soapy sponge. I could hear Xander turn on music in his room, the bass shaking the door frames. I knew I should remind him our upstairs neighbors would complain if we had the volume too high, but I wasn't sure I could face him. Instead, I let the music tremor up my legs as I made my way around the kitchen, wiping surfaces, once, twice, three times. My hands were shaky.

I wasn't feeling anything more for Xander than I always did. He was my friend. He was my confidante, my support system. I needed to talk to him, to watch TV together, to cook with him, to shop together. I needed him with me. But that didn't mean a thing.

It was much safer that way. There was no other option for us. I couldn't handle anything else.

# CHAPTER SEVEN

WHEN A SEASONAL WORKER had quit last-minute before Christmas, Scarlett asked me if I could fill in at her shop for a couple of hours every few days. She told me I was doing her a favor, but everything was better when I wasn't home. Holidays were never easy for the grieving. Everywhere I looked, I'd see something I knew Max would love. I'd see the decorations on the trees and think of how we used to watch the tree lighting downtown together. I'd hear Christmas music and think of how he'd sing *The Little Drummer Boy* off-key over and over to annoy me, knowing how much I hated that song.

The Christmas before he died, Max, Eloise, Xander, Scarlett, and I sat around the duplex eating a holiday dinner and exchanging presents. When Max handed me the little silver box, I felt my heart leap into my chest. I thought he was finally proposing to me after so many years together. After all the hard days we had together, he'd finally make our union official. I fluffed my hair in case Scarlett was going to take any pictures of the big event. Slowly opening the box, I found the most gorgeous sparkling pair of garnet earrings. I fought to keep my face composed as disappointment rolled over me. I loved the earrings. They were glorious. But it wasn't the engagement ring I hoped for. It wasn't the symbol of love I'd dreamed of. Now, every time I walk past a jewelry store with its holiday display of gleaming gemstones and precious metals, with its promises of everlasting love and happiness, I felt the pang of disappointment from that day. I relieved the embarrassment of hoping for something that'd never come.

I wore the earrings today. I touched them now and then as I busied myself straightening up a rack of cashmere scarves in the window display, reorganizing them so they were lying with clean edges in a neatly fanned out circle.

A few minutes before closing time, I was surprised to see Eloise walk into the store, glancing around skeptically. There was a time when I was concerned that she was going down the wrong path. Her clothes got tighter, she colored her normally blonde hair black. A few days before, I drove by and saw her smoking at The Hole. I wanted to help her, to assuage her pain, but who was I to do that? I was as bad, if not worse off than Eloise.

I walked around the counter to give her a hug. She was a few inches taller than me now. She would've been almost as tall as Max if he'd lived to see it.

"What brings you in?" I asked cheerfully.

"I was talking to Xander, and he said you were helping Scarlett today. So, I thought I'd stop by and..." she paused, looking away. "And well, I'm a junior now and I think it's dumb, but I promised Steph I'd think about going, even though I think school dances totally blow, but Homecoming is coming up..."

I clapped my hand to my chest, "Oh, Homecoming! I loved the dances in high school. It's so fun, Eloise, go!"

She glowered at me. "I'm pretty sure it's going to be a bunch of horny teenagers drinking watered-down Kool-Aid, dancing to Calvin Harris, and getting finger banged under strobe lights."

"Well, yeah. But I swear you won't regret it. Even if it is the worst night of your life."

"I have quite a few of those, so it'd take a lot to challenge that honor," she quipped.

"Well, even if it was, having a school dance story, especially a bad one, is a milestone of growing up."

"How would you know? I'm sure all your school dance stories are filled with romance and whispering sweet nothings."

I didn't want to tell Eloise that my best school dance story wasn't with her brother, but with Xander. Aside from the one formal school dance I talked Max into, on the condition that I paid for his suit, it wasn't the height of romance. Most of my dance stories with Max involved catching him making out with girls in equipment closets, him getting too drunk before we got there, or us fighting about some stupid thing and one of us storming off.

My smile faltered, but I worked at keeping it on. "So, I'm assuming you need a new dress? It's still a formal, right?"

Eloise held up a short purple dress, pinning it against her body and looking into the mirror. "Semi-formal, whatever that means."

I walked over to the rack of cocktail dresses, sliding them along the rod until I found one that'd look good against Eloise's patchy black hair. "It means you can wear a shorter dress if you want to."

Eloise took the dress from me, looking at it with suspicious eyes. "Well good, if I do this, I'm not wearing a long dress." She walked to the dressing room with the dress as I turned to the store, looking around for other options.

I handed her another dress over the top of the door. "Try this one on. I think it'd look good with your blue eyes."

The handle opened with a click and Eloise stood in the door frame, her round face serious.

"Oh, Eloise," I whispered, smiling. I stepped back and beckoned her to come out and see herself in the three-way mirror.

The top was a sheer illusion neckline, fading down into a sweetheart decolletage. The cobalt blue lace was tight over the body, stopping right above her knee. She looked like she was all grown up and, in her twenties, "Oh, you look gorgeous."

"I don't know, it seems a little..." she tilted her head to the side. "I think most girls are wearing something a little more..."

"Revealing?" I asked.

"Well, yeah. It's kind of long, isn't it?"

"Maybe the mini dress is more in fashion these days, but I bet they don't have a back like this." I stood behind her, turning her around. The back of the dress dipped low, almost to the base of her spine. While the front was demure, the back screamed scandal. "This is the type of dress you take with you when you go to college. You go on big dates in this dress, you go to Christmas parties in this dress. This is a woman's dress, Eloise."

"You think?"

"I bet the boys will go crazy." Snagging a pair of earrings off the table, I handed them to her. "You need something for your ears, no other jewelry. You'll look amazing. I wish Max could've seen you in it."

I expected the mention of Max to make me sad but talking about him to Eloise didn't have that effect on me. Maybe it was because we both loved him, or because she perfectly understood the pain of losing him. She reached for my hand and squeezed it. "I don't think he would've liked the back part."

I laughed loudly, shaking my head, "No, probably not. But you're seventeen, you're practically a woman now. It was bound to happen, eventually."

She reached down and grabbed the price tag, glancing at it before her face fell. "Of course. I find a dress that might make me consider going to this stupid dance and it's impossibly expensive. I should've gone to Goodwill and picked out a millennial reject gown."

I grabbed the tag, pulling it off with a quick flick of my wrist. "It's taken care of."

She looked at me, aghast. "No, Ana, you can't pay for it. It's over two hundred dollars."

I flapped my wrist at her. "Consider it bought. I only have one condition to paying…"

She rolled her eyes at me as she made her way over to the dressing room. "I bet I can guess what it is. Don't worry, I'll go to the dance."

I walked behind the counter as I rang up the dress. "And take lots of tacky pictures. That's all I ask."

She came out wearing her old jeans and a faded Ridgewood High select choir hoodie I recognized as mine. I must've left it at their house years ago. I was amazed it was still in one piece.

I handed her the bag. "Did you drive here? I'm about to close. I could give you a ride home."

"No, I drove old Clarence," she replied, referring to Max's old beater car. I couldn't remember why he called it that. But the ugly little car seemed like a Clarence and the name stuck.

"Well, wait a few minutes and I'll walk you out." Hurrying through the last of the drawer counts, I put everything back in the organized filing system I'd created for Scarlett during a sales lull. Locking up behind me, we made our way to the parking lot. I slid my arm through hers, pulling her close to my side. "I can't believe you're a junior already."

"Yeah, a few more years and I'll be out of here."

"Have you looked into colleges yet?" I asked, sidestepping a big slush puddle.

"Not yet, but my teachers said if I keep my grades up, they'll help me with the applications. So, I have a pretty good shot of getting in somewhere."

"I have no doubt."

"Honestly, I don't care what I do. I just want to leave. Why didn't you leave after college?"

We stopped in front of her car. The car's fading paint chips were larger than the last time I saw it. I picked at a small spot, scraping the beige paint with my fingernail. "Max was here. I came back for him."

"But he could've gone anywhere, too. I don't know why he never left either."

I shrugged, pulling my coat tighter around me. "I don't know. Probably in part because you were here, and he wanted to look out for you. This was his comfort zone. I don't have an answer for why we didn't go."

Eloise flexed her jaw. "I'm getting away. At this point, I don't care what happens with my mom. I don't need to be her keeper anymore."

"No, you don't. Max wanted you to leave. He talked about it all the time. Said you got the brains in the family. You have the drive, the talent."

"I miss him." It wasn't a sorrowful statement, just a fact.

I grasped her hand in mine. "I know. Me too. Every day."

We held each other for a moment as the wind picked up, a biting December chill swirling around us. "If I come over before the dance, will you do my hair? I can't afford to go to a salon like the other girls."

"Of course. I'd love to." I pulled her close, hugging her tight. I loved her with everything I had, and I hoped she could feel it.

# Chapter Eight

I STOOD IN FRONT of the bathroom mirror, adjusting my new dress over my thighs. The Spanx Scarlett swore I needed under this dress made my stomach feel tight and my constricted breathing. Scarlett insisted if wore a dress from the new spring collection before she put it on the floor, I had to wear it the right way. She made a big speech about being a walking advert.

In the lobby, Xander, Emma and Scarlett were getting us a table at Rêve de Vin. Scarlett tried to talk us out of such a swanky place, but we insisted. She deserved a big night out for her birthday.

I frowned at my reflection. Even though I'd tried to curl my hair before we left the house, my hair was flat. The wind from Xander's truck to the entrance of the restaurant was enough to blow away any semblance of a wave. I reapplied my lipstick to give myself a boost.

I enjoyed dressing up, despite complaining about the tight undergarments. It felt nice to wear something pretty—to do my hair and wear heels. And I liked Xander's low whistle when I came out of my room. For the first time in a year, I regained a part of myself I hadn't realized I'd lost.

We ordered different dishes and shared with each other, polishing off a bottle of wine. Scarlett was quick to order another one for the table. Xander retold his favorite story about Scarlett, when at the age of sixteen, she fell off a park swing, breaking her arm, and then tried to tell everyone she broke it in a wakeboarding accident. Halfway through dinner, I realized how happy I was. The thought made me stop mid-thought.

I was happy. I laughed at jokes and told stories about work. Since Max died, I hadn't had such a happy moment.

Scarlett and Emma left before us. Scarlett had an early morning doing inventory the next day. She leaned in and gave us both kisses on the cheek after Xander and I took care of the bill. She offered to pay, but we all shot her down. We wouldn't allow her to pay on her birthday.

I stood in the anteroom of the restaurant, tipsy from the wine, as I waited for Xander to get his truck. He insisted I wait for him and not walk to the icy parking lot in my heels.

"Hey, Ana."

I turned around to see Max's friend, Peter Jorgensen, standing next to the hostess booth. Beside him was a girl who didn't look old enough to vote. It figured. Peter always liked them younger.

"Peter!" I chirped, my voice choking into a high squeak.

"How are you? Come give me a hug." He opened his arms. I didn't really want to hug him, but I couldn't see a way to refuse. I leaned in with my upper body, keeping my feet back. He hugged me close, and I could smell the weed that always clung to his clothes.

"Long time no see, huh?" he remarked.

"Yeah, it has been."

"How long would you say?"

*It's been eleven months and seventeen days since Max died.*

"A year, probably."

He smiled big at me. "I'll be damned. So how have you been?" he asked, ignoring his date next to him.

"Fine. I've been okay, you know, considering."

He nodded, his face becoming more solemn. "Yeah, that's good. I was thinking about you a lot after it happened."

I wasn't sure if that was his way of giving condolences, or what, but I nodded anyway. "Thanks."

"So, what are you doing here?"

"It's Scarlett's birthday. We all got together for dinner."

"And who are we?" he smirked.

"Scarlett, her girlfriend Emma, Xander and I. It was Xander's idea."

Peter smiled, looking over my shoulder. "Is that so? That's nice of him. Are you two..."

I shook my head at him. "No, nothing like that. I can't imagine dating."

"I bet." Peter's eyes skated over my body, giving me chills.

I could feel the frosted air rush in as the door opened behind me. Xander came to stand behind me. "Peter. How you doing, man?"

They did one of those odd fist-bump, handshake things I never understood. Xander was pleasant enough as he talked to Peter, but I could sense his tension.

"After dinner, I was going to take Gail to the Skol House for a drink. You should join us," Peter invited.

"I'm sorry," I said, as genuinely as I could muster. "We'll have to take a rain check. I have an early shift at the hospital tomorrow and need to get home and in my pajamas."

"Yeah, I have to be up early too. It was good seeing you, though," Xander lied. He put a hand on my back, leading me away from Peter and his date. We walked to where he parked his truck at the curb, and Xander opened the passenger door for me to climb in. As he shut the door, I saw Peter jog outside to stand next to Xander.

"Dude, I got to ask—what the fuck are you doing?" his tone was playful, but a chill ran up my spine at the underlying menace.

Xander scrunched his eyebrows together. "What?"

Peter pointed at me sitting in the passenger side of the truck. "You and Ana."

"Me and Ana, what?"

"Are you guys fucking?"

"No, we're friends. It's Scarlett's birthday. A group of us took her out to dinner."

"So, it was you, Ana, Scarlett, and her..." he smirked, lasciviously, wiggling his eyebrows. I felt my lip curl at his expression. Had he always been this disgusting? "Girlfriend? I'd heard that Scarlett batted for both teams. Interesting." Peter shook his head at us. "I gotta say it sounds more like a double date type thing, if you ask me."

"Good thing I didn't ask you." Xander flexed his hand into a fist then relaxed it.

"It's shady looking, is all I'm saying, Xander."

"I don't know what you're talking about, Peter." Xander flexed his hand into a fist then relaxed it.

"Max was our friend. It's wrong to pilfer his girl. Have a little respect for the dead."

"I have plenty of respect." Xander shook his head at Peter.

"I'm just sayin' is Max wouldn't like it."

"Max isn't around, okay? Nothing is happening. We're just friends."

"That's not what it looks like. Taking her out to dinner, wearing a tie and shit. I know you always had a thing for her, but this is messed up. It looks like you're going after Max's leftovers."

Xander stepped forward, crowding Peter's space. "You need to stop talking. Right now."

Peter always talked a big game, but he was six inches shorter than Xander and had no bulk on his body. He was always a skinny little guy. I hadn't seen Xander fight in years, but I knew he'd have the upper hand. Stepping out of the truck, I walked to where they were standing. I put my hand on Xander's chest, pushing him away.

"Knock it off. Both of you." I scolded. "Xander, let's go home."

Peter laughed, "You guys live together?"

Xander tensed his jaw and looked away.

"It's none of your business, Peter. We haven't seen you since the funeral. You don't get to comment on our lives," I snapped.

He ignored me, staring at Xander over my shoulder. "Man, I'm telling you. Going out to dinner, living together. Doesn't look like nothing to me."

"Go back in the restaurant, Peter. Get back to your date before her daddy comes to fetch her for missing her curfew," I told him, pushing his shoulder softly toward the building.

Peter put his hands up in surrender as he backed up. "It doesn't look good. I'd think about what you're doing."

Xander's fists were clenched at his sides as he glowered at the door. I set a hand on his arm. "Hey."

He didn't respond to me. I slid my hand down to his hand, grabbing his fist, pulling it up between us. He looked down at me. "Sorry. I hate that guy sometimes."

"I know. But it's too cold to be standing out here glaring at the door. Let's go home."

His face relaxed and he squeezed my hand back. "Okay."

He held my door open for me, helping me climb into the passenger seat, before taking his spot beside me.

"He's right, you know," I said, staring out the windshield. Xander began to drive away from the curb. "About how things look. He's not the first one to say something about us living together."

"Who cares what Peter thinks, Ana? He's an asshole."

"It's not just Peter." I paused as the thought came to my mind. "What will people think of us? I don't want people getting the wrong idea."

Xander tightened his grip on the steering wheel. "What idea is that?"

"That we're together. People are going to talk and make it sound like..."

"Who cares what people think?"

"I do. You know I do. It's awful, but I care. I don't like thinking someone out there doesn't like me, or they think I didn't love Max. I can't have anyone question that."

"No one would question how much you cared about Max. That's ridiculous," he scolded.

"No, it's not! I'm going to date, eventually. Everyone says I'm going to have to move on."

He was silent for a while. All we had was the sound of gravel hitting the bottom of his truck. He reached over and grabbed my hand. I squeezed him back.

"I'm sorry the night had to end like that for you." He pulled into his parking spot, using his other hand to shift the truck into park. The truck was silent for a moment, and I moved to grab the door handle before Xander spoke again.

"You'd tell me if you didn't enjoy spending time with me, right?" he asked softly. "Just because we live together doesn't mean you have to hang out with me all the time."

"Of course. I love being with you. You and Scarlett are my family."

I opened the door and climbed out of the truck. He joined me on the walkway to our apartment.

"Family?" he asks.

"Yeah, of course you are. I mean it. I love you guys."

"Okay," he replied softly. "Good."

"Thank you for taking me out tonight. Aside from the whole Peter debacle, I can't remember the last time I had so much fun."

He put his hand on the door handle and paused. "I'm glad to hear that. That's all I want, is for you to have fun."

"I did."

He turned the key in the lock, swinging the door open. I ducked in under his arm, hanging up my coat and purse on the rack. Behind me, Xander crossed the room toward his bedroom door.

"Hey Ana?" he called from the doorway.

I turned to face him. His eyebrows furrowed. He seemed to contemplate what he wanted to say.

I stepped closer to him. He grabbed the neck of his shirt, unbuttoned the top button, and pulled his tie loose.

He opened his mouth, a haunted look passing over his face. "You looked really nice tonight. I like it when you wear that color."

I smiled at him. "Thank you. You looked handsome yourself."

We stood there smiling at each other, the light from the moon streaming in through our living room window. He stepped closer to me until he was right in front of me. Bending down, he pressed a kiss to my cheek. I closed my eyes, and a warm sensation flooded over me. He pulled away and looked in my eyes.

"I'm glad I got to see you smiling tonight," he whispered.

He left me standing there, my hand clasped to my cheek. The wine must have gone to my head. I watched his door, trying to place the feeling that washed over me. Why would I feel so guilty about a kiss on the cheek? And why, when his kiss lingered on my skin, did I almost turn my face to meet his lips?

# CHAPTER NINE

ARMED WITH A GROWLER of Sticky Cow's Freedom Bay Ale and her level, Scarlett walked around the living room, marking spots on the wall with a pencil and sketching out the general plan for what pieces would go where. I stood back with my beer, watching her. I knew better than to interrupt her while she was decorating.

At one point, I brought out a framed painting I'd stored for years in the back of my closet. In the painting, a woman stood at the bottom of a waterfall, looking up at the gray and black water cascading down to her. The only actual color in the painting were bright wings that sprouted across the woman's bare back.

I closed my eyes, laying my head against the back of the couch. "You know, the wall, clothes, the way you see yourself and know exactly where things go..." I trailed off, flinging a hand over the top of my head. "... knowing where you go. I wish I could do that."

She turned to look at me. "We're not talking about picture frames, are we?"

"No." My eyes still closed, I brought the pint glass up to my mouth, draining the beer. "I know that it's been long enough since Max..."

"Died," Scarlett supplied.

"I'm constantly worried about what he'd think of every choice I make. I'm exhausted from it." Keeping my eyes closed, as I talked, I didn't want to see the pity in her eyes.

Scarlett took the empty glass out of my hand. "Have you seen someone? Maybe you should talk to a counselor or something."

I waved the comment away. "I went to a few sessions with my mother's therapist. It was a colossal waste of time. I can't sit there and talk to some stranger. It didn't make me feel better."

Scarlett sat up straight and turned to look at me. "It's not about feeling better, Ana. It's supposed to hurt. Part of grieving is learning healthy limits to your grief. Setting healthy limits, period. Which, you know, has never been a strong suit of yours. Max walked all over you, and you know it."

I opened my mouth to say something, but no words came out. Scarlett shook her head. "Don't lie to yourself, Ana. He hurt you all the time. Don't pretend he was some saint."

"I don't want to pretend that, Scar! That's the opposite of what I want. But you have no idea how this feels."

She nodded at me, agreeing. "You're right. I don't. What I know is my best friend is suffering and I want her to feel better." She wrapped an arm around me and pulled me closer.

"I know you do." Hugging her back, I reveled in the warmth of her love.

She stood and went into the kitchen, refilling our drinks as the door slammed and Xander walked into the room.

Scarlett smiled at him. "Hey, late night? Did you have a hot date?" she teased.

He glanced from me to her, his eyes staying on hers for a minute too long. "Uh, yeah, actually."

A tightening in my chest took my breath. I had no idea he was seeing someone. He never told me. While I wanted to say that we talked about everything, this was one subject that never came up.

"And who is the lucky lady?" Scarlett teased. "And when do we get to scare her away?"

"Her name's Sherie. She works at the chiropractor's office in Anderlund Village. We got our coffees mixed up at the coffee shop. She grabbed mine by accident."

"Sure, she did." My comment came out more spiteful than I wanted it to sound. I pressed my lips together, my jaw tense. I coaxed a softer tone. "That sounds really cute, Xan."

"I guess." He ran a hand through his curls as he looked around the living room, nodding at the new decor. "So, you guys spent the day... uh..."

"Redecorating?" Scarlett supplied, handing my beer to me.

"Yeah, it's um..." He scratched his nose, looking around the room. "I guess it looks kind of nice."

"Oh, Alexander, you really know how to compliment a gal, don't you?" Scarlett teased.

I laughed, relieved we weren't talking about Xander's dating life any longer. "You don't like it?"

He frowned as he looked at the walls where we hung up a few pieces of art I bought in college. "It's different, is all. Where did you get this stuff?"

Seeing the painting on the wall reminded me of why I bought it in the first place—the sensation that came over me when I first saw it. I recognized myself in her—the thick feathered wings, the way she's partially submerged in the dark pool trying to bring her down, the flume before her cascading against achromatic foliage. Yet she was there, she wasn't down yet. It reminded me that the beating of my heart was all I needed. Maybe I could let the water lick my skin, but I wouldn't be towed under.

I pointed to the painting. "I've had that big one since I was at the UW. I never got around to hanging it up." Xander inspected it for a few minutes, his hand coming up to touch the right wing. "You don't like it?"

Xander stepped closer, looking over it. "No, I do. It's not what I expected from you, it's kind of..." Xander glanced at me, frowning, "Well, I don't get it, but if you like it, I'm cool with it."

I stood beside him, admiring the painting. The juxtaposition of Xander's reaction to having it in our living room compared to Max when it was in our bedroom was startling. I didn't want to take notice, but I couldn't help it. Max was not Xander. They would never be the same person. Stepping back, I left them in the living room.

Scarlett left to go see her new girlfriend and I retreated to my room. My legs were wobbly from the craft beer. Flopping onto the bed, I turned my head to glance at the closet. Scarlett had emboldened me. I could change things—I could make this place my own. But I needed to go through Max's things to do that. With everything else in the condo placed exactly where it should be, the boxes shoved in my closet mocked me every time I opened the door. There were a few times I tried to go through them, but opening them made me freeze, my heart beat faster, my breath came out in short blasts, and my vision turned to pinprick dots in front of me. I couldn't do it. So, I kept putting it off. I put it off until it was almost a year since they'd been put away. Almost a year since I'd smelled him on my pillow. Since I'd felt the fabric of his shirts against my skin.

I set the pint glass down on the floor and pulled the first box to me. Opening the boxes, a rush of cologne and stale air met me. I pulled out the shirt on top and I looked at the sweater I'd gotten him for his twenty-second birthday. Holding it in front of me, I rubbed the soft fabric between my fingers. I could picture exactly how he looked wearing them. The blue in the shirt brought out the blue in his eyes and he'd push up the sleeves on the sweater.

I set them aside in the keep pile and continued sorting through the box, placing items in one of two piles—keep or give away. Opting to keep a few things holding sentimental value, I sorted out old T-shirts reminding me of our time together. The fabric of some of his shirts was so old that little holes formed along the hem. I used to hook my finger through those little holes and drag Max closer to me. I let the soft cotton glide over my hand, lacing my fingers through the little holes. I sighed and dropped it in the keep pile. With one box left, I was doing better than I thought I would.

Between his shirts, I found a large manila envelope. Stuffed inside were letters—sheet after sheet of notes. All on different paper, all with different handwriting.

Pages and pages. Different handwriting. Different women. Different girls. Some were dated, some were not.

Letters. Written to Max when we were together.

The papers fell from my hand to the floor. A strangled sob escaped me. I sank to my knees—the shag carpet not nearly soft enough to cushion the fall. Xander must have heard me cry out. He rushed in wearing athletic shorts and his hair was still wet from the shower.

"Ana, what's the matter?" he asked fearfully.

I gathered all the papers and thrust them at him. Still sobbing, I watched as he read them, his face grew paler, his jaw tight.

"Where did you find these?"

I pointed at the box. "With his shirts."

"What were you doing looking through his shirts, Ana?" he asked softly.

Ignoring his chastisement, I kept talking, "I found these."

Xander sat down next to me, his long legs folding into a crouch. "You never should have seen those."

I thought about his words. He wasn't surprised by the evidence, or that Max cheated on me. He had no innocent explanation. No. All he offered me was—I never should've seen them.

"Did you know, Xander?" I whispered. He cleared his throat, looking away. I pulled back, looking up at him. "Did you know about this, Xander? Please tell me that the one friend I should've been able to trust didn't keep this from me."

"I wasn't sure."

"What do you mean you weren't sure?" I hissed.

"I suspected a few times. But he never admitted to it. I wasn't sure how to call him out. He was my best friend, Ana."

"But you were sure enough to suspect?" I asked.

He avoided my eyes, an afflicted grimace on his face. "I found out about one. She works at the hotel with Dana. I caught them together when I was doing some work in Manzanita."

"When was this?" I asked.

"After Christmas, a few days before…"

"But you never told me?"

Xander shook his head, avoiding my eyes. His voice got louder. "I told him he needed to tell you, or I would. I said he needed to end it with that girl if he wanted to keep you. He didn't deserve you. That…" he trailed off, looking at the letters scattered on the floor. "I mean, it doesn't matter anymore. He died before you found out. What am I supposed to say? Huh? *Hey sorry, but your boyfriend, my best friend, was cheating on you.* He made a fool of you," his voice softened. "He made us all look like fools."

"You should've told me. I should've known. If I'd known…"

Xander leaned back on his heels. "What? You would've left him? Would've made him leave? You took him back after he did it in high school." His words were harsh, but his tone soft.

I took the letters from Xander and sunk down onto the edge of my bed, staring at the words swimming on the paper. I tried to make sense of what I was reading. I needed to figure out how to connect the man I once knew with this man, the man who could say he loved me and then be with another girl—this man who told me I was the only one he loved and then gave himself to someone else.

Xander sat next to me, too far for me to lean on. But he put his hand in between us in case I needed to hold it.

"I trusted him. I wanted to trust him so much. I wanted it to be good." Not bothering to wipe my tears off my face, I knew Xander had seen me like this. He'd seen my worst.

"I know you did," Xander replied. He looked down at his empty lap.

"Why wasn't I enough? Why was what we had not enough? What is about me that made him need someone else? He was enough for me—he was everything to me." My sobs choked my chest and my shoulders heaved violently as I cried.

I felt Xander's arm snake around my shoulder as he pulled me closer to him. I shook against his side, wetting his bare chest with my tears.

"You are enough, goddamn it! Ana, you are so much more than enough." He pulled me away from him, looking me straight in the eye. "Ana, I swear to God. What Max did, it was never your fault. No matter what happened, it was him. It was always him."

"But if I'd just—"

"No!" Xander interrupted. "Don't you dare. Don't you take this on too. I will not let you try to take responsibility for Max's cheating. For what he did to you. For what he did to me, to himself. Some days..." Xander shook his head, his jaw tight. "Some days I wish I could punch him again for what he did to us."

"Again?" I sniffled. "When did you punch him?"

"When I found him with that girl. I warned him. He knew the consequences. But he couldn't help himself. He wanted everything. He always did. I warned him, and then I punched him."

I wracked my mind trying to place when this would've happened. "Wait, were you the one who punched him when he had that bruise on his cheek?"

He hesitated, "Yeah. I was."

"He told me he hit his face when he fell down..."

Xander leaned forward, lacing his hands in his lap. "No, it was me. I punched him. When I found them together, I told him I was going to tell you about it. He said some stuff, I said some stuff..."

"What kind of stuff?" I asked, putting my hand on his arm. He looked over at me, his stricken gaze boring into me.

"It doesn't matter. Not anymore. Just stuff. I hit him, I said awful things. I left..." he paused, tears filling his eyes.

He pinched the bridge of his nose, as if trying to keep the tears at bay. "That was the last..." he huffed loudly—his breath ragged. "It was the last thing I ever said to him and the last time I saw him alive."

I scooted closer to him, wrapping my arm around his waist. He hesitated for a moment before placing an arm on my shoulder. I leaned against him, fitting under his arm perfectly. "As bad as it sounds, I'm glad I'm not the only one with regrets." I murmured.

Xander snorted at me. "I shouldn't have punched him. I shouldn't have pushed him to the edge like that. If only..."

"That seems to be my mantra." I told him. "*If only*. If only I'd come home sooner, if only I'd talked him into staying sober. If only I'd been enough..."

"We're a fucked-up pair of kids, aren't we?" He tipped his head down and I could feel his lips on the top of my head, kissing my hair. Holding our bodies still, I savored the feeling of how good it felt to be loved in our fractured duplicity.

"Could you stay with me tonight?" I asked. "I don't want to be alone."

His lips moved out of my hair, his cheek pressing against my forehead. "Of course. Whatever you need."

# CHAPTER TEN

O NE YEAR.

Xander and I had made it through one whole year without Max.

We sat on the floor in front of the couch, a bottle of cheap whiskey and a two-liter of soda between us. I needed more of a chaser than Xander, but I'd always been a lightweight. The weather report forecasted an icy night, so we used up the last of our pellets in the stove. So far, the weather report seemed exaggerated.

Suddenly, I felt much more drunk than I did a few moments ago. The candles we lit in case of a power outage burned down lower, casting shadows on the wall as darkness fell outside.

"It's looking all *romantical* in here." I joked, reaching for the bottle of whiskey. The amber liquid still burned my throat, but it got easier the more I drank. I set the bottle down between us and wiped my lip with the sleeve of my sweater. "Do you want to call someone to come over and make use of the ambiance? What about that coffee-shop girl?"

I could hear my voice slurring the words, making 'ambiance' into an accented sound of pretension.

"Of course not, Ana," Xander scoffed.

"Are you sure? I wouldn't mind." Grabbing the hem of my sweater, I pulled it up over my head, the loose weave getting caught in my earring. My arms out of the sweater, I glanced at Xander as I set to untangling the earring.

He chuckled softly to himself but didn't comment on my wardrobe challenges. Instead, he leaned forward, carefully pulled the dangling earring out of my ear and laid the sweater on his lap. He worked deftly to untangle the loose threads from the wire. "I haven't even talked to Sherie since our date."

A rush of warmth flooded through me, knowing he hadn't called her. Bumping my shoulder against his arm, I said, "Well, you're doing better than me on that front. I don't know if I'll ever be ready to date again."

His jaw tensed for a moment, and he glanced away. "Let your mom know first. I'm sure she has all sorts of eligible bachelors to set you up with."

"I'm sure she has a list. Probably several lists. I swear she's omnipotent. Did you know the first time I tried to cut school she knew before I even got home?"

"I did."

"Some lady from her book club saw me and called her immediately."

"Yeah, I know. Remember? We were with you. It was you, me, Max, and Vanessa Charles."

"Vanessa Charles. God that's right." I wrinkled my nose. "I hated her. She was such a bitch," I grumbled.

"She wasn't too bad."

"She was awful—always pretending to be all tough, talking about all the skateboarding tricks she could do. I hate when girls do that—try to act all tough to impress a guy."

"I don't think she was trying to impress anyone. I think you were jealous because Vanessa had enormous boobs at fourteen, whereas you did not."

"I was not jealous of her boobs."

"Yeah, okay," he scoffed at me.

"Why would you even remember how big my boobs were?"

"I'm a guy, Ana. Of course, I remember how big your boobs were." He shook his head at me. "They were small. You didn't really get them until you were what, sixteen?"

I rolled my eyes. "God, you sound like such a pig right now."

"I didn't touch them or anything. I quietly noticed you," he coughed and took a sip from the bottle between us. "Them. Boobs, I mean. Any girl's boobs."

"Oh yeah? What else did you notice about me?" I teased.

"You had nice hair. It was shorter, remember?" He raised his hand up to touch two fingers to the top of my collarbone. "You used to complain that it was too short to put up and you could only use those hair snappy things."

"Barrettes," I supplied quietly. His fingers still rested on my collarbone. Warmth radiated from his touch, and I had the urge to lean in closer.

"Yeah, those," he breathed.

He looked down at his fingers on my bare shoulder. They left warm tracks against my skin as they moved. They moved so slow I could barely feel it, not stopping until they rested in the hollow of my throat. He wasn't looking at me anymore, instead watching his fingers.

I could feel my heart beating faster; my skin felt tight. I opened my mouth to say something, then bit my lower lip in my teeth, not sure what to say. His hand stilled and his eyes slowly met mine. In the candlelight I could make out the shadow from the scar below his left eye where a child at daycare had thrown a fork at him when he was four. I realized I knew that about him. I knew all the little things, like how there was a quarter sized birthmark on his scalp where a patch of hair grew white-blond curls. I knew the way he filled his bowl of cereal with milk first, then put in the cereal. I knew all these things and now I knew how his fingers felt against my skin.

I thought for a moment his fingers might dip lower and was surprised to realize I wouldn't push him away. But instead, the pressure gradually eased as he pulled his hand away.

"Sorry," he whispered. He picked up the whiskey bottle from the floor and I watched as he brought it to his lips. His lower lip was full, partially obscured by a few days' worth of golden stubble on his chin.

I looked away and grabbed the bottle away from him and took a long slug. "You want to know a secret?"

Xander leaned forward, a smile playing on his lips. "Sure, I'd love to."

"I hate lilies. Especially stargazer lilies. They shed their pollen all over the place. They're a church flower, an Easter flower. Lilies smell like a sweet rotting fruit."

"But Max..."

"Always bought them for me. I know. I never had to heart to tell him I don't like them."

"So, what is your favorite flower?"

Tilting my head to the side I considered his question. Max had never asked me what my favorite flower was. He assumed it was the perfect flower to give me at some point because I had lily in my name. But he never asked me. An inexplicable sense of annoyance simmered in my chest. Why had Max never asked? What else did he never know about me—what did I not know about myself?

"Dahlias. I like dahlias."

Xander's jaw tensed as he watched me. The air between us seemed to grow heavy. Max never knew what flowers I liked, but now Xander did. My hand tingled in my lap. What would he do if I reached between us and took his cheek in my hand? Would he push me away?

My gaze must've been too intense because he looked away, rubbing a hand over his face. The scratch of his calloused hand against his stubble was audible in the silence between us.

"I miss him every day, Ana. I do."

I laid my hand on top of his. He turned his palm up so that I could grip his fingers. "I know you do, Xan."

"For years, he was the only friend I had. He was the only kid from the neighborhood. He knew what it was like for us. I didn't have to worry about him judging me for how my house looked, because his house looked the same. We could eat our free lunches together. He got it. He got me; you know?"

"I do."

Staring at his hand over mine, our skin etiolating in the moonlight, I was struck by how well our hands fit together. "I don't know what I'd have done this past year without you. But with you here to support me... Just, thank you."

"Of course. You know, I'd do anything for you," he said, his voice lower.

He held tight to my hand. I tried to decipher his meaning. They seemed like headier words than we were used to, but we had been drinking, and it was a long day.

I tried to pull my hand away, but he held on tighter. "You know I mean that, right?"

"Mean what?" I asked, matching his whisper.

"I'd do anything for you…"

Suddenly, he seemed too close to me. His hand was too warm against mine and I could feel my heart beating hard in my chest. My ribs felt too tight, and I struggled to take in a deep breath. In the dark, I could feel Xander's eyes on me. What did he mean by that? Was I looking too deeply into his words?

"Did you hear me, Ana?" he asked, his voice louder this time.

I didn't like this feeling rushing over me. Anger bloomed in my stomach. Why was he making me feel this way? Why was I having such a visceral reaction to him? It wasn't right. I didn't want to want this. Clambering up, I retreated to the kitchen, where I filled a glass with water from the tap. Xander leaned against the wall of the archway between the kitchen and the hall. The only exit.

"I should go to bed." Walking to him, I waited for him to move out of my way. Instead, his arm slid up the wall, creating a space for me to duck under. When I was under his arm, his body turned to face me. Stopping, I looked up at him. My back against the wall, I opened my mouth, trying to find words I wasn't sure I had.

Slowly, his hand slid down the wall to rest above my shoulder. If I turned away, I knew Xander wouldn't stop me. But my feet were stuck to the spot. His eyes flickered to my lips for a moment before he took a step closer to me. My body felt warm, my skin tingling where his shirt brushed against my arm. He placed his foot between mine, his legs on either side of my knee. He was so close I could feel his breath on my face. Leaning down, he pressed his lips to mine softly. I could taste the whiskey and mint gum on his breath. He pulled away slowly, testing my reaction.

At first, I was too surprised to form a coherent reaction. When I didn't respond, he leaned down again. I was rooted there between his body and the wall. My mind was a rebellion of urges. I should kiss him harder. I should stop him. His lips felt soft against mine; warmth flooded through me. He deepened the kiss, and I brought my hand up, squeezing his arm. His hand came up to thread through my hair, pulling my face into his. My skin was on fire, my insides molten under his embrace.

My hand came up to tangle in his hair. In all the time I'd known Xander, I'd never really touched his hair. It was softer than I expected. The curls wrapped around my fingers as I moved my head to kiss him harder. His body was so warm against me. His hands wandered down my body to rest on my hip, pulling me closer to his body. I moaned at the contact, and his fingers dug into the bare skin of my lower back. Every glancing touch fanned a fever inside me. I hadn't felt this way since...

*Oh God, what am I doing...*

*Oh no, no, no...*

I pulled away, stepping into the living room. Frantically, I wiped my hand against my mouth, trying to wash away what I'd done.

"What the fuck, Xander? What was that?"

He blinked at me several times; the spell he was under was broken.

"I kissed you."

"Why? Why would you do that?"

He leaned against the door and stared at me; his hazel eyes boring into mine. "You know why."

"Obviously not, or I wouldn't have asked."

He scrubbed a hand against his face. "Please, don't do this to me, Ana."

"Don't do what?" I snapped.

"Act like you don't already know. Make me spell it out."

"Spell what out? I'm not following."

"Yes, you are. You know how I feel about you." His eyes entreated me to understand something.

"No, obviously I don't," I said, my voice wavering, breaking on *don't*.

He sighed loudly and threw his head back, hitting it against the wood with a low thud. "You're going to make me say it?"

"I guess I am," I said.

He stared up at the ceiling. An arduous minute passed as I waited. Every second felt heavier between us. Slowly, he lowered his head to meet my eyes. Something passed between us in that moment. My chest twinged, resounding with each breath.

"I'm going to go to bed," he said, brushing past me, heading for his room.

I grabbed his arm, pulling him back. "Hey, come back here! You can't kiss me like that and then walk away. Don't start this conversation and not finish it."

He shook off my arm and glared at me. "You have no idea how miserable this is making me."

"I make you miserable? How the hell do *I* make you miserable?"

He threw up his hands, his voice loud. "I love you, Ana."

I stared at him stupidly. "Well, I love you too, Xander."

"No, I mean, I am *in love* with you. You know I am."

"No, you aren't. You're drunk," I argued.

He shook his head at me. "I'm not drunk. And even if I was, a little whiskey has nothing to do with it."

"You *are* drunk. You're drunk and emotional and you don't know what you're saying right now."

He stepped closer to me, and I took a reflexive step back. "I know exactly what I'm saying. You just don't want to hear it."

"You don't love me," I said feebly.

"Don't you dare tell me how I feel, Liliana Pryce. I know what love feels like."

I turned away from him. "I can't do this right now, Xander. We're both tired. You're not thinking straight."

He tensed his jaw. "You kissed me back."

"I did not!" The words rang false against my lips. I could still feel his hand on the back of my neck, his fingers in my hair, his lips against mine.

"You did. I could feel it. If you want to pretend it didn't happen, that's one thing. But I felt it. You kissed me back, even if it was only for a moment."

"You're confused. It's been a long day," I retorted. "I'm emotional. We went through a traumatic thing together and obviously we're going to have some odd feelings coming out of that..."

"It's not that. This has nothing to do with—"

"Don't." I put my hand up. "Just don't say his name. You don't get to kiss me then bring up his name as some fucked up justification."

"I wasn't going to." He struggled.

I shook my head at him. "I'm going to bed. Tomorrow, we'll put all this behind us and keep going like this never happened."

"If that's what you want, I can do that. But it won't change how I feel."

I pursed my lips and closed my eyes, counting to three. I flexed my fingers, digging each nail into my palm.

"We'll see about that, Xander." I turned away and walked to my bedroom, pausing in the doorway. I could feel him watching me. My skin felt warm from his gaze.

Behind me, I could hear him in front of his room. "You can come up with whatever justification you need, Ana. It won't take this back. I'm still going to love you the same."

I fought the urge to give a retort, but what could I say? I was out of words.

Instead, I closed my bedroom door and made my way across the floor, sinking into my bed. Anger boiled in my veins. He was confusing our friendship with something more. We'd always been friends, and we'd shared something with love—we shared Max. I knew what love was. I loved Max. Didn't I?

In the dark of my room, what happened reverberated through me. His kiss had rocked me to the core, sending everything I knew about Xander away. I had no idea he could kiss like that. As much as I wanted to act as if I'd never thought about it, I had. But I never imagined he'd kiss me like that. And I never imagined I'd want him to.

Whatever this thing between Xander and I was, it stopped being platonic long ago. In that moment when his lips met mine, I knew there was something much more between us.

The recognition of this didn't clear up any of my confusion. If I thought I was miserable before, it looked like my pain was only starting. As I drifted off, Xander's kiss stung my lips, and his words echoed in my head.

# Chapter Eleven

WHEN WE WERE IN high school, Scarlett got into a nasty car accident. In a bout of misguided impulses, she leaned across the passenger seat of her car to grab a CD and her wheel caught the gravel shoulder. She panicked and turned the wheel too far in the other direction, crossing into the other lane of traffic. When she realized she was in the wrong lane, she twisted the wheel back the other way, causing her to skid over the side of a high embankment. Her little convertible flew through the sky, falling thirty feet into the greenbelt. Her car landed upside down, her life saved by the seatbelt that kept her suspended upside down but still inside the car. She climbed out and had to fight her way up a cliff through blackberry bushes and poison ivy to get back to the street.

She flagged down a passing motorist, who stopped to help her. When Xander and I arrived at the hospital, she still had dirt caked in her nails and small burrs stuck in her hair. If she hadn't been wearing her seat belt, she would have fallen out of the car and likely would have been rolled over. If it'd happened a few yards down the road, she would've hit the cement-lined drainage ditch. There were so many variables that could've stopped her from walking away from the accident with only a moderate case of whiplash, a sprained wrist, and some abrasions.

Years later, Scarlett would simplify the accident, saying she simply overcorrected, that a more seasoned driver would've reacted differently. But, at that moment her tire caught the edge of the rocks, she panicked.

My parents never fought in front of me and my brother, but they were rarely affectionate with each other. Their relationship seemed based on timid cordiality and a sense of duty to keep the family unit together. They acted like business partners, each with a role to play in creating a picturesque family life. My father worked hard at his practice. My mother volunteered for every PTA committee, she joined the gardening club, the local parade board, the board of directors for the library, and served as vice president of the local beauty pageant of which she was a former title holder. She was secretary for the Ridgewood Pearls, a local fundraising organization for various charities. She would have dinner on the table every night and kept the house running like a well-oiled machine.

Like every teen before, I swore I'd have something more than what my parents had in life. I would note their every flaw and never settle. I didn't have to look far before I found the opposite of my parents in Max Constantine. Max was the only boy I ever slept with, my first and only actual boyfriend, the only boy I ever said those three words to. For more than half my life, Max was my entire world. I would've done anything for him to make him happy.

In Max I found passion, I found fun and frivolity. All the things I detested about my parents were missing from what we had. What I never considered were the things that kept them working as a team. I missed the way my father respected my mother's work. He fostered her interests, allowing her to expand on them. My mother worked hard to make the house a welcoming place for him to come back to. Their mutual respect, the way they complimented each other. While their relationship may have seemed passionless, they were friends. They trusted each other, never doubting each other's commitment.

Until the day I found Max on our bedroom floor, I didn't fully understand what Scarlett meant about over overcorrecting. Our entire relationship was created in the panicked moments we careened across the street, trying to fix the wheel into the road, only to end up in the brambles. My affection for Max went too far. I placed too much trust in a man who would always, in the end, leave me. A man I could never save.

I spent years climbing through the bracken of everything Max had left for me. The other women, the debts, losing the man I thought I knew, finally accepting that I never truly knew him in the first place.

Lately, I've been feeling as if I'm almost out of the thicket, only to have a fresh fear come through me. *What will I find in this new world? Who am I now, that I have emerged with skinned knees and tainted skin?*

In the time that passed after Xander professed his feeling for me, I realized there might be something more—something Max or Xander never told me. I thought about that kiss often—the feel of his lips against mine, how my first instinct was to hold him closer, relishing the pull in my veins.

I spent long nights alone in my bed, reliving that moment standing in our kitchen. I tried to discern exactly how I felt in that moment when Xander leaned toward me, his body warm and his touch igniting feelings I'd buried long before. Everything I had said to him was true. I couldn't believe he would try to kiss me like that. I didn't believe he meant what he said. But in the dark of my mind, I felt doubt. I kissed him back. In that moment between us, where I had no thoughts clouding my true feelings, I wanted his touch. I craved his embrace.

I knew I didn't want Xander with someone else. But what could I offer him? I was too bruised to love again.

# Chapter Twelve

*"I don't get celebrity crushes." –Ana, age sixteen.*

I THINK MY HEART broke a little when the first crocus broke through the ground, its bright purple head poking through the grass at the base of my parent's plum tree. The first signs of spring brought the rains, the gray skies, and a freak snowstorm that incapacitated the town when they'd put away their snow tires weeks before. I was busy at the hospital with whiplash patients, stitches from falling on black ice, and one case of hypothermia when an extremely fortunate high school kid was found sleeping outside by his friends.

Scarlett and I set up a biweekly lunch date at The Cabin. I went out more and more. I had a quick coffee date with my high school friends. I met my college roommate, Chloe, in Belltown for dinner one night, even crashing in her spare bedroom overnight after I missed the last ferry. Xander and I had our weekly rituals. We'd go to the grocery store, alternating who paid for the total each week.

Over wasabi ahi salad and mini mahimahi tacos, Scarlett and I discussed our lives. She and Emma were serious now. Emma had asked Scarlett to move in with her. While she was fearful of the commitment, I urged her to consider it. Emma was an amazing woman, and I could see how happy she made Scarlett.

"Now, enough about my love life. Let's talk about yours," Scarlett said, squeezing a lime over her taco and bringing it to her mouth.

"What love life?" I laughed, nervously turning my water glass around on the table. "I can't even imagine what one of those looks like."

"So, there's no one you're interested in?" she asked, a devious flicker in her eye.

"Definitely not."

"Nothing's going on with you and Xander?"

I let out a strangled laugh. Did Xander say something about our kiss?

"What? No. Of course not. Like I told you, we're just friends. Like you and I are friends. You like the ladies, but you don't see me worrying about myself around you."

She rolled her eyes at me. "First, rude. I am so hot. You should be so lucky. Second, you are not my type, and third..." She picked up her soda and brought the straw to her lips, confusion passing over her face. "Um, I don't remember."

"You were asking me if I was interested in anyone."

"Right! If there's no one you're interested in, does that mean that I can set you up?"

Scarlett's eyes lit up at the possibility of matchmaking and I stifled a groan. "Ugh, I don't know. I mean, is it too..."

She put her hand up. "Don't you dare ask if it's too soon. It's been over a year. When's the last time you've been kissed? Year. Had sex? A year. It's ridiculous."

I thought of Xander's lips pressing against mine, the way his arms felt under my hands, the rush of heat and shame as I backed away from him. Scarlett kept talking, oblivious. "No excuses. It's a guy Emma knows from high school. Really nice. I think you two would be perfect together."

"Scarlett, I'm really not sure..."

She leaned forward; her eyes big in desperation. "Please, Ana, pretty please! Will you do this for me? I promise if he's a total ogre, I won't set you up ever again."

I sighed, looking around The Cabin, for some sign of how to respond. "Fine. But one date. That's all I'm agreeing to."

She clapped her hands together in glee. "Yes! Oh, thank you. You won't regret it. This guy is so perfect for you."

"I doubt that." I thought Max was perfect for me and look where I ended up—brokenhearted and pissed off. There was a flash of sitting next to Xander, our shoulders touching as we watched TV together. It was nothing special, nothing heart stopping. Only familiarity, the warmth of his body against mine. That moment felt perfect.

All day long, I was nervous about my date. Scarlett offered to come over and help me get ready. She even tried to get me to wear a new outfit from the shop on loan. But I refused. If I was going to go through with this date—and I still wasn't sure if I was, I changed my mind about every fifteen minutes—I needed to do it as myself.

I changed out of my jeans and T-shirt. Standing in front of my closet wearing only my underwear, I flipped through my clothes. Everything I had seemed too casual, or too nice, too old-fashioned, or just plain old. It'd been so long since I needed to dress up to impress someone. Taking out a floral print sundress, I studied it. If I wore it with a cardigan, it might work. Holding it up to look at my reflection in the mirror, I considered myself. It made me look like I was shooting a country music video. I put it back in the closet and pulled out a blue silk top. *If I wore this with black slacks, maybe?* I shook my head. I looked like my mother before her charity group meetings.

Glancing at the clock, I saw he was going to be at my place in thirty minutes and I still hadn't done my hair or makeup. Shoving the silk top in the closet, I pulled out a little black dress that Bronson's fiancée, Becca, bought me for my birthday last year. I had nowhere to wear it to before, so I almost forgot about it. I pulled the dress over my head, smoothing the lacy fabric on the skirt down over my thighs. Luckily it was an A-line skirt, so I didn't need to break out the slim wear. Scarlett swore by them, but I had a hard time relaxing with such constricting underwear.

Rushing through my hair, I opted to straighten the funny spots on my already fairly straight hair. I wouldn't try a new style tonight. I'd planned on trying out a cat eye look, Scarlett and I had been practicing the last time we hung out, but I was still perfecting the steady hand it took and knew I'd end up with raccoon eyes if I attempted it in such a short time period.

Troy McConnell was perfectly punctual, knocking on the door at 6:15 p.m. just like he said he would when he called to set up the date. Opening the door, I was surprised to see he was cuter than I thought he'd be. I realized I'd expected an ogre. His strawberry blond hair was cut into a perfectly gelled crew cut. He was a good seven inches taller than me—a good height, but not too tall. Xander was too tall. It was impossible standing next to a guy who was a whole foot taller than you. His dark purple button-down shirt with a black tie set off his green eyes nicely. He was handsome, and I was surprised at how relieved I felt about that.

"Hi, Ana? I have the right place, right?" he asked.

"If you're Troy, then yes, if not..." I trailed off, not knowing how to finish my joke. He laughed anyway, even though I hadn't really been all that funny.

He held out his arm to me. "Shall we?"

We enjoyed a nice dinner at Burrata Bistro, splitting a bottle of wine that he picked out. Over osso buco and olive bread, I felt myself relaxing more and more. I found him to be charming and kind. He certainly was everything Scarlett said he was. Handsome in a clean-cut, proper way, reminding me a bit of my brother. He was pleasant and gentlemanly, pulling out my chair for me and holding the door open. Though I balked, he insisted he pay for dinner, telling me, "I'll let you buy me dinner next time."

He drove me back to my apartment and insisted on walking me to my door and opening the door for me. Standing on the doormat, Troy tucked a strand of hair behind my ear.

"I'm really glad Emma told me to call you."

I nodded at him. "Me too."

He smiled, flashing me a straight white smile that only came from years of expensive orthodontia. "Could I call you? We could try out that new tapas bar. I've heard good things about it."

"I'd like that."

He bent down, pausing an inch from my lips, trying to gauge my reaction. I leaned forward and he pressed a soft kiss to my lips. It was a tender, perfectly pleasant feeling. But I couldn't help but compare the feeling to the last man who kissed me.

He pulled away, a goofy smile on his handsome face. As he withdrew his hand from the respectful spot on my upper arm, he pressed one more delicate kiss to my lips.

"I'll call you soon, okay?"

I let myself into the apartment, locking the door behind me. The apartment was empty as I made my way down the hall. I wondered where Xander was. He'd been seeing more and more of that Sherie girl. I tried not to think about what they might be up to.

I changed into my pajamas, washing the makeup off my face. My reflection looked about twelve years old compared to how I looked dolled up. Would Troy be shocked to see me without makeup? I had a feeling I'd see him again. He met all the criteria. He listened intently as I told him about the basics of my job. He asked the right questions, joked about whether the Huskies would make it to the Apple Cup this year. I knew my parents would like him. He was handsome, successful, and came from a nice family. He wasn't the type who'd beat up my classmates in a parking lot or get caught kissing another girl at a house party. He had the same job since he graduated college, a nice condo in Illahee with a partial view of the water. He drove a newer sedan. Thinking about Troy was like checking off little boxes in my mind.

Heading to the living room, I was surprised to find Xander on the couch. He must have come in when I was getting changed and I didn't hear him. His arm draped across the back of the couch and a nonchalant look on his face.

"So how was the blind date?"

"Good." There was a tick in his jaw as I spoke. "Did I tell you I was going on a blind date?"

"Scarlett told me. She brought me a coffee when I was working on the courtyard at the Winslow Pavilion."

"Oh," I said stupidly. I wasn't sure why I hadn't told Xander. I had ample time to mention it. "I guess that makes sense." I wasn't sure why I didn't want Xander to know about my date. Why I scheduled it for a night when I knew he'd be out.

He leaned against the counter and studied me. "So, it was good?"

"Yeah. It was fine. He's a perfectly nice guy. He has a good job and was respectful of me." I opened the fridge, grabbing a bag of baby carrots.

He leaned forward, taking a carrot out of the bag in my hand. "Is that what you want? Someone to be respectful? That's your type?"

Setting the bag down, I turned to get a bowl from the cabinet. "I have no idea what my type."

"So, you never thought about it?"

"I never thought I'd be single. Not again. Even when Max and I broke up, it was so short that I didn't have time to think about what I should look for in a guy."

"You haven't thought about it at all?"

I dumped the bag of carrots in a bowl and set them in the middle of the counter between us.

"I don't know. Not in a real concrete way. I mean, I've thought about guys, you know. First kisses and dates and stuff. But nothing real. Nothing like tonight."

"Did he kiss you?" Xander asked, his face blank as he waited for my answer.

I hesitated, my stomach churning. I looked away from him. "You don't really want to know what happened on my date."

"You're right. I don't want to know about another guy kissing you. But I need to know."

"Why?" I asked.

"So, I can know how serious you are about this guy," he explained.

"It's only been one date. I don't even know how I feel."

"But you're going out with him again," he finished.

I nodded at Xander. "Maybe."

"Do you see this going somewhere?"

I pushed my bangs out of my face, huffing loudly. "I don't know. He seems like he could have some potential. We need to see, I guess." I narrowed my eyes. "Why does it matter who I see? Aren't you seeing that one girl?"

He considered me, a grimace on his face. "It doesn't, I guess. I wanted to know."

"Well, now you know." I smoothed out the bag that the carrots came in, running my hand over it three times before folding it into a small square. Then I unfolded it and repeated the action. Again, and once more, before placing the folded plastic square into the recycling bin.

"Are you sure you're ready to date?" he asked me. I avoided his eyes. His question was a valid one. I wasn't sure, but I knew the acceptable time of mourning was over for me. Whether I was ready or not, I was getting pressure to move on with my life.

"Not really. But I think I have to," I confessed.

Xander stepped closer to me, his hand coming down to rest on the counter between us. "Sweet, you don't have to do anything you don't want to. Just because your mom, or Scarlett, or whoever thinks you should, doesn't mean..."

"No, I need to. Am I scared? Sure. But does that mean I shouldn't try to move on?"

If I was going to start dating again, someone like Troy seemed like a good start. He was the opposite of Max in every way. He wasn't especially suave; he was cute where Max was striking. He was college educated, respectable middle-class upbringing, a steady job. He was nice, sweet even. I knew the moment I met him my parents would approve. While I'd never tell Xander, I knew from our kiss that he could never break me the way Max did. I was at no risk of being hurt that way. Because I was at no risk of falling in love.

"Maybe being with a guy like Troy will help me move on." I met his eyes, shrugging my shoulders. "It can't hurt anything."

I stared at him as he stepped closer to me, his arm grazing mine. His foot between mine. He was so close I could smell the dirt on his shirt, see the few blades of grass that stuck to his collar. "I don't like it, Ana. I don't like the idea of you seeing some stranger."

"He's not a stranger. He's friends with Emma. Scarlett would never let me go out with some crazy random." My breath came out husky. I wanted to back up. I wanted to get away from Xander, but I also wanted to get closer. My eyes flickered to his lips. I took a shaky breath. "Anyway, why do you care so much? I don't get it. Did I give you a hard time about that loony girl who stole your drink? Aren't you seeing her?" I asked. A pit formed in my stomach. I didn't like the idea of him dating a girl I hadn't met.

With those words, the trance broke. He blinked at me quickly, stepping back. His hands shoved into his pockets, he rocked back on his heels. "Ugh, yeah, kind of. I guess I am."

"See, and that story is way crazier than mine. At least Troy has people to vouch for him. That girl took your drink, and you end up with her phone number."

He ran a hand through his hair, scratching his head. Silently, he looked away from me. When he said nothing, I turned back to the counter to rearrange the spices that lined the window. I could hear Xander turn away from me, his footsteps moving out of the kitchen. He stopped in the doorway and slapped his hand against the door frame.

I whirled around to face him. His jaw tight, he looked at me. "Why do I think I'm still going out with Sherie? Dammit, Ana, just..." He squinted his eyes tighter, pinching the space between his eyebrows. "Is this really what you want? This guy?"

I nodded at him. "It's only been one date, but yeah, Troy seems really nice."

"So, he's the guy you want?" he asked.

"For now, yeah. I think he is." I replied, cocking my head to the side. "I don't know what's going to happen, but he seems as good as any."

Xander closed his eyes, clenching his teeth. "Better than me?"

"What?" I asked.

"So, you'll kiss this guy and it's fine, but not me? I tell you that I love you and I hear crickets. Are we never going to talk about what happened?"

I wasn't ready. To acknowledge the kiss between us was to open up all the mixed emotions I had swirling inside me. Troy was safe. He was new and came with no guilt, no betrayals, just a clean slate.

Xander shook his head at me. "Just be careful, okay?"

"Okay," I whispered.

He turned to walk out of the kitchen, smacking the door frame one more time.

# Chapter Thirteen

*"I'll never kiss another." -Ana age twenty-four.*

I WAS THOROUGHLY EXHAUSTED after working my third twelve-hour shift in a row. Setting my purse down, I could hear Xander talking to someone.

A girly giggle breaking through the silence of the apartment. I was shocked Xander was talking to a girl. As I listened to them, I stilled, their voices too low to make out what they were saying, but there was a soft familiarity between them. I rolled my shoulders, trying to work out a tension that had suddenly formed as I pulled off my coat.

I rounded the corner until I was in the kitchen. Across the island counter, I had a better view of Xander and the girl sitting on the couch.

I had to assume this was the girl he met at Starbucks. I tried to remember her name but couldn't place it. She had curly brown hair half up in a big metal barrette.

I watched them as they talked, a malevolence rising in me. The last thing I wanted to see when I got home was Xander and this woman sitting on the couch together. He said something to her I couldn't catch, and she laughed. It was an annoying, aggravating sound. I pulled a glass from the cabinet, letting it slam loudly to signal that they weren't alone. She looked over her shoulder at me, a surprise passing over her face.

Xander didn't look the least bit ruffled by me showing up. His arm slung over the back of the couch, not quite over her shoulder but above her. The stark familiarity unnerved me.

"Hey, Ana-Sweet. You're home."

I filled up my glass of water, taking a big drink, my eyes on the girl. I took my time, setting the glass down before finally looking at Xander. "Yeah, long shift today."

The girl stood up, walking over to me. "I'm Sherie. You must be the roommate Alexander has told me so much about."

"I am the one and only," I replied. She stuck her hand out and it took me a moment to realize she wanted to shake mine. I brought my hand up and she took it, clasping her other hand over mine, enclosing it in hers. It wasn't a handshake—it was like an overly familiar hand-holding session. I struggled to smile at her.

She stepped back, motioning to the living room. "Sit, I want to get to know you too." She sat back down on the couch next to Xander, leaving only Xander's ugly rocking chair for me to sit in. Over the course of five minutes, I felt like an intruder in my apartment.

"So, you're the Starbucks girl?" I asked. "The one who took Xander's drink?"

"Ana!" Xander shot me a warning look.

Sherie didn't seem to catch my tone because she giggled. "Oh yeah, quite the meet-cute, huh? I was distracted and grabbed it off the counter, took a big drink and nearly spit it out on the floor."

"I assume his quad shot mocha wasn't what you like?" I wanted her to know that I knew his drink order.

"No way. Do you have any idea how much sugar is in chocolate syrup? So much." She pulled out the word "so," dramatically long for emphasis. "That's why people are so fat, you know. Sugar, it's the new drug of choice. That's what people should be worried about. It's going to kill our generation."

Chuckling more to myself than anything, her clueless comment bit deep. "I don't know, Sherie. I'm pretty sure actual drugs are a bigger problem."

"It's Shur-Ree," she corrected. I gave her my flattest look, my annoyance still simmering. "You called me Sherry, like the drink, but it's pronounced Shur-Ree."

"Right."

Sherie somehow snuggled closer to Xander. If she wanted to get closer, she'd have to sit in his lap. "So, do you have a boyfriend?" Sherie asked cheerfully.

"No. I don't," I answered, my tone all ice.

"You don't date? Alex said that you were dating some guy the last time we went out. He talked about it a lot, actually."

It had been a few weeks since I went out with Troy. He never called for a second date, and I was relieved to not have to decline.

"No. I'm not seeing anyone."

When I didn't elaborate, she changed the subject. "So, Alex said you guys grew up together?" Sherie asked me, her voice too cheery.

I cocked my head to the side as I considered Sherie, before shooting a glance at Xander. "Yes, *Alex*ander and I did."

Xander dropped his arm down from the back of the couch, placing it in his lap. He shot me a cautionary look. "Okay. Well now that you guys are acquainted, should we start dinner?"

She looked from me to Xander her face brightening. "Sure, that sounds great. Let me freshen up for a moment. Bathroom is where, again?"

Before Xander could respond, I told her, "Head into the hallway, first door to the left."

She gave me a strained smile. It felt good to reassert power over my place. This was *my* apartment. I wasn't going to have her come in like it belonged to her and Xander together.

Once we heard the door close, Xander leaned forward, his hands forming a steeple in front of him. "There should be enough for you, too. I figured you'd be hungry after work tonight."

I tried not to let the kind gesture get to me. It didn't matter if I had no right to be annoyed, I was going to relish in it. "I need to shower, and I don't want to ruin your date by third wheeling it."

"Of course. If you want any food, you know where to find it."

Getting up, I made my way to the hall before turning around. "You didn't make chicken parmesan again, did you? Because I was lying the last time I had it." I wrinkled my nose at him. "It is not up to "impress your date" caliber yet."

"You said it was good!" he said, panic crossing his face.

"I said it was better. It was just okay, to be honest."

"Well, I don't know how to make anything else."

"Serve the spaghetti. No harm in that, impossible to mess up. It'll be fine."

He nodded his head several times as if he was trying to psych himself up. "Right, okay, it will be fine."

"She obviously likes you. I'm sure you could serve her your soggy chicken parmesan and she'd still go out with you again."

He smiled, "You think?"

My chest felt too tight as I tried to force a smile. "Totally." I got up, making my way toward the hallway. As I passed the couch where he was sitting, he grabbed my arm.

"Hey, speaking of fine. Is this, okay? Bringing a date back here? I know before in the duplex you didn't really care, but things are a little different now that..."

"Yeah, of course, Xan. Totally cool. Nothing's changed." My voice went up too high at the end, betraying me.

"Are you sure? Because we haven't talked about it yet."

He was right. We've never had this conversation before. Now, with the prospect currently using my expensive lemon coriander hand soap, I felt a little sick.

Looking down at his hand on my wrist. I wanted to rip my arm away, and I wanted to sink down next to him and take his hands in mine. Meeting his eyes, we stood there, his fingers below my wrist as if he were taking my radial pulse. He squeezed slightly and I stepped closer to him, not breaking eye contact.

"I need to know this is okay, Ana." He whispered, so softly I had to watch his lips move. I thought of how I had traced those lips while he slept next to him that first night in the apartment. And then I thought about our kiss that I said was nothing. What right did I have to tell him not to date?

"Tell me it's not okay, Ana," he pleaded. I turned my hand until our palms met, the callouses on his fingers rasping against the back of my hand. "Tell me and I'll stop."

"Xander..." I started.

The slam of the bathroom door broke us apart. I stepped back several paces until I was a safe distance away. Sherie came back into the room, her lipstick refreshed and her hair now down around her face. Stepping around her, I made my way quickly to my room. "I don't want to impose on your date. I should probably take a shower, anyway, wash the stink of sick off my skin."

As I turned to walk away, I saw Sherie wrinkle her nose in disgust. As I closed the door to my bedroom, I heard her laugh and then Xander laughed. I thought it sounded strained, but I wasn't sure if that was wishful thinking.

In the shower, I replayed what happened on the couch, trying to piece together exactly what this feeling was coursing through me and what I'd been about to say to him.

I stayed in my room for several hours, attempting to read the latest thriller Scarlett had given me for my birthday, while listening for any unusual noises. After a chunk of time passed, my hunger pangs got the better of me wanting to avoid them.

I cracked my bedroom door to watch as Xander walked Sherie out. He opened the door for her, and she paused in the doorway, turning to him. He put his hand on the top of the frame as he looked down at her. She hugged the strap of her handbag to her side.

I could barely make out their conversation. I knew I shouldn't eavesdrop, but I couldn't help myself.

"I had a good time tonight, Alex."

I rolled my eyes at the nickname.

"Me too. Thanks for coming over."

She smiled up at him, her hand coming up to rest on his arm. "We should do it again sometime." She leaned forward, lowering her voice. "Maybe just the two of us, next time."

He dropped his hand down, covering her hand. I looked away. I didn't want to see him responding to her touches like that. "That sounds nice. Let me walk you to your car."

When she agreed, he put his hand on the small of her back. A heat flared in my chest from watching his hand touch her. Even though I was sure I'd been quiet, he glanced back at me as he walked out the door. For a moment, we held each other's gaze, my face flaming under his attention. I looked away, abashed. I didn't like this sick feeling in my stomach as I watched them walk away.

The entire five minutes they were out in front of the apartment, I sat at the table imagining what they were doing in the parking lot. Was he kissing her goodnight? Were they making plans to go out again together? Was he asking her to come back later when I wouldn't be home to interrupt them again? I pictured him leaning down and brushing the brown hair from her face, his hand resting on her shoulder. His head dipping lower as he lowered his lips to hers for a kiss.

Running a hand over my face, I tried to wipe away the images. From the living room window, I could see she still hadn't gotten in her car yet. Gathering up the plates from the table, I stacked them on top of each other to bring them to the sink. I turned on the water and poured in some dish soap. As I washed, I listened for the sound of her car.

A minute later, I felt Xander standing behind me, a dishcloth in hand.

"You don't have to do the dishes. I made the mess. I'll clean it up."

"I don't mind."

We washed the dishes together, quietly handing over the plates and cutlery to be dried.

"Are you going to see her again?" I dared to ask.

"I don't know, probably." I frowned into the sink, my skin feeling too tight suddenly. "Why? What's that face for?"

"She doesn't seem like your type is all."

"My type? I didn't know I had a type, Ana."

"She's a little, I don't know." I wave my hand in the air, trying to pull the least disparaging word out of thin air.

"What? Nice, pretty, well-employed, single?"

I groaned at him. "Silly. She seems silly. She is the type of girl who'll always be just that, a girl."

He raised an eyebrow at me. "And? I'm not into boys, *Liliana*."

I rolled my eyes at him before turning back to the dishes. "I know that *Alexander*."

"Then I don't know what your issue is with Sherie."

"Sherie," I snorted derisively. "What kind of name is that? *It's Shur-Ree, not Sherry,*" I mimicked.

"That's her name."

"Whatever." I pulled the plate out of the soapy water, scrubbing it with the sponge, dipped it in the water to rinse, pulled it up to scrub, and dipped it, repeat, repeat, before handing it to him.

"You know I don't need you to approve of who I date, Ana."

"I know that." A pit formed in my stomach, and I scrubbed the plate harder. The pain of the scrubbing pad rubbing my skin raw centered me. "That doesn't mean I can't be honest with you. I don't see it lasting with her. You would get annoyed with her way too quickly. She'd drive you crazy three dates in."

"You never know. She could be the great love of my life." His voice hardened as he spoke. I snorted at him, rolling my eyes.

He slammed a plate on the counter, the sound echoing in our small kitchen. I startled, my hand going to my chest. "Goddammit, Ana. You don't get to do this to me. You can't have me here for you all the time. We can't keep going out the way we do, spending all our time together, eating all our meals together, shopping together. You can't keep falling asleep in my bed anymore. You can't kiss me back and then act like nothing happened. It's not healthy. It's not right. Not unless..."

I stared at the murky water in front of me. The grease from the marinara sauce formed a film, casting a pinkish hue to the soap bubbles. Slowly, I popped a bubble with my finger. I hoped Xander would go on.

The silence in the kitchen felt crushing. I turned my head slightly to glance at him, fighting to keep my face straight. "Unless..."

His arms were tight across his chest, and he glowered at me. "Don't you dare, Ana."

Slowly, I turned to look at him. "Don't what?" I asked.

"You don't get to have it both ways, Ana. You can't keep me all to yourself. I have needs. I get lonely too."

"And you think I'm not lonely?" I laughed darkly.

He frowned at me. "I know you're lonely. I see how unhappy you are. Better than anyone, I know. Don't you realize that, Ana?"

I opened my mouth, wanting to tell him it wasn't like that, but I couldn't spare a lie.

"But I can't be the person to fill that loneliness you have. It's not fair to me. I deserve better than that. Now, if I want to spend some time with a pretty girl who, yes, might be a little silly, I should be able to. I'm not your boyfriend, Ana."

The truth sliced through me. I fought the urge to snort at him. "I know you're not my boyfriend, Xander. But you *are* my best friend."

He softened his glare. "You are too."

"So, I don't understand why…"

He stopped me, his eyebrows pulling together. "Yes, you do. I know you do. Don't act like we haven't talked about this. Like I haven't made myself perfectly clear."

"What are you saying, Xander? Tell me what you're saying," I asked softly.

"You know what I'm saying," he replied. "You know, it wasn't supposed to be this way, okay? I don't want to feel this way. I don't want to want you the way I do. Do you have any idea how much easier my life would be if you weren't in it? How much happier I could be? Of course not!" he spat.

I stood back, shocked. My mind whirled with his words. They stung across my chest, breaking me apart. Was that really how he felt? The night we kissed wasn't a fluke. I knew, I always knew it. How could I pretend otherwise? "Xander… I…"

"I know what you're going to say, Ana. And I got to tell you… I can't hear it. Not tonight. I can't stand here and be rejected by you again." He scrubbed his face with his hand. "I'm tired, and I can't keep having this conversation with you."

Before I could respond, he turned away and walked to the living room. I heard him sit on the couch and switch the TV on. Placing both hands on each side of the sink to hold myself up, I stared straight ahead, trying to garner the strength to step forward.

# Chapter Fourteen

S TANDING IN THE KITCHEN, I could hear Xander watching TV in the other room, a random show about woodsmen or fishermen or something that I would complain about typically, but if Xander got up, I would continue watching for a few episodes. I closed my eyes, thinking of how angry he seemed to be when confronting me.

I kept pushing him, trying to get the truth out of him. Not just his own truth, but mine as well. I expected him to show me how to feel, like Max did. I never had to doubt my feelings for Max. That was one thing I could count on. But with Xander? I felt so mixed up inside. I wanted to go to him. But I also wanted to walk out the door and run away from this whole place, with all its gnarled complications. All these goddamn emotions.

How long had I felt this way? How long did I linger too long on the image of Xander's smile? I couldn't fight against the way my heartbeat pulsed in my ears when he came into the room. How many times did I reach for him and hold onto his hand longer than what was appropriate? I felt my resolve unraveling before me. I knew. Of course, I knew.

Before I could talk myself out of it, I walked into the living room. Xander sat in the middle of the couch, pointedly ignoring me. Striding in front of him, he continued to look away from me as if I wasn't there. I sank down on my knees, crouched between his legs. Grabbing the remote from his hand, I muted the volume. Placing my hands on each side of his legs, I looked at him.

"Xan. I don't know what to do right now." I whispered. He sighed heavily, opening his mouth to speak. I shook my head at him. "Please, don't."

I closed my eyes, lowering my head and tapped my fingers on the couch next to him. "You are my best friend. Most days, you're the only thing I can rely on in this entire world. If I lost what we have... I've already lost so much, Xander. I can't lose you too."

"I'm not going anywhere, Ana," he whispered. He placed his hands over mine, stilling my fingers.

"I feel like..." I struggled with the words. "What if we screw this up?"

"We won't."

My eyes filled with tears. I looked away from Xander. "You can't know that."

"I do. Of course, I know that." He reached up and cupped my cheek in his hand. I turned my face into his palm. He wiped a tear off my cheek with the pad of his thumb. "I can feel it. Can't you feel this? Can't you feel..."

Placing my hand over the top of his. "I feel it, Xander. I do. But I don't know if it's enough..."

"It is enough. Trust me."

A warmth swelled over me as I laid my head on Xander's knee. He raised his hand to run his fingers through my hair. "Oh, Xander, what are we going to do?"

With his hand in my hair, I closed my eyes, trying to stop the tears. I thought of how. when I was a child, my mother put me in piano lessons, which I spent a few months failing at. She put me in softball, and that was a bust. I went through cheerleading, guitar lessons, ballet, swim team, soccer, sculpting, jazz dance. All to equally disastrous results. The only thing in life I could excel at was mediocrity. Complacency has always been a strong suit of mine. Why work hard? Why toil and burn at something that would never merit a single return?

Max was the one and only thing I could ever say I gave my all to. My relationship with Max was a singular focus for most of my life. I foolishly thought that it would be for all my life. I'd hoped maybe I could refocus my energy on being a mother someday—to mine and Max's children. But everything I wanted to achieve in life was not meant to be.

With my head on Xander's leg, I felt his hand on my hair, his calloused fingers catching against my scalp in a gritty way that stirred in my chest. I wanted so badly to believe in the way I was feeling. To fall into Xander's arms, to kiss him the way I wanted to. I wanted to lift my face to his, press my lips against his lips, and feel his hand on my waist, pulling me closer. I wanted him to push me down on the floor and press the weight of his body into me. I wanted to feel the score of his beard across my cheek as he kissed my neck. I wanted *him*.

But if the last year after Max has taught me anything, it's that I was a fool when it came to matters of the heart. I let my adoration blind me once and I can't let it happen again.

Xander was silent as the weight of what was passing between us settled. "What do you want to do?" he whispered.

The tears welled up again, surprising me. "I don't know."

"If you want me, I'm yours. You know that, Ana. Say the word." His hand stilled in my hair, gently brushing through the snarls.

I pulled myself up, my hands still on each side of his legs. I studied his face. It was such an honest face with his wide smile, his upper lip was a little too full to be symmetrical with the lower lip, his hazel eyes flared with little gold flecks. His blond eyebrows, his light-colored stubble. Xan's face had character. The scar on his chin, the raised keloid I'd brushed my finger against so long ago. Was that when this began? When did I start feeling this way?

I was still between his knees. It felt a little pornographic. I thought for a moment that if someone walked in at that moment, they'd get the wrong idea of what was going on.

I wasn't sure how I wanted to feel. I wasn't sure how to proceed with this.

"Xander," I whispered. "I don't…"

I shook my head, not trying to wipe off the tears coming now.

"Please, Ana, tell me. What are you saying?" He leaned forward, placing a hand on my cheek. "Tell me what to do."

"I wish I knew," I said, my voice low. He cradled my cheek in his hand so gently. Such a tender sensation made me despondent. His soft touch against my skin, his silky words, this realization that I'd developed feeling for him all overwhelmed me. Knowing that, with a single word, Xander would be with me was too frightening an idea.

I stood up. I needed distance from him. His warmth, his touch—it was too much for me. I shook my head. "I should go to bed."

He grabbed my hand, my palm fitting so perfectly in his grasp. His calloused fingers delicate against the back of my hand. "No, Ana. You can't go to bed, not after what's happened."

I shook off his hand, the absence of his touch burning. "I have to. I don't know what this is, I don't know what is happening here, but I have to go to bed before I do something I regret."

"You won't," He promised.

"Don't say that. You can't know that. I don't want to regret you. I don't want to regret anything about you Xander." I struggled to keep my voice level. "So please, let me go. Let me think on this."

His hands dropped between his legs as he leaned forward, letting my words sink in. I turned to leave, my hand on the wall steadying me. I didn't trust my footing. Behind me he called out. "Just tell me, here and now. Am I wasting my time waiting for you?"

Facing away from him I froze, trying to figure out the best way to answer his question. I didn't want to lead him on, but I couldn't tell him to forget about me. I didn't want him to leave me. I didn't want him to be with another woman. But I didn't want to say that what we were feeling was normal, that it was okay. I shook my head. "I don't think so."

I was almost to my door when I heard Xander walk down the hall. I could feel him behind me.

"Ana," his voice was a whisper.

I thought about staying faced away, as if we were some soap opera. I always thought scenes like that were ridiculous. Why would people talk away from each other? But in that moment, I understood why. I couldn't turn around and face Xander. I couldn't face the choice I'd be making if I turned to him. My hand would surely come up around his neck and pull his face down to mine, then his hands would grab my hips and bring me into him. My bedroom door would open, and we'd stumble through, our lips still locked together. Then he'd fall on top of me, and we'd come together.

I felt his hand on my shoulder. His forefinger rested on the side of my throat, and I stilled under his touch. "Ana, wait."

I wasn't sure if I wanted him to stop or keep going. I didn't know what I wanted anymore. Slowly his finger brushed against the hollow of my throat, and I let out a small gasp, my body warming under his touch. He didn't try to turn me around, letting me stay facing away as he bent down. I felt his breath against my hairline; a shiver of anticipation coursed through me. My traitor body reacted as he pressed his lips to the back of my neck. His hands dropped down from my shoulders and glided down my arm and to my hips, holding me steady. My insides felt like liquid, and I felt myself relaxing into his touch. Blood pounded in my head as I felt the long-forgotten tingle between my legs. His kiss against my neck deepened as he held me tighter, his fingers digging into the soft spot of my stomach. His hand covered my hip bones, his thumb rested above the top of my pants, pulling them down enough to touch the bare skin of my back. My head came forward, granting him more space to lean into me. I was a live wire under his embrace. I could feel his whole body behind me, strong and warm. He sucked the skin of my shoulder into his mouth, and I wavered on my feet from the sensation. His teeth dragged across the sensitive skin of my shoulder and shocks ran from my center down my body. Heat pooled between my legs, and I pressed my thighs together.

How easy it would be to move into him, to feel that mouth move from my shoulder to my mouth. To feel that tongue against my own. His strong hands held me steady as my hips moved back into him. I could feel the hard length of him pressing against my ass and I knew then exactly how well we'd fit together.

"I want." His words a breath on my shoulder.

I stiffened at the words. Want. Yes—I did want him. More than I allowed myself to admit. But what I wanted didn't matter. I couldn't allow myself to hurt him the way I had been hurt.

He must have felt the change in me because he pulled his lips away, his grip on my waist lessening. If I was going to turn, now would've been the time.

He waited me out as I considered what I wanted to do. Every physical part of me wanted to turn to him, wanted him to touch me more, to give him more. A rousing heat surged through me. In his taction I felt more alive than I'd felt in a long time.

But my mind stopped me. How could I turn to Xander? How could I respond to his embrace with my own when I didn't know what I wanted from him? When I didn't respond, frozen in my vacillations, he pulled away slightly. Against my neck I could feel his words, moving through me.

"I don't want to have regrets either, Ana. If I hadn't done that, If I hadn't made it clear just how much I want you, I knew I'd regret it." He stepped away, leaving me standing in front of my bedroom door. I listened as he got to his room and shut his door before letting out the breath I was holding.

My legs felt weak, my whole body was an inferno. I shook as I made my way across my room and into my bed. An unidentifiable feeling came over me. For so long, Xander had been such a big part of my life, that while I never took the time to consider it, he'd been there for me through everything.

I had no idea how I felt about him, about us. What were we, what did I want us to be? It wasn't as simple as this wantonness between us. It would've been so much simpler if it was. I wished I could have met a man I had no ties with—a man who could be a one-night stand.

The ease of meeting a stranger, having a few drinks. The liquid courage to let my inhibitions down. While I had my share of fantasies about sex, even when I'd be lying in bed, taking the matters into my own hands, the visions I had were no longer of a faceless man. They had taken a shape with blond curls, hazel eyes, and strong hands gripping me. The smile I had known for so long—I couldn't think of how long he'd been on my mind when I would reach my climax.

I wanted the way I was feeling to be because It'd been so long without the touch of a man. I wanted the pent-up lust to have no face or name.

Yes, I was reacting to his touch, but I had no way of knowing what the root of it was. I didn't want it to be Xander I was feeling this way about. Because he was Xander, he was my best friend, he was my partner in crime. I couldn't risk what we had for what could be just my lust. It wasn't fair to him. He deserved so much more than that.

I wasn't sure how I was able to finally pull the covers over me, or how I could close my eyes. But as I drifted off, the restless ache of lust continued to stir inside me. Something that I hadn't felt in years.

# Chapter Fifteen

Waking the day after Xander's date with Sherie, I wished I hadn't dreamt at all. I couldn't remember the specifics, but when I awoke it was with a deep longing in my chest, and a sense that I wanted to be near Xander. I wanted to wrap my arms around him and hold on tight. I laid there in bed, looking up at the ceiling and clutching the extra pillow to my side. Everything was supposed to feel better in the morning, but in the cold light of day I felt worse.

The stark realization of what had passed between me and Xander haunted me. We lived together, how could I blur the lines so readily when I knew I was taking a chance that could result in losing my home and my best friend in one fell swoop? While Xander seemed more than willing to push the boundaries of our relationship, I knew one of us needed to be practical.

After mulling my options over for a good chunk of time, I got up. I was no wiser on how to proceed with Xander or even what I wanted to say to him. The apartment was empty. I shouldn't have been surprised, he kept early hours for work. He was probably halfway through with his workday when I woke. I was relieved I had more alone time to figure out what exactly I was doing.

That night, Xander returned as I was getting ready for the night shift. I was packing up my snacks as he walked in the door. Our eyes met and he paused. I could see the doubt there. I had all day to think about it and I was no closer to figuring out what it was I wanted from him.

"You're leaving?" he asked, dumping his keys into the little bowl beside the door.

I nodded at him, trying to keep my gaze steady. "I've got to be there at six."

He glanced at the clock on the stove, not commenting that it wasn't even four yet.

He leaned against the refrigerator watching me as I mixed my yogurt with chia seeds. When I went to put the yogurt container back, he didn't move. He just looked down at me.

"How did you sleep last night?"

"Fine," I lied. When he didn't move out of the way, I yanked the handle harder until he jumped. I plunked the yogurt down and stuck my head into the fridge, looking around for something else I could use as a snack, the more complex the better, anything to distract me from Xander and his gaze.

He stepped back, now leaning against the stove, his arms crossed against his chest. "I slept horribly."

"Oh?" I said into the vegetable crisper drawer.

"Yeah, I did. And I think you did too."

I sighed heavily. I had hoped that Xander would let this go, at least give me a day's peace before he wanted to discuss it. I was obviously wrong.

Straightening up I leveled a stare at him. "I slept fine."

We stood there considering each other. His work shirt was filthy, covered with bark, grass, and dirt. He had a large yellow streak of something across his left shoulder. Dirt flecks clung to his day-old stubble. Still, he looked good. He looked like he'd worked hard all day. Like he was committed, responsible, and strong.

He was never classically as handsome as Max. Max was beautiful—something few men could pull off. Everything about Max was angles and contrast, with the blue eyes and the olive skin, the dark hair and the white teeth. Xander was never the guy who turned heads, not like Max was.

But I knew better than anyone that Max's beauty came at a cost to us all. When every door opens wide for your beautiful face, you never learn how to turn the key.

Xander was a different look altogether. He was naturally pale; in the summer his skin didn't tan so much as the freckles on his arms began to blend together. His face had a thicker, youthful look to it, despite how thin he was. But he'd grown into his lanky body, finally filling out in the shoulders and arms. His eyebrows were too blond, blending into his skin. His lax curls were too dark to be blond but too light to be brown. I glanced away, realizing I'd been appraising his looks.

"I can tell you're lying," he replied, picking an apple slice out of my sandwich baggy I set out.

"Hey," I snatched the bag from his hand. "That's my snack for work. Don't eat my food."

He put his hands up in surrender. "Sorry."

I zipped the bag up, indignant. "You know I don't have time to go out and get food when I'm at work."

He popped the rest of the apple slice in his mouth and chewed as he looked at me. "I know you aren't really snapping at me about an apple slice."

"Obviously, I am."

He stepped forward, cocking his head to the side. "Ana, come on."

"What? I really do need snacks. I can't have you eating the stuff I have to bring."

"You don't need…" he looked at the large bag I'd been packing sitting on the counter. "Five different items, in a single shift."

"Maybe I do," I retorted. His needling me was especially aggravating.

"If you're really that hungry, I can bring you food. Not that you're at risk of starving with this buffet you're bringing."

"I like options." I grabbed the bag off the counter next to him and turned to face the other counter, setting the bag down there. "Besides, I'd never ask you to bring me food. You have to go to sleep so you can get up early. I'm hungry at like two a.m."

"If you're that hungry I'll bring you food."

"I don't need you to."

"I know. But I'd still do it."

My hands shook as I set the yogurt next to the trail mix in my bag. Slowly I turned around to face him. His warm eyes were on me. My chest began to hurt, my heart was beating so hard in my chest as I stared at him. He took a step forward toward me.

"You know I'd do that right?" he asked softly. I nodded at him, too confused at how to react—I wanted to step away from him, I wanted to touch his hand, to pull him closer to me. He took my silence as encouragement, taking a small step forward toward me. "You should let me take care of you sometimes, Ana."

My heartbeat pounded in my ears; heat rushed through my body. Those words, so sweet, I wanted to believe them, but I knew better than to trust myself. "You do enough. You do more than enough for me Xander. I ask too much from you," I replied, trying to get us on even footing.

"You're wrong. I don't do enough."

"We're not talking about fruit anymore, are we?" I whispered, stupidly.

He shook his head. "You deserve so much more. You deserve to be put first."

I could sense where this was going, and I wasn't ready to hear it from Xander.

He stepped closer still, closing the space between us until I could feel his heat against me. "You know, Max never respected you. He always allowed you to come second to his wants. He never put you first."

"And I let him," I finished. "Don't make me a victim here, Xander."

"He never respected what you wanted and I..."

Suddenly I was angry. How was what Xander saying any different from what Max did to me? I needed time, I needed to figure out exactly how I felt before I let him swoop in. One of us had to be rational about this.

"You what? Is this you respecting what I want right now?" I shot back. "Maybe, right now, what I want is some goddamn space. I'm starting to feel like you're trying to do exactly what Max did. You're not letting me have a choice in this."

He stepped back as if the words stung. "Yes, I am. You are always going to be the one to decide how this goes. Whatever you want..."

"Maybe what I want is some peace. Can you handle that?"

"Of course..."

"Maybe what I want is to date another man, could you respect that?" I asked. I felt emboldened by my words.

"If I..." he trailed off, I could read the pain on his face. "If you needed that, then yes."

I gulped, as I studied his face. The heartache written all over it. "I'm not saying I'm going to date someone else right now, Xander."

"You're not?" he asked softly.

"No. But..." I stepped closer to him, putting my hand on his chest. "Look, whatever this is between us? I don't know what it is. But I can't risk you over my loneliness. I'm just now accepting that I'm going to have to put myself out there. For so long I thought Max was going to be the last man I'd ever kiss. I still need to get used to the idea that I'm going to meet someone new, that I'm going to kiss another man."

He was silent, allowing me to explain myself. "Does that make sense?"

"Yeah," he sighed. "I guess it does."

"I need time. I need to know that how I feel is real. That it's not unsatisfied urges and a lack of human touch. I need to know this is more than a physical need."

He placed a hand over mine, gripping my hand in his. "But you do feel something? Last night wasn't some fluke?" he asked, his voice quavering.

"No, there's something. I feel it too. I do."

"What do you feel?" he asked expectantly.

I smiled at him, "Do you need me to say that last night I was attracted to you? Is that what you want? Because I was. It took all I had not to turn around when you stopped me at my door." I thought about his mouth on the back of my neck, the way his hands felt against my skin. Tingles ran through my body.

"I feel like you and I have been dancing around this for a long time. There's been something between us, and I feel like I screwed it up that night we were drinking whiskey. So, when you came to me last night..." he trailed off.

"I'm scared, Xander. I'm really scared. There is a lot to consider here. And no matter how physically attracted to you I may be, you're still my friend. If this didn't work, what would that leave me with? I'm not ready to risk it yet."

"I will take whatever you want to give me. I'm okay with that now. If you don't want to be more than friends, I can handle that. I'll spend a long time getting over you, probably always consider you the one that got away, but I'll do it. For you, I'd do it."

I couldn't look at him, couldn't hear the declarations he was giving me. I glanced at the clock behind him. "I need to get to work. But we're okay, right?"

He nodded at me. Obviously torn at wanting to say more, but not wanting to scare me. "Yeah, we're okay."

I gathered my stuff together, throwing my jacket into the bag for later. I headed to the door, about to leave when I paused. I could feel his eyes on me as I stood there. I needed to give him more. He said he would be okay if we were just friends, but I knew we were past that point already. We had been for a while. I didn't realize it until I was knee-deep in it. We might try to trudge back into a platonic place, but I didn't want to. I couldn't be "just friends" with Xander, not anymore.

I dropped my bag at the door, turning back. His eyes lit up when I faced him. I took the three steps to get to him and he met me in the middle. I reached down between us to take his hand in mine. I brought it to my mouth, pressing a kiss to his palm. His callouses scraped against my lips in a way that churned deep within me, liquefying my insides. I breathed in the smell of sunshine and grass on his skin, savoring him. My eyes closed and I spoke into his hand. "I'm not going anywhere, I promise. I need you to wait for me, okay?"

Slowly I opened my eyes to meet his. He was staring down at me. I felt my whole body unfurl in his gaze. The ground shifted beneath me and all that was keeping me upright was his gaze upon me, his hand in mine. His other hand came up to tangle in my hair, pulling my head toward him. He leaned forward, his forehead resting against mine. Our breaths were ragged. I struggled to get a hold of myself. We stood like that for a minute until our breaths synced together and I could open my eyes. He was staring at me with such intensity I gasped. Pulling away slightly, he brought his lips up over my nose to rest on my forehead, where he pressed a kiss to my hairline. Squeezing the back of my neck slightly, his touch sent shivers down my spine.

"Do you remember our first kiss?" he asked me. I nodded against him, as I closed my eyes, remembering what I never told Max.

# Chapter Sixteen

I N THE SUMMER BEFORE seventh grade, I returned to Ridgewood a week early from the summer camp I'd been attending for the fourth year in a row. Summer camp made me miserable. I was impossible on water skis. My decoupage was a sloppy mess that only a mother could compliment and even then, was relegated to the upstairs bathroom where no one would see it. I had no interest in any sort of competitions, opting instead to read thick Fear Street books in the bunker while all the other girls were playing beach volleyball. The last time I tried the game, someone yelled at me for not blocking a shot and I got so frustrated I walked off mid-game, calling the girl a bitch.

Despite my best intentions of avoiding camp activities, my downfall came in the form of a trust activity where we led a blindfolded teammate around the campground. My partner was a rail-thin girl from Utah. She led me off a small embankment where I tripped and sprained my wrist. She told me later she thought I could see out of the bottom of the blindfold like she could and assumed I'd see the drop-off before I stepped.

I spent the first two days home wearing an ace bandage and my mom bringing me lemonade. My time away from Ridgewood had done nothing to ease my issues with meeting new people and making friends. I longed for the comfort of being around Scarlett and Xander, but most of all I'd missed Max.

I called Max a few times but each time he was out. With different girls each time, according to his mother. I hadn't realized how much it stung until I heard it myself. All that previous school year I watched as my classmates began to show signs of puberty and interest in the opposite sex.

From the moment I realized boys and girls were different, the idea of kissing a boy wasn't completely disgusting to me and I knew I wanted Max to be my first kiss. I saw the way girls looked at him—the flirtations, chasing him around the playground, kissing him and then running away. I stood back and watched it all. I watched as Tracey Penrose pinned him against the recess wall and pushed her lips against his before turning away, giggling. I caught sight of the women on Max's naked girl magazines that he hid under his bed—the puckered nipples and swollen breasts, the nipped waists, and long legs. All the things I could never be. While the other girls in class were allowed to wear short skirts, I was still in knee-length dresses with thick stockings. The other girls got to wear heeled jelly sandals while I had flat black Mary Janes. They got the chunky blonde highlights, straightened to a glossy shine. My mom still put my hair into two plaits each morning. Every day I felt as if I was getting farther and farther away from the other girls in my class.

Despite not hearing from Max since I'd returned, I made my way over to Queenie Hill Road once my mom begrudgingly gave me the go-ahead. I knocked a few times since the doorbell broke years before. After a few minutes and a loud crash inside followed by yelling, Dana answered the door. She looked me up and down, frowning.

"Liliana."

"Hi Ms. Franklin. Is Max here?" I asked, trying to keep my voice as polite as possible.

She pushed the screen door open further, stepping out onto the front porch. "No, sweetie, he's not. He might be at Xander's, might be with that tart, Hallie next door."

I glanced at the house next door. Max mentioned there was a girl who lived there, but I couldn't imagine why she'd want to hang out with Max. She was fifteen, a whole three years older.

"Okay, thank you" I turned to walk away before Dana coughed behind me.

"That boy has been a whole lot of trouble for me, you know that?" she asked.

I turned to face her, biting back a retort about her lackluster parenting in my throat. Max was always babysitting Eloise while Dana was out drinking. My years of lessons on manners stopped the words.

She kept going. "He keeps it up, he's going to end up like all these other stupid kids out here. A loser. Or worse, like his good-for-nothing father."

*You're one to talk about being a loser,* I thought.

After nodding at her I made my way across the street to Xander's house, hoping Max was there playing video games or something. Xander's dad didn't love having me in the house, but he didn't seem happy about anything, so I didn't take it personally.

I knocked on the door several times before giving up and heading to the other house. I could at least check and see if he was there. The peeling paint and cracked cement walkway were almost identical to Max's house. Just as I was about to knock on the edge of the ripped screen door a girl opened it, her eyes getting big as she looked at me. Her eyes were dark with thick, smudged eyeliner and she wore a ripped T-shirt that hung off her shoulder and was tied right below her boobs showing off her stomach. Her jean shorts were so short the pockets hung out of the bottom. Behind her was Max, a bottle of something in his hand.

"Can I help you?" she asked disdainfully.

"Uh," I stammered.

"Hey Ana! It's cool, Hallie. She's a friend."

Hallie eyed me cautiously, obviously not liking what she saw. When I left the house, my flower tee and white shorts felt so nice. Now, standing in front of Hallie with her cleavage and curvy hips, I felt like I was a preschooler. Hallie gave me a chin nod that I assumed was a greeting.

Max stepped around Hallie and onto the front porch. "Uh, so Hallie and I were going to go..."

"Don't tell her! God, Max, she'll probably tell her daddy."

"No, I won't," I interjected though I had no idea what they were going to do.

Hallie pushed past me, stomping down the driveway. Max looked from her to me and back to her. She paused at the end of the walkway, glaring back at us in that cool bitchy way I knew I'd never pull off no matter how old I got. "Are you coming or not?"

Max stepped down toward her, sparing a glance back at me. "Sorry, I got to get going. I'll see you at school, okay?"

I stood there stupidly standing on the front porch for a few minutes, watching them walk down the middle of the street. Slowly, I made my way down the walkway, stepping over the cracks and pits.

Once I got to the street, I considered my options. I could go home, where I'd have to avoid my mother who'd ask me about the visit. I could walk around town until I was feeling better and buy myself an ice cream at Dairy Queen. I could see if Scarlett was home from her cousin's wedding in Phoenix.

Instead, I sank down on the curb, buried my face in my hands and began to cry. I don't know how long I was sitting there crying before I heard the tinny chime of a bike riding toward me. I lifted my face to see Xander pulling up.

"Ana? What are you doing here?" he asked, hopping off his bike. He tried to kick out the kickstand several times but from the looks of it, the metal had rusted in the up position. He huffed loudly, dropping it to the mottled grass behind us.

I opened my mouth to speak, but all that escaped was a loud wail.

Xander sat down next to me, his knees folded up almost to his shoulders. "Whoa. You okay?"

*Obviously not.*

I wiped my face, nodding my head. "I'm fine," I sobbed.

He folded his hands in front of him, looking down at the sidewalk. "You sure? You don't really look..."

I took a shaky breath, willing myself to stop crying. "Yeah, I'm good. I came over to see Max but..."

Xander looked up the walkway between Hallie and Max's house and then down the street where Max and Hallie had disappeared into the woods. "Oh."

"I'm an idiot. I don't know why I'm crying about this." I sniffed, looking down at the ground. I kicked a small patch of grass that was growing through the cracks in the sidewalk, nudging the shallow roots until the patch was shredded under my sandal.

"About Max?" Xander asked. I nodded at him, moving a rock into the hole where the grass had been growing. "He steals some of his mom's liquor when she's not looking, that's why they're hanging out."

"Oh," I said stupidly.

Slowly Xander put his arm around my shoulder without moving his body closer to me. His hand rested awkwardly on my upper arm. "You like him, don't you?"

"Of course, I like him. We've been friends for a long time."

Of course, Xander was too perceptive. He always had been with me. "No. You like, *like* him. You want him to be your boyfriend."

I considered lying but, in the end, I couldn't do that. I nodded, somehow hearing the words made it ache that much more. "Not that it matters. He's never going to like someone like me."

Xander tightened his grip on me, pulling me closer to him. It felt good to be close to someone. I found myself leaning into him.

"He's a dumb guy."

"No, he's not. Max is—"

Xander pulled away to look down at me. "Trust me, Ana. I'm a guy. I'm a dumb guy. We're all dumb guys. And Max is the worst of us all."

I stared at the spot in the woods where they disappeared, willing him to come out, knowing that the longer they were back there, the farther he'd go with this older girl.

"Just once, I wanted him to look at me like that. To see me at all. It's like he still thinks I'm some little kid with ruffled socks."

Xander rubbed my arm softly and I tilted my head against his shoulder, closing my eyes. He cleared his throat but didn't speak at first. "He does see you like that. A lot of guys see you differently. You just don't realize."

I scoffed loudly, keeping my eyes closed. "Yeah, whatever. You're trying to make me feel better because Max is off doing, you know, *stuff*, with Hallie." I couldn't even say the words for what they were likely doing.

"No, I'm not," Xander asserted.

I pulled away, wiping the tears off my face. "Thanks for saying all that. But it's okay, you don't have to lie."

He kept his arm on me but let me straighten up. "I'm not lying. I don't think you're some little kid, Ana. I see you."

I stared up at his face. Over the summer he'd grown much taller. He used to be around the same height as Max but now he was shooting up, lanky and awkward. A small pimple marred his babyface cheek. He needed a haircut badly; his loose blond curls hung slack in his eyes.

"You see me?" I whisper. "What do you see?"

He didn't break eye contact with me. His eyes the same mix of colors as the water in Freedom Bay. He focused on me in a way that made my cheeks flame pink. "You're nice, and really super smart, and pretty..."

"You think I'm pretty?" A small smile crept across my face. "No one has ever told me I'm pretty before." Which was true. It was the first time I had heard a boy say that about me. I'd heard "cute" before, but always from adults. This was different. This was a boy—a boy my age. Pretty girls got kissed, pretty girls got boyfriends, pretty girls got dates to school dances.

He looked away, redness blooming across his face up to his ears. "Well, yeah, I mean... I guess I do."

Without thinking I leaned forward into Xander. I pressed my lips against his, my eyes screwed up tight. He felt warm against me, his lips tasting sweet like fruity gum. He lifted his hands and then they fell to his side as if he didn't know where to put them.

I pulled away, to study Xander. His eyes were still closed with a big smile stretched across his face.

"Sorry," I blurted. I jumped up, dusting off my butt. It was a mistake to kiss Xander. I had always envisioned my first kiss would be so romantic, that we'd be somewhere nice, maybe slow dancing together to a pop ballad. I'd be wearing a nice dress, and he'd say all these sweet words and after the kiss we'd be boyfriend and girlfriend. But most of all, I always pictured my first kiss to be with Max.

Xander furrowed his brow at me as I finished cleaning off the back of my shorts. "But..."

"I..." I looked down the road at where Max had gone earlier, guilt pounding in my chest. "I'll um... see you at school?"

He stared up at me as I shifted my weight from foot to foot. I wanted desperately to run off, but I needed Xander to reply first. I could see the hurt pass over his face. Xander never was good at keeping his emotions inside, at least not to me.

"Right," he said.

I bent down to grab my backpack off the curb, avoiding his eyes. "So, I'll see you in school, if not before, right?" I laughed again, my voice too high, all wrong.

Before Xander could say anything else I turned away, speed walking down the road and back to my house where I'd collapse on my bed and not get up until it was time for dinner that night.

I now realize that I should've known there was something more between Xander and I that day. My choice to lean forward to kiss him, the flutter in my stomach, the way I replayed that moment over and over in my mind. Even the way it was the first thing I thought about when Max and I finally kissed. Instead of thinking it was everything I'd been wanting, my first thought was to compare his kiss to Xander's.

I wondered what would have happened if I'd stayed behind that day. Would Xander have asked me to be his girlfriend? Would I have ended up with Xander in the end? What kind of heartbreak could I have avoided? What kind of happiness would I have sacrificed if only I had stayed?

There was no way of knowing, then. All I could see was Max. Xander was right, there never was room for another. He filled up my vision, blurring out the rest. But now I could think back on that one moment sitting on the curb of Queenie Road, my cheeks tight from tears and Xander's lips against mine. The thought that I never could explain away. The secret I never told Max.

*So, this is what a kiss is. Will anything ever feel as good as this, right now, right here?*

At the time, I didn't want it to be Xander.

I couldn't accept that I had control over what I did. That I could've chosen differently. It was so much easier to go along with what Max wanted. Max wanted me to want him, so I did. He wanted to be with me, so he had me. I allowed it to be as simple as that. Because the truth was so much more complicated.

Never did I imagine I'd have to face these truths. I'd felt something that day with Xander. Throughout our friendship there were fleeting moments where I'd catch him looking at me and instead of being bothered by it, I would smile to myself. So many things. The way I watched him too. That his hand on my wrist, his arm against mine, that his lips against the back of my neck and his body pressed against my back made me feel alive. That he gave and gave to me, and I wanted more. I wanted him too.

I couldn't explain away this pull I had toward him. Denying how I felt about Xander was making a liar out of me.

# Chapter Seventeen


*"I know exactly what I want." –Ana age twenty-four.*

Every night as I made my way down the hall to my room, I would pause in front of Xander's door, placing a hand on the flat surface. I'd picture what he would do if I opened the door and made the next move. I'd close my eyes and think of the sweet pressure of his hand on my hip, his lips against the back of my neck. I wanted him more each day. But I couldn't bring myself to take that irrevocable step toward him. So, I'd pull my hand off his door and make my way down the hall to my own room, alone for yet another night.

In the morning I'd wake to his noises in the apartment—the shower turning on, the coffee grinder going, the opening and closing of doors. Before I could fully process where my thoughts were taking me, I'd think of what these noises would sound like if I woke in Xander's bed instead of mine. What would he do? Would he kiss me on the head before leaving for work? Would he get dressed in the dark or turn on a light?

Xander wanted more from me than I was ready to give. Weeks went by and there were moments where we'd brush against each other in the hall, his hand gliding against mine. I'd be cooking and feel his eyes on me, burning into my skin. I used to have the sensation of him watching me before, when we were still in the duplex. Before that even, in high school. Then, when I would look over at him, Xander would look away so quickly I'd wonder if I imagined it. Now he'd hold his stare, unabashed by being caught. Every time I'd feel the same heat flowing through me, my heartbeat hammering in my chest.

While he hadn't tried to kiss me again, there was freedom between us that I wasn't sure I wanted. When I was in the kitchen, he'd touch my arm as he walked by. He'd grab my waist, squeezing me as he reached to get a glass from the cabinet. Before, when we would touch, one of us would pull away, the sensation being too much. Now we'd stay where we were, not moving past lingering touches, but not pulling away either.

We were sprawled across the floor in front of the TV, watching the end of some World War Two documentary. It was the first time in weeks we both had a free night. When the documentary ended, Xander handed me the remote, letting me pick the next show to watch.

As I flipped through the options, he cleared his throat. "Do you remember that time we were hanging out at Scarlett's house?" Xander asked, his arm resting against mine. I could feel his warm touch through the fabric of his thermal.

"Senior year. It was spring break." He paused, his eyes growing wistful.

It was during the brief time Max lived in Idaho, when he'd left me, and I wasn't sure I'd see him again.

"Yeah, I remember." I replied. The three of us watched an action movie in her basement. Scarlett stretched across the love seat, leaving Xander and I on each end of the couch. At some point in the movie, our feet rested against each other, but neither of us moved away.

"There was a moment..." he trailed off and I knew what he was talking about. Scarlett had fallen asleep halfway through the movie and when Xander got up to cover her, he grabbed a big blanket for us to share. I watched as he tucked the blanket around Scarlett tenderly.

I asked if he missed being with Scarlett and he laughed, saying that her dumping him was the easiest rejection he'd ever had. I asked him what the worst rejection he'd ever had was, and he got quiet. He sat next to me, his hand on my foot as he gazed at me. "I'm still waiting on that."

We sat in silence looking at each other, the cacophony of two actors battling it out in a kitchen, a low buzz in the background.

Neither of us moved toward the other, but there was a charge between us. Something drawing me closer to Xander. I don't know how long we stared at each other, neither of us getting closer than our seated positions, but a palpable longing hung between us. Xander was the first to look away, his eyes settling on the television. He didn't look back at me the rest of the night.

Looking at Xander all those years later, I couldn't help but think of that moment when he stared at me from the other end of the couch and how I thought, *if he tries to kiss me, I'd kiss him back.*

Xander cleared his throat. "I've thought about that day a lot."

I couldn't look at Xander. I didn't know what to say, or even how I felt about what he was telling me.

"No matter how much I wanted to kiss you, it wouldn't have made a difference. Max came back. He couldn't help himself with you."

"What does that mean?" I whispered.

Xander glanced over at me and back at the ceiling. "I told him, before prom. I told him that I was going to ask you out. I told him that if he really cared about what was good for you, he'd stay away. That he needed to allow you to move on."

I rolled over on my stomach to face him. "That wasn't your choice to make, Alexander."

"And it was yours?" he smirked at me, but it didn't feel cruel, more sad than anything. "Anyway, he didn't take my advice. It probably made him come back sooner to be honest. I think he could handle the idea of you dating some stupid collar-popping friend of your family. But me? No way."

My forearm lay next to his arm, our bare skin touching. I thought of moving away but I didn't, instead I leaned a little closer to him. "Isn't there a guy rule about that?"

"That has nothing to do with it. If the situation was reversed, he'd have swooped in as soon as I left town."

I wanted to tell Xander that he was wrong, but I knew it wasn't true. Max knew what he wanted. When he desired something, he went for it. It wasn't always a good thing. It made him a tragically impulsive partner. There were so many times I had to apologize after Max. But being around someone who had that level of confidence was intoxicating. He never doubted himself, he always acted as if he deserved everything that came to him, and then more. For someone who lived in a perpetual affliction of self-doubt, it was a heady sensation to be in his presence. I fed off his confidence to bring me up.

"No, it wasn't some morality issue. He couldn't stand the idea of you thinking of me that way. Because he knew." Xander turned his head to look at me for what felt like the first time in our conversation. "He knew that I'd be better for you, that I could make you happy. He knew that and it terrified him."

I shook my head at him, frowning. "That's an awful thing to say. Max loved me. You act like he didn't want you to win or something. Like I was the spoils of your war. I wanted to be with Max. I loved Max."

"Ana, I know you did. I'm not saying you didn't love him," he whispered.

"Then what are you saying?" I snapped, annoyed.

He rolled over on his side to face me, propping himself up with his arm. "I'm saying that I told him as much. I told him that I knew I could make you happier. That I cared about you. That if he really loved you, he'd let you find your way back to him. You know what he said to me?"

"What?" my voice low. I wasn't sure I wanted to hear it. I felt like all I had of Max these days were revelations and denouements of the man I thought I knew.

"That it didn't matter if you would be better with me. That you belonged with him. That you belonged *to* him, and he wasn't going to let me try. He said that if he wanted you, he could have you."

I thought about his words. They were identical to the ones he'd used the morning he showed up on my porch with a bouquet of lilies.

*You belong with me.*

*We belong to each other.*

*All I want is you.*

*I know you need me too.*

At the time those words sounded so romantic, so mighty in the face of the pain I'd faced in losing him. I wanted to believe in those words—that he came back for me, that he came back because he loved me and couldn't live without me. But once again, there was more to the story than I expected.

"Max never saw what he had. He never appreciated all the amazing gifts in his life. If I could've been as charismatic as Max, as funny, as confident—the things I could've done with my life. Then maybe I would've gotten the only thing I ever really wanted. Yeah, Max had a shitty childhood, but so did I. But at least he had you. You were the only good thing he thought he had. When are you going to see the truth, Ana? He was never going to let you be free of him. You know that, right?"

I pulled myself up until I was sitting back on my heels above him. "You don't get it. Back then, I didn't want to be free of him."

He lay prone next to me, staring at me straight on. "I know you didn't. I knew that. I'm not telling you that I expected you to choose me. I'm not an idiot, Ana. I'm telling you that you deserved better than Max. You deserved better, and he knew it. You need to think about that while you're dragging his ghost around with you everywhere you go."

"I am not dragging..." I blubbered, shocked. "You are being such an asshole right now. I hope you know you've ruined a perfectly pleasant night for me."

He tucked his hands under his head and looked back at the ceiling. "It's worth it. I don't care if you're mad at me, Sweet. I'm tired of lying to you. I'm tired of holding in Max's secrets. It's not worth it to me. Not when I know you aren't letting him go."

"This isn't a three-step process, Xander. This," I hit my hand against my chest. "How I'm feeling, this is grief. I don't know how I can let it go. You make these comments like they're going to help me get over it. But I don't know if they will. All they do is make me feel worse."

He propped himself up, leaning back on each elbow. "I don't want you to feel worse, Ana. I want you to understand the truth."

"You know, hearing these things, finding out about the girls, the drugs, the money issues. It's like I never really knew him. And do you know where that leaves me?"

Xander had the good instinct to stay quiet as I continued talking. "I lost Max—I lost the person I loved more than anything in the world. And then the farther away from his death becomes the more I find out about him, and every time I find out something new, it's like I'm losing him all over again. Because that means I never really knew him. Every time I learn something new, I have to reconstruct the man I lost, and I feel the ache of his dying all over again."

He looked stricken at my words. "That wasn't what I meant to do, Ana. I wanted you to understand the truth about him."

"You can't love a man you never really knew. That's the only conclusion I can come up with. So more than anything, that is what I'm grieving. The loss of the love of my life. The death of the man I never wanted to be free of."

"Do you *now*?" Xander whispered. "After all this time do you still love him?"

I set my jaw looking down at Xander, his face so open and honest. While I allowed myself to be blind to Max and his fallacies, I knew, that no matter how much Xander's words stung, he would never delude me. I owed him the same as much as I could offer. "I am always going to love the man I thought he was. I don't care how much it hurts to hear, it's the truth. I need you to know that the person I considered him to be, the one he let me see—I am always going to love that man."

"Even if it isn't the real Max?" he asked.

I shook my head as I clambered up onto my feet. "Have you considered, if I didn't know him, then you didn't either?"

He seemed unperturbed by the remark. "You're probably right. But I don't have my whole identity wrapped up in his deception. Like I told you, I refuse to keep his secrets anymore. Not when you deserve the truth."

"I can't believe how you're being right now. I'm going to bed."

Before I slammed my bedroom door, I heard Xander yell across the condo, "Still worth it."

# Chapter Eighteen

GOING TO THE MALL was never a pleasant experience for me. Without Scarlett as my buffer, I felt especially exposed. While I considered buying my mother's birthday gift online, I knew she appreciated the little touches that only came from setting foot into a store—taking the time to go through the wares, feel the fabrics, smell the candles—before deciding on a gift.

By the time I had my presents in hand: a set of blown glass earrings and her favorite scented hand cream, my nerves were shot. I decided to treat myself to an overpriced coffee. Waiting for my order to be called, I glanced around. So far, I'd avoided having to make awkward small talk with anyone making this overall, a successful shopping trip. As long as I could make it to my car unscathed.

"Venti americano for Cherry."

A woman brushed past me, huffing, "It's Shur-Ree."

Sherie grabbed her drink and turned toward the condiment bar which unfortunately was directly behind me. I considered taking off, but still had to get my drink and I was certain that leaving would cause more of a scene than staying put. Sherie saw me, a toothy grin breaking across her face.

"Ana? Right?"

I struggled to find words. I was never any good at making small talk with people, and talking to the woman Xander was potentially dating? No way. "Hi Sherie. How are you?"

"I am so good! I got a ton of shopping done. It's so nice to get away and shop, have a little me time, don't you agree?"

"Yeah, sure," I agreed halfheartedly, sending a perturbed glance across the counter at the barista. Why was my drink taking so long?

"You know I'm so glad I ran into you. I wanted to ask you something," she said, ripping the top off four Splendas at once and pouring them into her drink. Behind me they called out my drink. I grabbed it off the counter, heading to the bar to dump in some cinnamon and sugar. Sherie watched me as I fixed my coffee as quickly as I could.

She motioned to the pastel packets of sweeteners on the bar. "You really should consider a substitute to sugar. Like I said last time, it really is a drug epidemic. Big sugar is going to kill a whole generation if we aren't careful."

I set the sugar canister down to look her in the eyes, my words as carefully as I could muster. "I think actual drugs are a lot worse than a little sugar."

"Oh, no. You have no idea. I was just certified as a personal trainer and..."

I interrupted her. "I'm a nurse, and my boyfriend, Xander's best friend, died from a drug overdose a year and a half ago, so I'm telling you that real drugs—actual drugs—are a much bigger threat than sugar."

Sherie had the decency to look abashed.

"I'm sorry, I didn't know. Alex never said..."

"It's not really first date conversation, is it?" I put the lid on my coffee and turned to walk away. "I need to get going. I have to drop off something on Queenie Hill, so I should be…"

"For Alex?" she interrupted. I frowned at her as she surged on. "That's where his father lives right? He mentioned that. I can't imagine it, can you? Ugh. That place is such a dump. I hate even going over to that side of town after dark. Too many shady people."

"That's where he grew up, you know that right?" I asked, perturbed.

She scoffed, "But he doesn't live there anymore. You know what I mean. Alex said your father's a doctor."

Instead of responding, I stared her down. While that area had never been my favorite, and my mom didn't like me going there after dark when I was growing up, I felt a certain sense of fealty to defend the neighborhood that raised both Max and Xander.

"I really do need to go, Sherie. Good to see you." I lied. I turned to walk away but she caught up to me as I made my way out the double doors.

"I'm leaving too. I'll walk with you, I had something to ask you."

I sighed as it didn't look like this girl was going to take a hint. We walked to the parking lot, her chattering beside me all the way.

Later, after dropping off the new shirts I bought for Eloise, I found myself sitting back in my car, my hands shaking. My conversation with Sherie was bothering me more than I expected it to. Besides her snotty attitude about Queenie Hill, I was annoyed that she knew that Xander was from that area, that she would know something about Xander.

As I was about to turn my car on, I saw Xander come around his father's house, a stack of lumber under his arm and a hammer in the other hand. I remembered he said he needed to fix his dad's fence after the dog chewed a hole in the wood and kept running off. I watched him working, his long-sleeved shirt straining against his shoulders as he set the wood down on the ground. His faded yellow beanie pulled down over his head. The weather was too cold to be doing this kind of manual labor, but I knew that wouldn't stop Xander from helping.

I pictured Sherie stopping by, coming up and talking to him, touching his arm the way she did at our apartment. Flirting in that effervescent way of hers. I didn't want her there. I didn't want her anywhere near Xander. I didn't want her to know anything about him. She could be the nicest girl in the world, and I still wouldn't want her to know him. I had a sense of dominion over him, that I knew I had no business of feeling. He'd told me that earlier. I had no rights over him, who he dated or who he talked to.

Before I could stop myself, I climbed out of the car and crossed the street to stand next to him. I thought I saw a flicker of joy cross his face as I approached but it could have been wishful thinking.

"So, I ran into Sherie at the mall today," I said without preamble.

He set the hammer down and picked up a new nail from beside him. "Is that so?"

"Yeah, she asked about you."

He glanced at me, the nails in his teeth. "What did you say?" he asked, his words garbled.

"I said, you're doing fine." I paused, leaning down and picking up a nail he dropped in the grass. I tried to keep my voice flat. "She asked me if I thought you were going to call her again." He looked back at the fence, lining up the nail to hold the board. "I told her I didn't know."

He drove the hammer down, sinking the nail into the wood. He turned to face me, setting the hammer down on the bench next to him.

"Are you saying I should call her?"

"No, of course not," I blurted. "That's to say, if you really wanted to call her you should. I mean, like I said before, I don't think you two are right for each other."

He crossed his arms against his chest, appraising me. "If you don't want me to call her, I won't."

"It isn't up to me, Xan." I replied quickly, the words tumbling out of me before I could take them back.

He chuckled at me, scrubbing his hand across his face. "Fuck."

He picked up the hammer and another nail and turned back to the fence. I watched him work, trying to decipher what he could mean by that four-letter word. I wanted it to be up to me, but at the same time I didn't want to feel the weight of that. If I had to power to tell Xander I didn't want him seeing someone else, that meant we were moving on to something more, that we could be more than we had been. That meant a commitment to something I wasn't sure I trusted in myself.

In the minutes it took him to finish, my fingers and toes were tingling from the cold. He gathered all his stuff up and headed to the back shed. I silently followed him.

I stood back, watching as he put everything back in its correct place before locking the shed up with a heavy-duty padlock. He didn't invite me inside his father's house, but I followed him in anyway. When we were growing up, I hardly ever spent time at Xander's house. We ended up Max's most of the time because he was constantly having to watch Eloise while Dana was off doing other things. Xander's dad never outwardly complained about us spending time there, but he was a quiet man who had little tolerance for teenagers infiltrating his house. Walking in after being gone for so long I couldn't help but notice how little the place had changed. The chairs and couch were in the same place. The same round dining room table with its three mismatched chairs sat in the kitchen.

I walked over to the wall where Paul had taped up a newspaper article featuring Eberhardt Landscaping and Gardening a few years ago. "You should have this framed for him." I motioned to the picture.

Xander glanced at it. "You think? It's three dumb lines and a picture."

I glanced back at the picture. In the picture Xander and his father are the exact same height, their faces wearing the same look of annoyed compliance with the picture taking. "It's three years old and it's still up? He wants it kept."

Xander stepped closer to me, looking at the paper. "Maybe you're right."

I could feel him next to me. Without thinking I reached down and took his hand in mine, squeezing it. "It really is amazing what you've done for the company, Xander. In such a short time you guys went from barely able to pay a single bill to having an actual crew."

"We hired some new guy the other day too. Cocky kid, but he seems like he'll be a hard worker so who cares if he runs his mouth a little."

"It's because of you. I hope you know that." I assured him, tilted my head so he had to look at me.

He shook his head at me. "Nah."

I looked from him, dropping his hand, and walked over to the table sitting in a chair. "I wasn't very nice to Sherie today."

He raised an eyebrow but didn't remark as he opened the fridge and grabbed a soda out and cracked the top. He took a long drink before offering me the can.

I took it, studying the bargain brand label as I talked. "She has a knack for saying the wrong things. I know I shouldn't be bothered by her, but I can't help it. Something about her just..." I groaned shaking my head.

"She's harmless, Ana," Xander told me, sliding into the seat next to me. "She doesn't mean anything by it."

"I don't appreciate hearing her talk about you like she knows you." I cast my eyes down, the admission stinging.

Xander sat back, his arms crossing against his chest as he appraised me. "But she doesn't know me. We only went out a few times."

"It doesn't matter. Xan. She wants to know you. That's enough." I glanced at him for a moment before looking away, the strength of his stare too intense for me.

"She's not the one for me, Ana. I think we've already established that."

His words brought a tremor through me, sending a heat in my chest. Breathless, I leaned closer to him. "Then who is?"

He leaned closer to me, taking my cheek in his hand. "You know the answer to that."

"I need to hear it," I admitted.

He didn't say it, instead he leaned closer to me, his lips getting closer to me. He ran his thumb over my jawline, sending shivers down my spine.

"I want to kiss you so bad right now."

My breath hitched at the words, my eyes flickering to his lips. I wanted to tell him not to, I knew I should tell him to wait, but instead my traitor body leaned closer to him, my hand finding his free hand. Slowly, I nodded my head.

"Tell me to stop, Ana. Tell me to stop and I will." He stared into my eyes, allowing me the time to respond before slowly coming forward until he was so close, I could count the flecks of gold in his eyes. His eyes flickered down to my lips, and I closed my eyes as I leaned into him.

Xander dipped his head down, pressing his lips to mine. Unlike the time in our doorway, I didn't freeze. I ran my hands through his hair, pulling his face closer to mine. Not breaking away from our kiss, I rose slightly from my chair to climb on his lap. I straddled him, both of my hands in his hair, our lips fused together. He grasped at my waist, pulling me into him. Our bodies melded together as he kissed me. I could feel him all over me, his heat pulsing through me. I was on fire from his touch. His hands ran up my sides, his strong arms wrapped me closer and yet I wanted more. I pulled away and his kiss trailed across my jaw to my neck. I tipped my head back and a loud groan escaped my mouth. The sensation was intoxicating. He shifted under me, and I could feel all of him, strong and hard.

He moved his hand under my shirt, the difference in temperature a shock against my skin. That was the reality check I needed.

"Wait, no, we can't..." I pulled away to look down on him. I couldn't do this, it wasn't right, I wasn't sure what I wanted.

Xander's hand dropped down to his sides. Slowly I climbed off his lap, standing above him. "Sorry," he whispered. "I got carried away."

"Me too," I murmured, rubbing my arms with my hands, trying to tame the goosebumps that erupted from our kiss. While my mind was telling me to back away from Xander, my body was craving his touch. I wanted to sink back into him. I wanted to devour him.

Xander leaned forward a pained expression on his face. "That was..."

Breathless, I sank back into my chair, scooting it back so I wouldn't be tempted to climb on top of him again. "Yeah, it was." I agreed. "Still, it was a mistake."

He looked up at me, his eyes torrid. "Not to me."

"It's too soon," I whispered. "For me, I'm not ready."

"Too soon in general, or too soon for it to be me?" he asked.

"I don't know," I admitted. "I can't help but feel a little weird about it."

"What is it that's holding you back? Is it Max?" he asked. I winced at his casual use of Max's name.

I hesitated. "Xander, it's one thing to date some random guy, to kiss some stranger."

He held up a hand. "I don't want to hear about you kissing another guy."

"But you. To do that with you..."

"You don't think it's right," he offered.

"I'm messed up," I admitted, sheepish. "I wish I weren't. I wish I could give you what you want."

"You're what I want Ana." He leaned forward folding his hands in front of him. He looked down at the floor, nodding his head as he was thinking. "But you already know that. If you said the word, I'd forget all about every other woman out there. Forget Sherie..."

"Don't say her name," I snapped quickly, surprising myself. I turned red at my outburst. "Sorry, I don't want to talk about her anymore."

"How much did it bother you?" he asked. "Seeing Sherie today? Talking to her about me?"

"More than I wanted it to," I confessed.

"Does it hurt?" he asked. My eyes snapped up to meet his, a look of icy truth in his gaze. "Knowing that someone else might like me like that? That she might want me? That she could know me? Does it hurt?"

I nodded at him, not trusting my words at all. His tone seemed too calculating. The question too sharp to understand what he was asking.

"So how do you think I feel, having to sit back and know that someone else gets to know you? That someone else gets all of you, day after day. Can you imagine how that feels at all?"

"It's not the same thing..." I began.

"No, you're right Ana. It's not. Because as nice of a girl as Sherie is, nothing serious was ever going to happen for us. You can have your fleeting moment of jealousy with her but in the end, you know, deep down, that I don't feel that way about her."

I sat there, transfixed as he leaned closer to me. Instinctively I moved forward until our knees touched. "I didn't know that, though."

He shook his head at me. "Yes, you do, Ana. Yes, you do. How I feel about Sherie... it's nothing compared to how I feel about you. And you know that. I told you as much. But comparing yourself to how I felt..." he scrubbed a hand over his face. "You have no idea what it was like for me, Ana. You have to idea the pain of watching the person you want to be with more than anything, constantly choosing another."

Nothing I could say would help this—I didn't want to hear what he was saying but I couldn't help but lean forward, needing the biting words. I never wanted this truth, but I knew I needed it. "And what's worse, was having that person be your best friend. That person was the guy who depends on you and to develop feelings for the woman he considers his girl? Every time I looked at you, every time I thought about kissing you, I felt guilty."

"You never told me…" I stammered.

"Of course not. When could I?" he asserted. He leaned forward taking my hands in his. I looked down at our fingers entwined. "It wouldn't have mattered anyway, I knew that. No matter how *I* felt about you and Max, I know you love him."

"I do," I whispered. I wanted to pull my hands away, but his touch soothed me, somehow having him near while I heard these words, having his hand against mine as I said what I needed to say, made it easier. "I did," I corrected.

"Trust me when I tell you, I will never be Max. I know what he was to you. Better than anyone, I understand. But give us a chance. Let me show you that while what we have isn't what you had before; it could be something else."

"Something more?" I asked skeptically.

"I'm not trying to replace anyone. But we can be more than what we are. For now, can that be enough?"

I squeezed his hands in mine, running my thumb over his rough skin, brushing over a scab that'd formed on the back of his hand, likely a work injury. Still looking down I nodded at him.

I could feel him smiling, his shoulders loosening with relief. He brought my hands to his mouth and pressed a kiss to each of my knuckles.

# Chapter Nineteen



*"I can quit whenever I want."–Max to Eloise*

I FOUND MYSELF SITTING on the side of the road, steam pouring from the hood of my car, and a loud sizzling noise each time I turned over the engine. Still in my scrubs after working a night shift, I had to admit this was beyond the scope of my skills.

I gave it ten minutes of sitting in my car, watching the steam dissipate before I tried to turn it on again, only to have the same sputtering and sizzling. I knew then I had to call Xander.

After our revelations at his dad's house, we hadn't talked about what was going on between us. We hadn't kissed again. I wasn't intentionally avoiding him, but I wasn't seeking him out. I had successfully spent a week finding excuses to keep myself busy. I knew I was procrastinating because despite saying I'd give him a chance to show me we could be more, I still wasn't sure I was ready.

I got lucky. He was only a few miles away, at the local shopping center. He pulled in behind me in his work truck, all his tools crammed in the back. Through the windshield I saw another guy sitting in the front seat next to him. Xander climbed out, pulling a bright yellow beanie out of his coat pocket, and shoving it on his head. The other guy followed suit, stepping down from the truck to look at me. I stepped out of the car, standing between the door and the car.

"So, you finally blew it up?" Xander teased as he sauntered toward me.

I crossed my arms and narrowed my eyes at him. "This car has never done this before. It's always been reliable."

Xander put one hand on the top of the car, right next to my shoulder. I looked up at him. His cheeks were flushed pink from the chill in the morning air. He hadn't bothered shaving. His scruff had grown in golden thick. "You want me to take a look, or did you already call AAA?"

*AAA, shit. Why didn't I think of that?* My parents had been paying for my membership since I was eighteen.

"You can look, though I doubt you'll be able to do much. I was driving down the road when steam started pouring out of the hood. I had to pull over it was so thick. I shut the car off but when I tried to turn it back on the steam started even worse and—"

He stepped closer to me, placing a hand on my hip. It rested there for a moment, his touch burning. I gulped loudly. My breath hitched. He squeezed my hip briefly before nudging me out of the way so he could lean over to pop the hood open. I stepped out of his way, watching him as he opened the hood and looked around. Xander never was the car expert in our friend circle. That was Max's domain. Xander was handy enough to fix little things, but I doubted he could do much for my little coupe.

He poked around a bit, checking various places with a flashlight. The other guy came up to stand next to me.

"Car trouble?" he asked.

I fought the urge to roll my eyes at his question, nodding instead as I watched Xander pull the dipstick to check the oil. I tried to remember the last time I'd checked the oil and came up short. I hoped I didn't accidentally blow the engine.

"That sucks, good thing we were around the corner, huh?" the guy said.

I glanced at him, chewing my lips. "Yeah, I guess?"

He stuck his hand out to me. "I'm Cory, the new hire."

I took his hand, shaking it quickly before turning to face Xander. "I'm—"

"Ana, yeah. Mr. Eberhardt told me. Ana the roommate."

I glanced at Cory, wondering what exactly Xander had told him. "Right." I didn't like the sound of being called *the roommate*. But what else should I be called? It had been weeks since we'd talked about what was between us. Neither he nor I made a move forward.

"That sucks about your car. Were you heading to work?"

"Leaving actually."

"Yeah, Mr. Eberhardt said you're a nurse, that's cool. I like nurses. Kind of hot, you know?"

I looked over at him, my eyes wide. Did he really say that? "Good to know." If Scarlett was here, she would've thought of something scathing to say. But with everything that'd happened today, I didn't have the energy to come up with a witty quip. I looked back at Xander as he put the tension rod down, letting my hood drop.

"Well, it looks like you have a busted radiator hose. I can tape it and add more water to get you back to the apartment, but I don't know how long that fix will last. You're going to need to get take it to a shop."

I grunted in annoyance. "How much will that cost?"

Xander shook his head and shrugged his shoulders. "No clue."

Cory chimed in. "My brother-in-law works at Bayview Auto. I can call in a favor, have him take a look."

I looked at Cory surprised. "Really? That would be really—" I furrowed my brow, not sure what word to use. "Um. That would be great Cory, thank you."

"Anything for a pretty woman," he said, winking at me.

Xander frowned at the compliment, turning to me. "So, you want me to call a truck, and have it towed?"

I frowned, trying to figure out how much repairs at a shop would cost me. "I guess I don't really have a choice, do I?"

"Not really." He said shaking his head. "It's now or a few days from now."

"Go ahead," I sighed. I opened my door and sank into the driver's seat, annoyed. Xander pulled out his phone and asked for the tow truck, giving the dispatch our exact location much better than I could. I never was good with gaging distance. The way he said '*a mile and half southbound Fredrick Road off 407*' sounded better than the '*halfway between the big highway and the old elementary school*' that I would've said.

Hanging up the phone, he shoved it back in his coat pocket, looking from me to Cory. "Why don't you go hang out in the truck. I'll be there in a minute."

Cory nodded, considering Xander for a moment, "Will I still get..."

"I'll pay you your same rate, Cory," Xander growled. "Now go get in the damn truck."

Cory did a little mock salute before jogging back to the truck, leaving me and Xander alone.

"That kid, I swear," Xander mumbled under his breath before turning back to me. He stepped closer to me, placing a hand on the roof of my car.

He looked down at me in my seat as I rubbed my arms, trying to keep the cold away. All I had to keep me warm was my thin cardigan from the hospital. "So, this sucks."

Bending down to crouch between my legs he took my arms in his hands, rubbing them up and down quickly. "A little, yeah."

His touch warmed me, but I had a feeling it was more my reaction to him than the friction he was causing. Crouched between my legs, he caught my eyes. If I leaned forward, I knew he wouldn't pull away. I could kiss him again. Didn't I want to? I closed my eyes. I knew exactly how his lips would taste, the way his hand would feel against my hair. I could imagine the flush of heat from his body against mine. It'd be so easy to give in one more time.

I pulled away, as I moved my feet inside the car, where it was slightly warmer. Xander frowned as I moved. He sighed before getting up and coming around to the other side, getting into the passenger seat.

After a minute of shaky breaths, I turned to face him, resting my head back. "I'm sorry I made you come out here for this. I didn't know who else to call."

"Hey, I'm glad you did. I told you, I want to be here for you." He leaned his head against the headrest, so we were at the same odd angle facing each other.

"You really don't need to wait with me. You've already missed enough work and now you have to pay that guy to sit in your truck listening to the radio."

"It's not a big deal, Ana. I'm not going to leave you on the side of the road."

"But..." I stammered.

He shook his head, taking my hands in his. "No. Not happening."

Seeing I was losing the battle I nodded, squeezing his hand back. I considered pulling away, but he held them so tight I couldn't. "How long do you think it'll be?"

"They said twenty minutes. Hopefully it won't take that long." He glanced back at the truck before returning his eyes to me.

I glanced away to look back at Xander's truck where Cory was sitting in the cab looking at his phone. "That was nice of Cory to offer to call his brother-in-law."

Xander scoffed. "He's trying to impress you. He obviously has a crush."

"What? No way," I peeked back at the truck to see Cory waving at me. I offered a little wave back.

"Don't encourage him, Ana." Xander said, trapping my free hand. "He's a kid, you'll devour him."

I laughed at his analogy. "Please, like I'm even remotely capable of doing that."

"You absolutely are. How do you think I feel?" His face clouded as he stared at me, causing me to stop laughing. "My crew can only take one heartbroken employee at a time, Ana. You'd wreck him."

I leaned forward, my voice barely above a whisper. "Is that what you think I'm doing to you?"

"I know it is." He wasn't trying to be cruel, his face open to me.

"I don't want you to be heartbroken." I said, my chest splintering at his admission. We stared at each other for a long moment, the car suddenly feeling far too small to hold everything we had between us.

"I've felt this way a long time, Ana. I know how to cope," he assured me. "I can function with it."

I pulled away, closing my eyes. "I know what you want from me Xander. I don't think I'm ready yet."

"I know you aren't there yet."

I turned my head to study him. "This could go wrong; it could go so wrong and then where would that leave us?"

"It won't, Ana," he whispered.

"I can't lose you. I can barely keep myself together these days. Don't ask me to risk you over something that you're not sure of."

He sat up, his mouth in a grim line. "But I am sure. I've always been sure of us."

"You say always, what does that even mean? How long could that be, really?" I ask. I wasn't sure I wanted to hear the answer, but I couldn't help myself.

He leaned forward, tucking his knee up closer to his body. He rested his elbows on his knees as he considered me. "Since our first kiss, probably. On and off through the years. But it became real when we were freshmen. We were partners for that history project, remember?"

"We wrote a play where time travelers went through American history and explained the significance of events to the people they met," I recalled.

He smiled at the memory. "You remember what the teacher wrote on our final draft?"

I laughed. "Yeah, *great work Liliana! I wonder what portion Alexander contributed?*"

His smile faded. "There was a moment when we were researching, both of us were on the floor of your living room, books all around us. You rolled over and closed your eyes and started complaining about how much work we still had to do.

You threw your arm over your face and pretended to sleep and even though you weren't being funny, I laughed. Without thinking I offered to finish the research for you. I realized in that moment I'd have done anything for you. I wanted to kiss you so bad, but you were dating my best friend. So, I sat up and grabbed all my things and made some excuse about needing to get home."

"You never told me," I murmured. "In all the time we've spent together when we were young, you never told me."

"When could I? You were always with Max, or getting over Max, or mourning Max. There was never room in your life for anyone else."

"But if you would've told me sooner... Who knows what would've happened if you would've kissed me that day, or that day on the couch at Scarlett's, or all those other times you could have? Maybe if you had..."

"It wouldn't have made a difference, Ana. Not then. I'm not going to delude myself into thinking that if I'd been more forward, you would've chosen me over Max. I knew better than that. If he hadn't left us, you guys would still be together, and I'd still be on the sidelines watching you."

I thought about contradicting him, but I couldn't. He was right. Max was never going to be done with me. What we had was too strong. He was so big in my life; I couldn't see anyone else. "You're probably right."

He leaned closer to me, cupping my cheek in his hand. "I'm still waiting Ana. Until you tell me to stop, I'll keep waiting for you."

I dropped my eyes to his lips, they looked so smooth. Hadn't I been thinking about kissing them? Hadn't I wanted to feel him against me? In the breadth of my car, with all our admissions between us, I couldn't remember why I didn't want to kiss him or why I was holding back.

Slowly I leaned forward to press my lips against his. He froze for a moment, and I wondered if I'd misjudged the situation entirely. Then he pushed back with his mouth, meeting me with renewed vigor. His kiss deepened and his tongue came out to brush lightly against my lower lip. Slowly he rubbed his thumb under my chin, coaxing me closer, to give myself over to him. Without breaking our kiss, I folded my legs up underneath me, leaning across the console to get closer to him. He grabbed my hips and held them steady as his kiss slowed. I gripped his forearms, strong and thick from his job.

Blood boiled under my skin as I fought to be closer to him. His hands came around my waist, his thumbs above my hip bones. I dug my nails into his jacket, losing myself in him.

A horn honked, breaking us apart. It was the tow truck coming to rescue me. We stared at each other, breathless, as the sound of the tow truck parking in front of us became a cacophony inside my car. He pulled away dropping his hands.

"I'll go talk to the driver real quick," he said, his voice husky from my kiss. I nodded at him, glad for the sudden reprieve. He hesitated for a moment, his expression torn, before he cupped my cheek, his thumb rubbing against my lower lip. I sat, breathless as he clambered out of the car.

Through my windshield I watched as Xander motioned to the car, discussing where to take it. The driver handed him a paper and I saw Xander fold it up and shove it into his wallet. Sauntering back to me he motioned for me to get out.

"Okay, they're going to take the car to the shop. I'll take you home."

I looked back at the tow truck, the driver working with the large metal hook. "But don't I need to sign something, or pay or anything?"

"I got that stuff. We'll figure it out later." He rested a hand on the small of my back and led me away to his truck. I tried to not smile at the use of the word *'we,'* but failed.

Back at the apartment, I came to the sad realization that when it came to Xander, it'd be hard work keeping my wits about me. I wasn't sure what came over me whenever he was around, but all reason seemed to leave.

I blanched as I thought about how I acted in my car. I made out with Xander in a broken-down car on the side of the road, and I liked it. It didn't matter that my emergency brake was digging into my stomach as I kissed him. It didn't matter that he needed to get back to work. It didn't matter that his employee was only feet away probably watching everything we were doing.

It didn't matter that if it all went wrong, I'd lose my best friend, and I still wasn't over what happened last year. In that moment all I wanted was Xander's lips on mine, his hands on my skin, and his breath at my ear. I wanted more—more than he could give, more than I could ever ask for.

# Chapter Twenty

**X**ANDER LOOKED AT THE cart, then back at the list in his hand. "I forgot the ketchup. I'll be right back, wait here."

I leaned against the cart, pulling my phone out while he ran to the next aisle. Another cart started down the aisle and I moved out of the way, not glancing at the other shopper until they stopped beside me.

"Ana?" I looked up to see Troy standing in front of me, still wearing a suit, obviously just off work.

"Oh, hi Troy," I stammered.

He smiled at me, shaking his head. "What are the chances! I was just thinking about you." He laughed. "I was about to call you when I got home tonight."

I set my phone back in my purse and turned to him surprised. I had thought I'd scared him away for sure. "Really? Because I didn't hear from you after we went out. And it's totally cool, I get it. I was a little..." I whistled and waved my finger around my ear. "You know. I didn't think I was going to hear from you again."

He blushed and looked away, embarrassed. "No, nothing like that. I'm a little ashamed to be honest. Could I take you to coffee sometime? Explain myself for being such an ass?"

I hesitated, looking down the aisle for Xander. "I don't know…"

"Look, I get it. I said I'd call and then I didn't. I swear, I'm not that kind of guy. Let me buy you a cup of coffee. One cup, is all I'm asking."

I chewed on my lower lip, considering him. Xander rounded the corner and saw me talking to Troy. He narrowed his eyes at us but didn't say anything as he saddled up to me.

"What's up, man?" Xander asked, putting his hand out. "Alexander Eberhardt."

Troy took his hand and shook it, grimacing slightly at what was likely Xander's overly strong grip.

"Troy McConnell." He cocked his head to the side. "Wait, Alexander, like Xander, you're the roommate, right? Ana told me about you." His face relaxed slightly as the apparent threat seemed to disappear.

"Something like that," Xander replied, his jaw tight.

They stood there, quietly staring each other down for a moment. After a long awkward moment, I took the ketchup from Xander's hand and threw it in the cart. "We should get going if we're going to make it to the party," I told Xander.

His narrowed eyes moved from the clueless Troy back to me. "Yeah, we should." He glanced back at Troy. "Good to meet you, man."

"Same," Troy replied. "Ana, I'll give you a call about that coffee, alright?"

Before I could tell him no, Troy pushed his cart along, leaving us alone in the aisle.

Xander turned to face me, both hands on the cart in front of me. "What was that all about?"

"Nothing. He wanted to meet up for coffee and explain why he never called me."

"Did you say yes?" he asked incredulous.

"I didn't say anything. You walked up as we started talking." I shifted the items in the cart around, sorting them in order of how I wanted to load them at check out.

"Were you going to say yes?" he asked.

"I don't know." I glanced at him.

He glanced down to the back of the store where we last saw Troy. "I thought you didn't want to see him again?"

"What I don't want, is to have this conversation in the middle of the grocery store," I said, putting an end to the conversation.

The next day I found myself at Checkers Cafe, sitting at my favorite glass-top table in the corner, and looking over the cobblestone alleyway. Troy walked in scanning the small room until his eyes found me, a big smile crossing his face. He approached the table shoving his hands in the pockets of his jeans. In the time we spent together I'd never seen him in anything aside from nice slacks and a button-down shirt.

"You already got a drink?" he asked, nodding to the latte in front of me. "There goes my first act of gallantry."

I smiled at him, opting not to comment on his attempt to win me over. "I got here early."

He took it in stride, leaving for a moment before coming back with his own large mug of coffee.

"Thanks for agreeing to see me again. I've been feeling like a total ass for not calling you." He cupped his hand around his mug and leaned closer to me.

"Troy, I get it. We didn't click, or you met someone else, or you weren't into me."

Troy took a drink of his coffee and grimaced before reaching for the sugar on the edge of the table and dumping in a packet. Some part of me found satisfaction that he didn't take his coffee the same way as Max. He stirred the coffee slowly, watching it instead of looking at me.

"The thing is, I really liked you. I liked you from the moment you opened the door. We had a really good time and I wanted to go out again. But I got home after our date and I was thinking about what you said, about how long you guys were together. And then I bumped into Emma and Scarlett and Scarlett kept going on and on about how you were so crazy in love with this guy and then he just dies. She made him out to be this mythical person and it made me worry that I'd be a rebound for you, and it freaked me out. So, I took some time to myself and then some more time and then I felt like it was too much time, and I blew my shot."

"You didn't blow your shot with me..."

His eyes lit up at my comment. "Really, because..."

I shook my head at him. "You're a great guy, Troy. To be honest, you are exactly, and I mean *exactly,* the type of man my parents would want me to end up with. If my mother could have met you, she would have flipped out. But..." I groaned, wiping my face with my hand.

"You're not interested," he finished.

"Not like that, not romantically. I should be. You have no idea how much I want to be interested in you, Troy. But I can't be. Not like that. And you're too great of a guy for me to waste your time."

He chuckled low, "It's not you, it's me?"

"Troy," I sighed. "We went on one date. You were the one who didn't call me. Let's call this one a draw. Neither of us came out with anything worse than bruised egos."

He nodded at me, a pained expression on his face. "One question, before I go." He hesitated, looking down at his empty cup. "That guy, your roommate, are you guys..."

I bit my lip and looked out the window, unsure of how to respond. "I don't know. Maybe? It's too soon to call it anything. We've known each other forever. I've known him for as long as I knew Max. Longer, I guess."

At that moment, I realized Xander would know more of me than Max. Xander and I had the time to know each other. The thought took my breath away. Could I chance this? Xander did know me. He'd always be a part of me just as integral as Max was. Could we be more?

He pursed his lips. "I figured, the way you were talking about him on our date and the way he was looking at you at the store the other day."

"There was nothing going when we went out, if it's any consolation," I admitted.

"But that's changed since?" He laughed to himself. "You know, what, it's really not my business. I guess I really missed my chance."

"Troy—" I started to say but he held his hand up to silence me.

Standing up he shrugged his jacket on and grabbed his wallet off the table. "It's okay, Ana, really. You were right before, just a bruised ego. I'll survive."

I nodded at him, not sure how to make him feel better. I hated disappointing people, especially someone as sweet as Troy.

"Friends?" I asked.

He gave me a small smile. "Friendly acquaintances?" he quipped.

"That works."

Xander was home already as I pulled in next to his truck. I considered sitting in my car and listening to another episode of my favorite true crime podcast instead of going in the house.

Never before had I turned a man down while I was single. I didn't count the slight flirtations from other men when I was dating Max. Having a boyfriend made me impervious to guilt in saying no. But now? This was different. I'd become my own person, completely in charge of my romantic choices.

I realized I'd developed a sick sense of satisfaction from being the scorned girl. For so long I was so innocent with the big, bad Max Constantine corrupting my poor, fragile mind. He was Lieutenant Wickham to my Georgiana Darcy. It would be so much simpler if I was a victim of all this pain.

I didn't regret one minute I spent with Max. But after reading those letters I found in his clothes, I realized I could begin to let him go—I can yell, I can scream, I can cry. Then, I can know that I loved him.

I used to wonder how Max could be so callous to hurt me that way. He let me believe I was the only one who could love him. I now understood how easy it is to break another person.

I could see it in Xander—patient, sweet Xander. I knew he wanted me. He told me he loved me. I wasn't sure what'd be worse: pushing him away to spare him further pain or giving it a shot when I wasn't sure I was ready.

I knew how much it hurt to give yourself to another person. It's the raw vulnerability of losing yourself. Now I knew how it felt to receive it, to look at another person and think *I don't deserve this kindness from you, this devotion. I'm not worth it.* And that felt so much worse. It's one thing to be the victim, but there's a new level of anguish when you become the villain.

Xander gave me permission to choose where this relationship was going to go, and I was afraid I was going to choose wrong. Every day the chasm in my chest felt deeper when I looked at Xander.

Eventually, I got out of my car and made my way into the apartment. As I rounded the corner into the living room, Xander looked up from his phone to me. He set his phone down next to him and studied me as I set my purse down. I could hear him getting up off the couch and walking up to me.

"How was your date?" he asked, standing behind me.

I turned to face him as I struggled with the zipper on my jacket. "It wasn't a date."

"Meeting a guy by yourself for coffee to talk about your relationship? Sounds like a date to me," he sneered.

I ripped the zipper down and tugged my jacket off forcibly, instead of hanging it up the way I normally would I twisted it into a ball. "Don't be a jealous asshole right now, please. You're not that guy."

"You'd be surprised." He took a step closer to me, took my jacket from my hand, smoothing it out and hanging it on the hook. "There might be a lot of things you don't know about me."

I rolled my eyes. "Please, Xander. Don't do this. I'm feeling bad enough about Troy right now, without you giving me a guilt trip over whatever this is."

"Whatever this is?" he asked. He placed a hand on the wall above my head and looked down at me. "So, you still don't know what to call it?"

I looked up at him, meeting his eyes. "You know I don't. You know I'm still confused…"

"No, you're not. You know how you feel. You aren't ready to admit it yet," he assured me, stepping closer until his foot was between mine and my back was against the wall.

"I don't know what you're talking about." Breathless from his heat, I looked away. "Wherever this conversation is going, we can't do this right after I broke it off with Troy."

"That's a bullshit excuse. It was one date. He was never a boyfriend. You're looking for whatever excuse you can come up with, so you don't have to make a choice. You need to decide what you want us to be. What do you want from me? Am I your friend…" He stepped closer, putting the other hand on the other side of me, bracketing me in between his arms. He dipped his head lower, his lips inches from mine. "Or am I more?"

I fought against the urge telling me that every kiss with Xander would make it more difficult to make a reasonable decision. When I was away from him, I could rationalize it. But here, in these moments where his body was so close to mine, where his gaze fixed on me, I wanted to surrender to him. Before I could think better of it, I stood on my toes and pressed my lips to his.

He pushed against me, pinning me against the wall. His fingers threaded through my hair, pulling my face to his. Gripping my hip, he brought my torso flush to his hips. His tongue traced my lips, and I opened my mouth to meet his. Grabbing the bottom of my shirt, he pulled it up, holding it tight to my lower back. I lowered my hands, pulling his shirt up, urging him to take it off. He pulled away long enough to rip his T-shirt off before his lips came crashing back down on mine. With only my thin T-shirt between us, I could feel his heart beating, the steady thrum of what we were doing.

His hands came up my back, his thumbs resting right below where my bra stopped. Breaking our kiss, I pulled my hands away to grab my shirt and pull it over my head. His eyes were glassy with lust and lingered over my body, his hands moving over my bare skin. His fingers slid across my stomach, tracing lines up over the swell of my breasts. His fingers dipped into my bra and brushed against my nipple. I gasped at the contact; he watched his hands as they explored further. My skin felt tight and hot from his touch.

"You are so beautiful," he whispered. He looked up and our eyes met. He cupped my cheeks, pulling my face closer to his. He didn't kiss me. Instead, his eyes bore into me. "I want you so much, Ana."

"I want you too," I whispered back. Locked in his gaze, I couldn't be anything but honest.

He pulled away from me and dropped his hands. "I'm sure I'm going to regret this." He scrubbed his hand over his face as he took a step back. His hands shook as he slowly opened his eyes to meet mine. My breath hitched as the ominous tone began to sink in. "But we can't do this right now. I want you. You have no idea how much I want you. But we can't…"

I nodded at him as I bent down to grab my shirt off the floor, clutching it in front of me. "I get it," I whispered.

"No, you don't." He took a few deep breaths to compose himself before stepping closer to me, catching my eyes. "When we do this, I want all of you. You understand? When we make love—and that is exactly what it will be—there is no going back from that."

"I know," I murmured as he stepped closer. He took my hands, pushing them down until he could look at my body again.

I was on fire under his gaze. Everywhere his eyes went it felt as if it was his hands, or his mouth, trailing across my skin. Slowly he brought his eyes back up to mine. "When you finally let me love you, Ana…" he dipped his face down to press a small kiss to my lips. "You're going to love me back."

He stepped away, leaving me breathless. I closed my eyes, listening as he retreated to his room.

# Chapter Twenty-One

STANDING AROUND A LARGE bonfire with a bottle of cheap beer in my hand, I wondered what the hell I was doing at a party like this. I didn't like these types of get-togethers when I was in high school, back when drinking with a large group of people only made sense twenty miles from civilization and any discernible police force. Now that we're adults, being here felt even more ridiculous. But Xander had agreed to go and when he asked me to come with him, I couldn't say no to him.

When I got there, I was shocked to see Eloise standing next to the keg, a red cup in her hand. In the flickers of the oversized bonfire, I could see she was wearing a tight pink sweater that looked too thin for spending a night outside. Xander and I exchanged a wordless glance, agreeing to look out for her.

She told me that one of her friends dragged her to the party so she could spend the night with her boyfriend who seemed to be friends with Cory. I fought the urge to lecture her on underage drinking and tried to keep a close eye on her.

I felt Cory sidle up to me, two beers in his hands. He held one out to me and I took it, twisting off the cap. "So, you're not dating Mr. Eberhardt, are you?" Cory asked.

I took a swig of my beer, glancing at Xander who was talking with Eloise. "No, I wouldn't say that—"

"Good," Cory interrupted.

I raised an eyebrow. "Okay?"

"Cause if you're not seeing him, I can take you out," Cory finished. Didn't he see Xander and I kissing in my car?

I could sense Xander coming behind me, his hand resting on my shoulder. "You're not taking her out, Cory."

I glanced up at him, torn between being annoyed that he spoke for me and thankful I had an excuse not to go out with this kid.

"She said you guys aren't—" something in Xander's face stopped Cory from continuing. "Right, sorry boss. I'm going to get another beer. That girl in the pink sweater looks like she might need a refill too."

Xander looked over at Eloise and shook his head. "Don't even try with her."

Cory frowned at Xander but didn't question him. When he walked away Xander took his hand off my shoulder. The absence of his touch left a pang in my stomach. I turned to face him.

"You scared him away quick," I teased.

Xander looked at his retreating employee with narrowed eyes. "Little weasel. I told you, he likes you. He was asking all sort of questions after the other day."

"Like it matters, Xander." I rolled my eyes. "I'm not interested."

"I hope not." He responded quickly. His gaze was so intense, that I had to look away or I'd get caught in it.

"Where's that girl you were talking to?" I asked, trying to keep my voice as nonchalant as possible.

"What girl?" His eyebrows furrowed together.

I waved a hand in the direction he was standing earlier. "That girl. The pretty one. I saw her flirting with you."

He glanced around the party, the same confused look on his face. "Who? Do you mean Eloise's friend? She's a kid, Ana."

"Seems like you two were quite chummy over there." I tried to sound blithe, but I couldn't help my acrid tone.

He shook his head, frowning. "I wouldn't flirt with her. She can barely buy a lotto ticket."

I quirked an eyebrow at him. "Well, she was sure flirting with you."

"She was not. We were just talking. Eloise was there the whole time."

"So, you can't flirt with other people around?" I asked.

"No, that's not what I'm saying but…" He stopped, cocking his head to the side slightly as if something finally occurred to him. "Are you jealous?"

I stepped back, shaking my head, "No, of course not."

He stepped into me, closing the gap between us. "You are, aren't you?" His face broke into a huge grin at the idea.

"I'm not jealous! And besides, you're one to talk. Scaring off Cory like that. You know, I could've told him no myself. I didn't need you to—"

Xander's eyes snapped to mine, and I stopped speaking, too caught up to continue. "I did need to. He knows better. It's obvious that you're…"

I stepped closer to him, resting a hand on his arm. "I'm what, Xander?" I asked, my voice low.

He stared down at me, the air around us thickening with tension. "You're not for him. You might not belong to me Ana, but I…"

I could feel my heart beating loud in my ears, my breath catching with each moment that passed between us. He glanced down at my lips, and I licked them in reflex. It was going to happen. I was ready. I wanted this. I didn't care we were at a party in front of all our friends. I needed his lips on mine.

"I belong to you," he said, tilting his head down, his breath against my face. I pulled myself on my toes to be closer to his mouth. His hand slipped from my arm to my back pulling me closer. I closed my eyes and leaned in, feeling the warmth of his body.

A loud crash sounded, ripping us apart. We both jumped back looking toward the sound. Next to the keg, Eloise laid on the ground, sprawled out. We rushed forward, pushing past everyone else to get to her. Xander took one arm while I took the other. We pulled her to her feet, brushing the chunks of moss and twigs from her hair.

We walked Eloise to the closest bench, her feet dangling as we went. Sitting between us, Eloise groaned loud, leaning forward.

"I'm fine," she slurred.

"Obviously not," Xander replied. He kept a hand on her arm to steady her and smoothed her hair from her face.

"Why don't you come home with us? You can crash on the couch. We'll take you to breakfast in the morning." I asked.

She nodded at me, and we hefted her up between us. As we made our way to my car, I prayed that she wouldn't throw up all over my interior.

"What is going on with you two?" Eloise asked from the back seat. Her eyes were closed, the seatbelt catching her as she leaned in her seat. "You guys are acting weird."

"What are you talking about?" I asked, not trusting myself to look at either Xander or Eloise.

"You guys aren't fucking, are you?" Eloise slurred.

"No!" I snapped. Xander glanced at me, his jaw tense.

"Good, because that would be so weird. I mean, Xander is my brother's best friend. Practically my brother. It's like, incestuous, or something…"

"Go to sleep, Wheezy." A waver in my voice giving me away. If Eloise were sober, she would've caught it, but in her drunk condition she only shrugged.

We set her up on the couch, wrapping a big blanket around her. She turned her head and buried her face into the overstuffed cushions. Minutes later her drunken snores reminded me of Max.

Xander glared at me, then motioned with his head for me to meet him in the kitchen. I followed him in, an ominous feeling settling over me.

"What was that in the car?" Xander hissed.

"What?" I asked. I bent down to pick up Eloise's shoes off the floor.

"You know what. Not answering her question. You should've told her. Eloise has a right to know."

"A right to know what? I don't even know what's going on here. What am I supposed to tell her? Sorry, but I've been fooling around with your brother's best friend?" I walked to the hallway closet and set Eloise's shoes down.

"Is that what you call what we're doing? Fooling around?" he asked.

I bit my lip. The words sounded all wrong. Whatever was going on between Xander and I, it was far more than a simple physical connection.

"You know it's not like that for me. And three kisses hardly substantiate fooling around," he growled.

"Oh, I'm sorry," I mocked. "In all my vast experiences with men I didn't learn that making out isn't fooling around. Last time I kissed someone, other than Max, it was."

His eyes softened, "That's not what I meant, Ana. What this is between us? It's not about fooling around. I mean the kissing is amazing." He smiled at me. "But it's not about that for me."

"What did you expect me to say to her? It would crush her."

"It's going to hurt her a lot more to know you've been keeping it from her. That we both have. I think we should tell her, and Scarlett too."

"There's nothing to tell them, Xander."

"That's a lie and you know it." He stepped toward me, cupping my cheek in his hand. He leaned forward about to kiss me. I stuck my hand against his chest, establishing a boundary. He frowned at me. "You know where to find me, Ana. Goodnight."

He left me wordless, standing in the kitchen with a passed-out Eloise in the living room. I listened for the click of his door closing before going to Eloise. I rested a hand on her back, counting her breaths. I grasped her wrist, took a quick ulnar pulse, before feeling satisfied that she'd be okay. I made my way toward my room, pausing at Xander's door.

He was right. It would hurt Eloise to find out later. Every time I kissed Xander we got deeper and deeper into this game we were playing. Every time I got farther away from escaping culpability. If I didn't want anyone else to get hurt, the smart thing to do tonight would be to continue down the hall, go into my room and close the door. To stop kissing Xander, to stop thinking about his touch.

If I was smart, I'd leave him alone. But I was drawn to him. I needed him. When I was near him, I felt powerful, I felt emboldened. I felt things in my body I'd long ago thought were dead. I liked the way he made me feel.

I rested a hand on his door, fingering the grain of the fake wood, trying to decide what my next move should be. I tapped my fingers softly on the door in beats of three. I pulled my hand away, about to reach for the knob when the door flew open with Xander on the other side.

We stared at each other, both surprised. Without any more thoughts I stepped forward, stood on my toes, and grabbed him by the neck, pulling his mouth to mine. He responded by wrapping his arms around my waist, pulling me closer. His kiss was firm. There was an intoxicating urgency in his embrace. I stumbled against him, my hand raking through his curls. In one fluid moment he picked me up, his lips never leaving mine as he made his way across the room to his bed. Together we fell backward, his weight landing on me. His hands tangled in my hair as he crushed his lips to mine.

His hand moved from my hair to rest on my leg. Slowly as he kissed me, he slid his hand until it was between my thighs. I moved against him, urging him on. He reached down the front of my shorts, moving my underwear to the side and he slid his finger inside me as we kissed.

"I want to make you feel good Ana," he whispered against my skin.

I turned my head away gasping for a breath. Xander's fingers were inside me, his kisses on my neck. It was all too much, the brutal pleasure of it all. His hand moved against me, the pad of his thumb rubbing against my clit, sending sparks of pleasure through my body. His long fingers touched me exactly where I needed it and I felt myself getting closer. Gripping his arms, I gyrated on his hand, edging myself to release. His thumb brushed my clit one more time and I felt myself constrict around him.

"That's it. Beautiful." He murmured as I fell apart in his arms.

Blood pounding in my ears, I took in a shaky breath as his lips trailed from my mouth down my throat. With only a thin layer of cotton pants on, the hard length of him was pressed against my leg.

"Wait," I mumbled.

He pulled away, panting as he looked down at me. "What?"

"We can't do this," I whispered.

He groaned, his head dropping against my shoulder. "No, don't do this..."

He pulled his hand away as he started to roll off me, but I ran my hand through his hair, keeping him close to me. "No, stay."

He turned his head, so his mouth was on the base of my throat. "But you said..."

"We can't do this with Eloise out there." I explained. "It doesn't feel right."

He groaned louder but didn't try to move off me. He ran a hand across my stomach, sending shivers through my body. He raised his head to look me in the eye. "I guess, after the verbal lashing we got tonight, it doesn't seem right, does it?"

I shook my head. I propped myself up on my elbows. He slid closer to me, kissing me again.

"We'll continue this soon. But for now, I don't think we should say anything to anyone. Please?" I begged.

He sighed, tucking his face into the nape of my neck. "Why?" he asked, trailing feather soft kisses along my collar bone. "Why should this be a secret?"

I closed my eyes at the sensation, sinking into the mattress for a moment before remembering myself. I pushed his shoulder, making him roll off me. "No. We can't."

Xander stared at the ceiling, running his hand through his hair. "No, you don't like it or..."

I glanced over at him as he turned his head to look at me. "I like it. Trust me, I like it too much. But..."

Xander rolled to his side to face me completely and sighed. "I know what you're going to say Ana."

"I'm a mess and I'm stringing you along. I know I am. It's not fair to you. I don't know when I'll be ready..." Xander pulled my hand to his mouth and kissed my palm, calming me.

"What can I do? What will it take for you to trust we can be good together?"

"Trust?" I laughed. "Honestly? I don't trust anything about this." I admitted.

"You don't trust me? Is that the issue?" he asked, incredulous.

I scoffed. "Of course, I trust you, Xander. I don't trust myself—I don't trust that the way that I'm feeling is real. I don't trust that I'm making the right choice."

"You don't think I'm right for you?" he asked softly.

I wanted to lie and tell him he was hearing me wrong, but I couldn't lie, not to Xander. "I don't know. I don't know anything anymore. After everything I found out about Max, I don't feel like I'm the best judge of character. If I could trust him so explicitly and he could do all those things—if I could stand back and let him—it makes me question my judgment. Does that make sense?"

He shook his head. "I'm not Max. You know that. I've never been Max."

"I know you're not Max. But I'm still me. Or at least part of me is. I don't feel like *I* know who I am now."

"I know who you are," he whispered. "If you need to be reminded, ask me."

# Chapter Twenty-Two

*"I didn't hear my phone ring." –Ana to her mother.*

I STOOD IN THE bathroom in my bra and underwear, brushing my damp hair. I glanced at the clock on my phone where my carefully curated "getting ready" playlist was mid-cycle. I still had thirty minutes before I needed to leave to meet Scarlett for coffee. I tipped my head upside down and started blowdrying my hair.

"Hey," a voice yelled.

I dropped my hairdryer on the ground and whirled around. Xander stood in the doorway to my bathroom, leaning against the door jamb.

"You scared me!"

"Sorry." He glanced away and I realized that I was only wearing my underwear. He'd seen me like this before. It covered as much as my swimsuit would, not to mention our make-out session had veered in that territory. Still, I grabbed a robe off the wall and shrugged it on quickly.

"What's up?" I asked, trying to keep my voice as calm as I could.

"I...um. It's nothing, forget about it..." he went to turn, and I grabbed his arm, pulling back.

"No, what's up? It's obviously important." I bent down to pick the hair dryer up off the floor, winding the cord around my hand in a figure eight.

He sighed heavily. "I was thinking about what you said the other day." I furrowed my brow and waited for him to go on. He grimaced, then spoke quickly, as if he needed to get the words out fast or they would disappear. "I want to make sure you know that you deserve better. You deserve to be cherished, Ana, to be adored."

"God, Xander, why do I keep hearing that? Why does everyone feel the need to explain to me what I deserve or what I want?" I sat down on the edge of my bathtub and looked up at him. "I don't need to be taken care of, Xander. I mean it when I say I can take care of myself. What I need is respect. I'm not perfect. I'm not this angel you've built up in your mind. I don't want to be cherished. Did you ever consider that?"

He was quiet for a moment as my words sank in. He walked over, sitting on the edge of the tub with me. I took his hand in mine.

"I don't know what to say to that."

"You think I don't know how people see me? They think I was blind. Poor little Liliana Pryce. So blindly in love with that awful boy from the wrong side of town. It's a cliche, fodder for the town gossip mongers at a hushed Ridgewood Pearl lunch conversation when my mom leaves the table to use the bathroom. I'm sure it's all exciting for everyone else, but to me.

"For so long I thought that what Max and I had was kismet. It didn't matter what I wanted. Or even what you wanted. If Max wanted me, then Max had me. It was bigger than all of us. In the end, our opinions never mattered."

Xander pressed his lips together as he ran a hand through his curls, mussing them up. I reached over and smoothed a particularly unruly section. "Xan, don't act like you don't know that it's true. He didn't have any more control than you did. He probably had less. It's like it was never up to me. It was never up to either of us. Max, me, you... this always how it was, this is how it had to go."

"But it's us. Now it's you and me."

I stared at his soft hazel eyes. "It is, isn't it?"

Xander shook his head. "It's not like it was. Now it's up to you. You need to stop being so afraid of what others expect of you, Ana."

"I know," I whispered. "I do. I just can't help it."

He leaned forward and for a moment I thought he was going to kiss me, but instead he pressed his lips to my forehead, lingering a little longer.

His words were soft against my skin, I closed my eyes to the sensation. "I don't believe in destiny. We all have choices, Ana. Please make yours soon."

I was so lost in thought about my talk with Xander I didn't see Scarlett until she sat down at the table without even a hello.

"Ask me," she demanded.

"Ask you what?"

She scoffed loudly. "Ask me if there's anything I need from you."

"Nice to see you, Scarlett. I'm so glad we could meet up. I've been super busy at work too." I said sarcastically.

She waved her hand at me, flicking my comments away. "We're too close for that kind of small talk. Ask me."

"Okay." I played along. "Scarlett, is there anything you need from me?"

"Yes, Liliana Pryce, there is." She gave me a mischievous smile and slapped her hand on the table between us. On her finger was a large black stone on a thin platinum band. I stared at it for several seconds trying to figure out what she was showing me. She wiggled her fingers and I realized what finger the ring was on.

"You're engaged?" I exclaimed.

She laughed, wiggling in her chair. "Isn't it amazing? I was so surprised. We haven't been together that long, and I knew how I felt, but I've always been a headfirst type of gal so I figured she'd come around, eventually. I thought I was the one who would propose but..." she gazed down at her ring and let out a giddy laugh. "I am so excited."

I grabbed her hand to inspect the ring. "You should be. I am so excited for you."

"We already discussed it and it's going to be in May at her family's home in Illahee. It's not going to be a really big thing, only about fifty guests or so."

"You don't want a big thing?" I laughed. "You?"

She shrugged her shoulders. "Might be bigger than that." Her smile got bigger. "Emma wants a small thing, we'll see."

"No matter the size of the wedding, I'd be honored to be your maid of honor."

"You know, Troy will be there too." She quirked an eyebrow suggestively.

"Troy and I are not going to happen. I told you what a fiasco that was."

"So, you don't think you'll bring anyone as your date? Not even..." She pursed her lips theatrically. "Xander?"

"What does that mean?"

Scarlett peered at me over the top of her coffee mug. "Nothing. I've just observed that you and Xander have been spending a lot of time together."

"We live together," I said, chuckling. I tipped my cup up to my lips, the hot coffee scalding my tongue. I'd felt shaky since my conversation with Xander. "We've always spent time together. We've known each other since we were ten."

She raised an eyebrow at me. "And that's it?"

I looked away, not trusting myself. I didn't want to lie to Scarlett, she was my best friend and I desperately wanted to tell her everything. I had all these resolute emotions that were frightening the center of who I thought I was. I wasn't supposed to feel this way—not about Xander. I did the best I could to reroute the question.

"What are you saying, Scar?"

She placed her cup delicately on the table and smiled at me. "You know what I'm saying."

We stared at each other, a silent conversation going on with just one look.

*Don't make me say it, Scarlett.*

*Quit lying to yourself!*

*I don't even know what this is.*

*Yes you do. You're just scared.*

*I am, aren't I?*

"I don't know how it looks from your point of view." I demurred.

"Xander is a great guy. You know that. You are a really great woman. You probably have no idea how great."

"I am not."

She rolled her eyes. "Shut it with the false modesty. You can admit it. It's extremely important for a woman to know her faults and what she can offer the world. If you haven't taken an inventory of yourself lately, you should. It'd do you a world of good."

"That's quite new age of you." I wanted to change the subject, though I knew Scarlett wouldn't let it go.

"It's something Emma told me about. I liked the idea."

"And what did you find out about yourself?"

"Oh, tons." she waved her hand in the air dramatically. "I'm driven and artistic. I worry too much about other people and try to help them even when they don't ask for help. I tend to be a little overbearing in that sense. I'm messy." I laughed at her and she shot me a look, "Hey, I can laugh about that, you can't."

"You are all those things," I agreed.

"Now you," she prompted.

"Umm," I looked down at my hands, twisting around the handle of my mug.

*Selfish, lustful...*

"My cleanliness thing is excessive, I know that. Um, I'm a consummate people pleaser... uh... I don't know... this feels weird." I groaned.

"Good. That's a good start." Suddenly she slapped her hand on the table. "Oh. My. God. Did I tell you about book club?"

"No." I leaned forward, pleased the conversation was turning away from me.

"It was Taylor's turn to pick the book. So, she picks some sappy coming of age book, the kind where everyone learns a lesson in the end through the magic of hand-holding or some shit like that."

"A Lifetime movie script." I supplied.

"Worse, more like Hallmark, ugh." A glimmer lit in her eyes, and she leaned closer. "But she gave us the wrong author's name, so we all bought another book with the same title."

She looked around and pulled a small paperback out of her bag. As she slid the book toward me, I assessed the cover of a man's hand grabbing a fishnet clad leg. "Flip through it for a minute."

I read a few passages. My cheeks flamed on fire from the explicit lines. I glanced up at Scarlett, her shoulders were shaking as she suppressed a laugh.

"That was…"

"Deliciously twisted, right? That is some hard-core f-ing going on."

"I don't know how that is even physically possible," I whispered. "Is that a real fetish?"

She shrugged her shoulders. "Probably. There's a fetish for everything. The best part was when we all showed up at the book club talking about the book. Seeing poor Taylor's face when she realized we weren't going to be talking about a baker who saves a small town from bankruptcy with her magic cookie recipe was priceless."

I slid the book back over to Scarlett. "I wish I could've seen that."

"It was great." She took a sip of her drink then set it down, fixing her eyes on me. "Now are you sure there's nothing you want to tell me?"

I hesitated. I'd never lied to Scarlett before. But if I said the words out loud, it'd make what was happening that much more real. How could I talk to Scarlett about Xander? I had no clue what I was doing. "Nothing at all."

She smiled at me in that knowing way. I think she might suspect what's going on, but she gave me a pass and didn't press me further.

Xander wasn't home when I got back. In the darkness of the empty apartment, I hung my coat and purse in the closet. I could hear the soft buzz of electricity in the walls, the murmur of television in the other apartments.

I wondered what problems my neighbors had. Everyone has secret heartbreaks inside them. I felt like I was a visible wreck, lost between an old friend and the ghost of a lover. I was still alive. I had a future. I still had hopes and could feel. I could lean across a tiny kitchen table and kiss another man.

I found myself on the couch, lying against the pillows and closing my eyes. The coffee I had with Scarlett sent caffeine singing through my veins. My clothes felt too tight, my head was a thundercloud. I rubbed my hands over my arms trying to scratch the rolling tingles on my skin.

I heard the door open and shut. Xander's boots thudded down on the linoleum. Not moving from my spot, I pictured him as he took off his coat and hung up his keys. Next, he'd pull off his beanie and run a hand through his hair, mussing the curls haphazardly, making them stick up from static in the air. He rounded the corner and halted when he saw me on the couch.

"Why are you sitting in the dark?" He flipped on a lamp, dousing the room in yellow light.

"Thinking." I stared at the window, trying to make out the lights across the street.

"In the dark?"

I turned toward him. His brow furrowed as he looked down at me. "Yeah, it sort of… happened." His expression was so full of concern I had to look away. "I came home, and I sat down. I don't need to turn on a light to think, and it wasn't that dark when I sat down. Then I guess night came…" I trailed off.

Xander sighed as he sank down next to me on the couch, flinging his arm over the back. His fingers brushed my shoulder, combing through the ends of my hair.

"What's going on?"

I wanted so badly to look at him and tell him everything I was feeling. I wanted him to know how strong I felt when he looked at me. I wanted him to place his hands on me and never let me go. In the past two years, what had started as clinging together in grief had become a connection more sacred than anything I'd ever felt.

I wanted to tell him how, the entire time I was with Max, I felt like a *girl*. Part of me will always be that scared little girl sitting on the curb watching the boy she loved walking away from her. The girl standing in the doorway of a house party watching that boy kiss another girl. The girl lying in her parent's summer cabin, under a scratchy blanket, trying not to cry in pain as she gave herself over to him. Being with Max, I was always going to be that girl.

I realized, I had no compulsion to stay and take care of that boy, because I would never again be that girl.

When I was with Xander, I felt like a *woman*. The moment Xander told me to make my choice, he gave me back my ability to choose. I was in awe over the trust he placed in me, the way for the first time in my life I felt like I truly had a choice. I felt in charge of my own life. I could walk away from Xander, right that moment. I could pick up and leave Ridgewood forever.

"I was wrong earlier." I closed my eyes, trying to muster the courage to continue.

Xander turned to face me. "About what?"

"Earlier when I said none of us had a choice. I was wrong. I know that."

He pursed his lips, not responding. I could tell he wanted to speak but he let me go on, anyway.

"The thing is, it's so much easier when you can blame someone else for your life turning out a certain way, isn't it?"

"Yeah, I guess so..." he murmured.

"I knew what kind of guy Max was. I may not have admitted it, even to myself. But I always knew, deep down. I knew what I was getting myself into. You know, he tried to talk me out of being with him a few times, when we were younger. It made me so mad." I laughed at the memory of us in my bedroom, my mother standing outside the door, furious that Max was in my room.

"I knew what I wanted, and I wanted him. I'm not an idiot. I knew exactly what was waiting for me in a relationship with Max. I knew he'd break my heart. I knew he'd hurt me time and time again. I knew. And yet, I chose to love him. I chose to stay."

"You shouldn't have," Xander said.

"Maybe. But the thing is, I did stay. We can go round and round about the how and why of me staying with Max through everything. But in the end, what matters is that I stayed. I'm not the person you have built up in your head."

Xander leaned forward, resting his elbows on his knees. He scrubbed his hands over his face. "I know who you are, Ana."

"Do you? I spent so long feeling as if I had no power over myself. As if someone else made my choices for me. I mean, it's so much easier to be the victim, isn't it? It's so much easier to say that he controlled us, controlled what we would become. But I'm just as guilty as Max. There were two of us in that relationship. You can't act like he took advantage of me. I made mistakes too. I made a lot of mistakes. So many things I should've done differently, words I can never take back, or words I never said…" I trailed off. I didn't want to think about it. I couldn't go to where my guilt really laid.

"We all have regrets. That doesn't mean you deserved how he treated you." Xander said softly, he turned his head to meet my eyes.

"You say you know me. But I don't think you do." I leaned forward, placing a hand on the side of his cheek. "If we're going to keep going in this direction, I need you to understand that. I'm not a glass toy about to shatter. I can never come close to that girl you've built up in your mind. I can see who you think I am."

"But I do see you. I know the *real* you. I know the way you hum that angsty song from the 80s when you're in the shower. I know when you get stressed you clean." He leaned closer, his lips inches from mine. "I know you have a little freckle behind your left earlobe. I know that you have a scar on your ankle from a bike accident. I know the way you gasp a little every time I kiss you."

I closed my eyes, taking a deep breath. "Don't distract me from my rant, Xander. I need to say this. You need to hear it."

He pulled away enough for me to breathe steadier. "Okay."

I looked down at the floor, counting the swirls on the rug until I got to fourteen. "I can't be whatever this image is in your head. All I'd do is disappoint you. If you care about me the way you say you do, believe me when I say, I'm not that girl."

"Do you want me to insult you? Do you want me to name all your bad traits? I'll do it if it'd convince you I know what I'm doing here."

I laughed a small laugh. "No, I don't think my pride could handle that."

His expression turned somber. He reached forward and took my hand in his. "My eyes are wide open. If I want to love you, I will. Maybe you can't see what I see; you're blind to all the wonderful things about you. And that's okay."

He leaned over and kissed me. I wanted to pull him closer, pull him on top of me. But he pulled away. He fixed his eyes on me. I sat there breathless from his kiss.

"Don't tell me I don't know you, Liliana."

I was struck by how bare he made me feel. He didn't shy away from honest questions no matter how loaded they could be, how one wrong word could end us so quickly, whatever us was. I could break him with one word. That power sickened me, and yet I was drunk on it. In all my years with Max I never felt that. I had no power over Max.

Was this what Xander meant when he said I didn't understand love? Is it trusting that the other person wouldn't break you? Could loving someone mean deciding that the pain could be worth it all? A steady faith in another person's choices? Could it be that simple?

# Chapter Twenty-Three

WHILE I DON'T WANT to go to my parent's annual New Year's party, the idea of going to the bar was even worse. I couldn't venture out after hours anymore and be around people who barely knew Max drunkenly reminiscing about the past. I hated all the questions and the way people could simultaneously be careful and cruel.

This year, I'd finally cowed to my mother's insistence I go to their party. When I got off the phone with her, I looked up to see Xander watching me, surprise in his eyes.

"Did I hear that right?" he asked.

I set the phone down and leveled my eyes with his. "It would seem so. My mother said it'd mean a great deal to her to have me there. I think she wants to show me off to some of her friends who are parents of eligible young men and try to marry me off."

He raised his eyebrows. "How old-fashioned. I hope she's been saving up for your dowry."

"Yeah. That's not how she framed it, but I know her." I grabbed a rag off the sink and began wiping down the counter, scrubbing at a small spot of dried coffee. "She thinks I should be moving on by now."

"So, I'm guessing you haven't told her about us?" he asked, stepping around the counter to stand by my side.

I slapped the rag down in the sink and looked up at him. "We don't talk like that. She means well, but…" I sighed. "You know, Scarlett and her mom are best friends. She tells her mom everything. I think she told her mom about Emma before she told me. I wish I could say my mom and I have that type of relationship, but we don't."

I turned to face him. "I wish I didn't have to go, but I know if I don't, my mom won't let me hear the end of it."

"What if I went with you?"

"Like a date? Because I certainly didn't tell my mother we've been making out on the sly."

He frowned at me. At first, I thought he'd be mad about how I made our relationship sound casual, but instead he leaned closer to me. "It could be whatever you want it to be. We can be just friends, or it could be a date. It's up to you."

"Okay," I said, looking away from him.

"Okay to friends, or okay to it being a date?" he asked, nervous.

I knew I couldn't decide. I knew I'd vacillate between what I wanted until we walked into the party.

"Just okay," I said, not meeting his eyes.

The dress I borrowed from Scarlett was a black V-neck sheath with a silvery overlay. It was too tight in the bust, too loose in the hips, and a little too long on me to be fashionable.

I walked into the living room where Xander was sitting on the couch. He glanced up from the TV to me. His mouth twisted up into a large grin.

"Whoa, you look amazing."

I glanced down at the dress and frowned. "You think? I'm not so sure. It's a little low cut with my...you know."

He stood up and walked to me, placing a hand on my cheek. "I know I said we'd go as friends but seeing you in this dress is giving me some very unfriendly thoughts."

I handed Xander a flute of champagne. "So, my mother, in a stroke of uncharacteristic familiarity, just cornered me in the bathroom and asked if I brought you as my date."

Xander raised his eyebrows and tried to hide a smirk. "Did she? What did you say?"

"That we've been ripping each other's clothes off every chance we get," I rolled my eyes. "What do you think I said?"

"That would be an over-exaggeration of how far we've gone, unfortunately." Xander grinned.

I glared at him. "You know what I mean." I sighed loudly. "I played dumb."

He glanced over my shoulder at where my mother was visiting with a fellow Ridgewood Pearl, Liz Hansen. "I think your mom wants to set you up with Matt Hansen. Looks like she's trying to get you a piece of the great Hansen Outdoors Center fortune."

I grimaced. "After what happened to him and Cami? No way in hell." Our classmates, Cami and Matt Hansen recently separated, and I suspected Matt's roving eye was the cause.

I swallowed the last of my champagne and grabbed his glass out of his hand, draining his glass. I looked over at my mom.

"Sorry, I get anxious at these things. Being here reminds me of all the expectations I haven't lived up to. The constant questions from all their friends about my life. After they figure out I'm not that interesting they all want to talk about my brother. How his residency went, how successful he is."

Xander stepped closer, resting his hand on my arm. "Hey, I don't know if it makes you feel any better, but I think you're the most fascinating person here."

I laughed up at him. "That's all that matters, right?"

His hand didn't leave my arm. Seeing the serious look on his face I stepped closer to him, resting my hand on his chest. Gazing down at me, he covered my hand with his.

"You know, you're the only one who matters to me."

I glanced around the party, before grabbing his hand and pulling him behind me. I led him down the hall and around a corner. As we approached the stairs, I looked back. The party was in full swing, with no one watching us as we ducked away. We snuck into my childhood bedroom and closed the door.

"I haven't been here in a long time. Not since..." he trailed off, but I knew he was thinking the same thing I was. The last time Xander was here, he'd come over after I caught Max kissing Carrie Semple at a high school party.

"Still looks the same. I thought my parents would've cleaned it out by now, but they haven't gotten around to it. I'm pretty sure they won't consider me an adult until I get married. Until then, the shrine of Ana remains." I walked to my vanity. Pictures surrounded the mirror, the tape holding them up had begun to turn yellow from the years. I touched a group picture of all of us together on a camping trip. Even stupid Peter Jurgensen was in the picture. In it I'm where I always was, tucked under Max's arm, smiling up at him.

"Thank you for coming tonight. If I hate these things, you must be in hell."

"I'm surviving." He stepped closer to me and gently cupped my cheeks. I stared up at him, transfixed. Slowly he bent down to kiss me. My arms wrapped around his waist, pulling him closer. He walked backward until we fell onto my bed. His hands came down my legs and grabbed my thighs, bringing me closer to him. I could feel all of him against me. I slid my hands down to tug his shirt out of the front of his pants. I needed him desperately. A fever awakened across my skin, his kisses scoring along my neck. I started sliding my hand down the front of his pants, but he stopped me.

"We can't Ana," he whispered against my lips.

I pulled my hand back and leaned away from him, breathless. "Yeah, you're right, we just got…"

"Carried away."

I smiled at him. "Yeah." I climbed off the bed, straightening my dress. "We should get back to the party. We don't want my parents coming to look for us."

He laughed. "You go on ahead of me, I need a minute before I can go out there."

I looked back at him, confused. Then I saw him reach down and adjust himself in his pants. I clapped my hand over my mouth and giggled before scrambling out of the room.

Back at the party, I tried to keep my distance from Xander. I did impulsive things when I was too close to him. I couldn't risk having all the guests see me mauling him. Counting the time until the New Year's, I made painful small talk with my parent's friends, relaying the same tired information.

*Yes, these canapes are delicious.*

*No, I don't see my brother very often these days.*

*Yes, I still live in town.*

*I'm proud of my brother, yes.*

*Ridgewood General, in the emergency room.*

*My soon to be sister-in-law is lovely, for sure.*

*No, you heard wrong. I'm a nurse not a doctor... no I don't know why you'd think that either.*

*Yes, my brother will be very successful.*

*No, I don't know what's in the peanut sauce.*

I got lucky the guests never asked me about my dating life. I knew if I was forced into giving a straight answer, I wouldn't be able to honestly say there was no one in my life. I couldn't define what Xander and I were, but it was definitely something.

At one minute to midnight, I locked eyes with Xander across the room. He stared at me, a small smile on his lips. He didn't move toward me, respecting my wish to keep us a secret. Thirty seconds left on the television. I watched as people began to drift closer to their significant others, preparing for the big kiss. Though I knew I might regret it, I stepped toward Xander, clutching my champagne glass tight in my hand and stopped in front of him.

He took a step closer to me, took my glass out of my hand and set it down on the side table. Around us everyone was shouting the countdown. They must be loud, but locked into his gaze, the cacophony fell away. Fireworks erupted from the top of the Space Needle to the sounds of the local indie station but all I could sense was him.

As he leaned toward me, I decided I wouldn't turn away. I wanted to kiss him. I wanted to feel him against me, and I didn't care who saw us. In that moment, as the new year began, I wanted nothing more than to have his lips against mine. I closed my eyes, and everyone cheered around us. His kiss was featherlight, enough to look innocent but sent waves of heat through me, nevertheless. His face skimmed against mine, his lips moving across my cheek to rest on my ear.

"Happy New Year, Liliana."

I gripped his elbows as he leaned into me. The way we were standing no one could see his face, which was lucky, because he gently nipped at my ear lobe with his teeth, sending a shockwave through me. My knees weakened. He pulled away enough to press a quick kiss to my cheek. I saw the fire in his eyes, and my cheek burned from his touch, the place he held my arm seared under his embrace. I stared up at him, not able to keep the stupid smile off my face.

"Happy New Year," I whispered back.

He raised a hand and slowly brushed aside a lock of hair that'd fallen out of its twist. I brought my hand to rest on top of his, never breaking eye contact.

"Hey, guys." Matt Hansen interrupted us. We both jumped back, our hands dropping between us. He grinned. "Nice party, right? I used to hate when my mom insisted I go to these things. But now that I'm older, it's like I don't have anything better to do."

"Right, nice party." Xander answered.

Matt glanced between us, a smirk on his face. "So, are you two, like, doing it or something?"

I opened my mouth shocked at his crudeness. I shouldn't be all that surprised to hear him talk like that. Before I could respond, Xander cleared his throat, sparing me a small glance. "Nah, we're just friends man. No big thing."

"Uh-huh." Matt chuckled as he took a swig of his beer. "If you say so." He looked around the party. "You guys want to head to the Skol House? I'm sure they'll still serve us if we hurry."

I grimaced. "Not really. I'm not in the mood for the bar scene tonight." I looked at Xander. "I can crash here if you want to go, though. I don't need a ride."

He shook his head at me. "No, I'm good. I'm done with the Skol House too. I just can't hang anymore, I guess."

Matt drained the last of his beer and set it down next to my champagne glass. "Well, you change your mind, you know where to find half our graduating class." He laughed loudly, clapping Xander on the back. "See you guys."

I turned back to Xander. "Are you sure? It might be fun for you."

He shook his head, laughing, "No way would that'd be fun." He leaned closer to me, his lips against my ear again. "Speaking of fun though, we should get out of here."

Pulling away I smiled up at him. "I'd like that." I glanced around the party where everyone was still having a good time. "I'll grab my stuff quick, meet you at the door?"

I should've known better than to think my mom would let it go. My kiss with Xander at midnight still lingered on my cheek when my mother stopped me. I was about to leave when she pulled me into her bedroom. The door was barely shut before she got to her point.

"Darling, Alexander is a sweet young man. But I'm not sure he's the right person for you."

"Who says I'm seeing Xander?" I asked, knowing the crack in my voice gave me away.

She raised an eyebrow at me. "I'm not blind Liliana. You ignore that perfectly nice boy Matt Hansen all night to whisper and laugh with Alexander."

"First of all, Mom. Matt Hansen is not a nice boy. Trust me. I'm friends with his ex-wife. And second…" I sighed. I couldn't lie convincingly so I decided to switch tactics. "Why would Xander be so bad to date? Because he was Max's best friend? Because he doesn't have a mother who's a Pearl? Or is it because he doesn't have a mother? Is it because he grew up poor?"

She frowned at me. "You make me sound so shallow when you ask me that. I'm thinking about you, Liliana. You're a sensitive girl. After everything Maximilian put you through, I want to see you happy, I want you to have security."

"Xander is secure. I feel completely safe with him. He'd never do anything to hurt me. I thought you liked him."

"I do. Your father and I both admire him a great deal. He's a hard worker, and obviously a loyal friend. I know he has done a good job in helping support you after Maximilian passed away."

"He did more than help support me. He was my entire support system." I laughed. "When Max passed, Xander was the only one I could turn to. He was the only one who understood what I was going through. He was the only person I trusted. Mom, I was hurting so much, and the only thing that helped me was turning to someone who cared for Max as much as I did. Max was Xander's best friend. They were practically brothers. I know how you felt about Max. No offense Mom, but I couldn't turn to you for support when you spent our entire relationship barely tolerating his presence."

"Ana." She sat down on the edge of her bed, sighing loudly. "You think I never had someone like Max? I was young once too. I dated the wrong guy a time or two. I know how appealing someone like Max can be. But if I was cold to him, it's only because I knew how much you were going to get hurt. I wanted to protect you."

I sank down next to her. "I know you did."

"You are so much like your father, always seeing the good in people, wanting to help them. Giving and giving. There were nights your father didn't come home until late at night because he was treating patients, waving away money. A person like that in the wrong hands..." She looked down at her hands, playing with her wedding band. "It can go so wrong. I worry you'll be hurt again."

I grabbed my mother's hand, squeezing it gently. "Mom, I know you mean well, but you have to trust me to make these decisions myself."

She sat back, staring out the window. In the daytime it would've been a picture of rugged mountains jutting behind Freedom Bay, but at the midnight hour it was a blacked frame. "I worry about you, is all. If he's your boyfriend now—"

"He's not." I interrupted, the words stinging against my tongue. "He's not my boyfriend, Mom."

She sighed, casting me an impervious look. "If you say so."

The car ride home was quiet. I knew I should be thinking about the conversation with my mother. Instead, I kept replaying the moment Xander answered Matt, saying we were friends. Despite the fact I'd been so adamant about taking things slow, and I was so convinced we shouldn't let anyone know about us, the words stung. I didn't want to hear him say them.

Once we were inside the apartment, Xander walked to his room and opened his door before he turned to me. "I don't know what you want to call tonight, but thanks for inviting me. Even if it was just as friends, I had a better time than I thought I would."

He stared at me, and I willed myself to step toward him. He seemed to sense my reluctance and nodded slightly at me, giving me permission to stay away. He turned away, closing the door behind him. Still gripping my little silver clutch, I walked down the hall into my own room. Slowly I pulled off my dress and hung it carefully back into the closet. I'd need to dry clean it before I gave it back. I kicked off my heels and felt the blood rush back into my toes. I glanced at the door, knowing Xander was only a few steps away from me.

I did my going-to-bed routine slowly, taking my time washing the makeup off my face, applying lotion, brushing my teeth. I pulled on an old concert T-shirt and ratty sweatpants with snowmen on them. I picked up a comb and began to work through my hair. With every stroke of my comb, the words echoed through me.

Just friends.

No big thing.

The way his lips felt against my skin, the pull of his gaze across the room. I couldn't pretend that I didn't want Xander anymore. I couldn't stand next to him and not want to touch him. I was tired of fighting it. I couldn't hold on to my silly excuses any longer. They seemed trivial against the desire I had for him.

Staring at my reflection I grimaced. My face was scrubbed bare, my hair was fluffy from the vigorous brushing I did. I grabbed some tinted lip balm, sliding that on my lips so they didn't blend into my skin tone. I patted my hair, trying to tame the frizz. I snagged a cotton nightgown out of the drawer. It was too cold to wear it, but seduction could be a chilly business, I reckoned. I thought about whether I wanted to put on underwear. If I was sleeping, I wouldn't put anything on under my pajamas, but I wasn't planning on sleeping. I weighed the options before grabbing the first lacy thing I could find and pulling it on before I could change my mind.

With one last backward glance I walked out my bedroom door on shaky legs. The hallway was completely silent. I could see a crack of light under Xander's door. Taking a deep breath, I opened the door to his bedroom. He lounged on his bed, reading a book on top of the covers. When the door opened, he sat up straighter, setting his book down next to him. "Ana…"

I climbed on the bed, leaned forward, and put a finger to his lips, silencing him. He watched me as I swung a leg over each side of his hips. Straddling him, I leaned down, inches from his face. "I was thinking about what you said to Matt tonight. I hope you only said that because you thought I wanted you to."

Beneath my thighs I could feel how strong his legs were. He had taut muscles from hours of manual labor. His shirt had ridden up and I could see the flat expanse of his stomach. It was pale with the lightest trail of gold-blond hair. He furrowed his brow and I leaned closer to him. "The thing is, I don't want to be your friend."

"You don't?" his voice throaty.

I shook my head, "No, I want more."

"Whatever you want, Ana." His voice got husky. He kept his hands laid flat on the bed next to him.

"You mean it?" I whispered.

Slowly he brought his hand up and cupped my cheek. In the low light of his bedside lamp, his eyes were hazel pools. "Anything. Anything you want, I'll give you."

He laced his hand through my hair, bringing my lips to his. I bent down, meeting his lips for a kiss. "For tonight, all I want is to not leave your bed."

# Chapter Twenty-Four

I N THE DAPPLED LIGHT of his lone lamp, Xander kissed me back, digging his fingers into my hips. I could feel how warm his skin was through my nightgown. At some point his shirt came off. He slid his hands from my face to rest on the back of my thighs, bringing me to rest right against him. All that lay between us was flimsy fabric.

Every kiss before tonight had an edge of urgency behind it, as if we were one moment away from being permanently torn apart. This was a different kind of kiss. It was slow and indulgent. Every dip of his tongue against my lips, every brush of his fingers across my skin; a sweltering pain coursing through me. He took his time moving his hands gently up my thighs, his fingertips tracing lines on my skin. My hands were in his hair as I ground my hips into him. Beneath me I could feel his body reacting. I deepened our kiss, moving with him.

Groaning into my mouth, he moved his hand over my ass, up the back of my nightgown to rest on the small of my back. My nightgown bunched up around my waist. His hands roamed all over my back, his fingers pressing into my skin. A galvanic urge thrummed through me. I wanted more of him. Now. I pulled him closer, needing his body against me. His tongue traced against my lower lip; my hands were in his hair. His hands traced over my tighs and then bare waist, pushing my nightgown higher. His thumbs resting below my breasts. I ran my hands down his throat, moving them lower until I paused on his bare chest.

I broke our kiss, pushing against his firm chest to straighten up. Grabbing the hem of my nightgown, I started pulling it over my body. Xander stopped me with his hand.

"Wait."

I stilled, looking down at him. "What?"

He gripped the bottom of my nightgown, crushing the lace trim between his fingers. "Are you sure about this?"

I bent down, pressing a reassuring kiss to his lips. "Yes, I'm sure."

He cupped a hand around my throat, his fingers on the nape of my neck. "We can't go back from this."

"I don't want to go back. I just want you," I whispered.

For a long moment he stared at me, all the fears of what could be between us swimming in his eyes. His hand slid down from my neck, slowly trailing down the front of my body. His gaze didn't break as he gripped the bottom of my nightgown and in one fluid motion, he pulled it over my head.

He leaned back, looking over me with a fire in his eyes. I should've been self-conscious, but something about the way Xander's hand splayed across my hip, the way his gaze roamed across my body emboldened me.

He grabbed my hips and rolled me over, his hands running down my side stopped at my underwear. He kissed me hard as he pulled first my underwear off and then his. A condom appeared, and we came together. I gasped as he slid into me, the sensation building as his eyes connected with mine.

His touch was fire coursing through me. The flame was steady in a way I never knew possible. Every kiss, every caress felt true. The careful way he hovered over me and the way his lips felt against my neck, the way his hands gripped my hips, my thighs. In the way we moved together, a perfect synchronization. While it wasn't familiar, I knew it was right. Every move called out to me.

*You thought you knew pleasure?*

*This is what you've been waiting for.*

*This is trust.*

*This is the beautiful burn.*

*This is everything you'll need.*

I cried out, as we crashed together, our bodies slick with our exertion. I bit down on his shoulder, tasting the salt on his skin. His fingers dug into the back of my thighs, pulling me deeper to him. Our breaths were ragged when he pulled away to look down at me.

A smile stretched across his face and my heart leapt at the sight. He opened his mouth as if he were going to say something, but then closed it, ducking his head down to rest in the hollow of my neck. I ran my hands through his hair, the sweat from the nape of his neck slick against my fingers. I closed my eyes, savoring the feel of his breath against my collarbone and his weight on my chest.

He spoke into my neck, a wisp of air cooling me. "Stay with me tonight?"

I pulled his hair enough to get him to look up at me. His eyes bored into mine. I rubbed my thumb along the spot where his ear met his jawbone. "I'm not going anywhere."

In the morning, the light was all wrong, waking me as it fell across my face. I sensed Xander beside me, his face buried in my neck, my feet were wedged between his legs. I sighed as I savored the weight of his arm across my waist.

Slowly I opened my eyes. Xander's room got the early morning sun. I realized he was typically up before the sun rose, getting ready for work as the light began to filter through his thin blinds. I decided that next time we needed to sleep in we'd spend the night in my room where my black-out shades kept the room in darkness.

I rolled over to my back, struck by the thought. *Next time.* Did I want a next time? I ran a finger over my lips, still tasting him on my skin. I couldn't doubt the way I felt any longer. There were so many things that tried to break me recently. Being with Xander was a balm for my pain. I couldn't stop if I wanted to.

I glanced over at Xander's sleeping face. I thought of the first night we spent in the apartment, and how I studied him as we lay sleeping. I was struck with how I felt by just looking at him. Even if I didn't want to admit it, I was losing myself in him. I turned to my other side and faced him completely. He didn't stir, but his hand slid against my body as I moved. Slowly, I brushed an unruly curl from his forehead.

The feeling washing over me was different from anything I'd ever experienced with Max. I thought I loved Max. For so long I thought Max loved me. But lying next to Xander I realized how little I understood about love.

In the end, I never knew Max. And how could I love a man I never knew? When you don't have all your heart to give, can you say it's real? Max never knew me. He knew what I wanted him to know. I tried so hard, for so many years, to be the kind of woman he could love. I'd stuff down parts of myself and try to erase the parts of me he wouldn't like. I tried to become the woman I thought he could love. By doing that, I was as culpable as he was. How could I say Max and I loved each other if we never truly knew each other?

I laid my hand on Xander's cheek, feeling his skin soft under my fingertips. My chest hurt from the contact; my breath caught in my throat. His eyelids were bleached lilac in the morning sun. His eyelashes were white-blond at the eye line, curling to a russet brown at the tips. I could feel the tears threatening my eyes, so I closed them, willing myself to regain composure.

I took a deep breath and counted to three as I let it out.

I took another breath, counted to three.

I took another breath, counted to three.

Slowly, I opened my eyes. Xander was looking back at me. I gasped, surprised. I wanted to say something, but his gaze held me transfixed. His lips parted slightly. I thought of what those lips did to me last night, and warmth flowed through me. He brought his hand up, gently brushing my hair from my face.

When Xander looked at me like that, it was as if I truly was the person he claimed to love. I wanted to be that woman. His trust in me made me want to be more. If only the woman he saw was real, if only I could measure up. The thought felt like a weight bearing down on my chest. If he truly knew me, he wouldn't be staring at me with such adoration. I didn't deserve someone so emphatically good.

"Why are you sad?" he murmured, a line forming between his brows.

"I'm not," I sighed. "I'm so happy."

I wasn't lying, I was happy. But every breath of happiness was tinged with an unyielding truth. How long until this fell apart and Xander realized I wasn't the girl he thought he knew? How much longer until I screwed it up? Because, if I was the taker in this relationship, if I was Xander's Max, I knew it was only a matter of time.

A slow smile spread across his face as he stared at me. "Me too." He leaned forward to press a kiss to my lips. "I never thought I'd have this. I never thought I'd get to wake up with you in my arms. I never thought I'd have you."

There were no words to say. I wanted to tell him everything. I wanted to stay here with him all day, savoring this night in our consecrated bed and the down of his hair.

"Before I forget," he murmured into my hair. "Happy Birthday."

I smiled into his skin. "Thanks."

He nuzzled into my neck, his words at my throat. "Can I give you your present now?"

"You didn't have to get me anything." I pulled away to look up at him.

"But I already got it." He sat up, reaching behind him into this nightstand to pull out an envelope. He handed it to me with a hopeful look on his face.

I sat up next to him and opened the envelope, pulling out the papers inside to study them. "You got me admission to the Lisandre exhibit?"

He gave me a small smile, still nervous. "Is that okay? I was thinking about how much you loved that painting in the living room and so I looked up the name of the artist. She's coming to town in November. We could go to Seattle and make a whole day of it."

Throwing my arms around his neck, I hugged him. He wrapped his arms around my waist bringing me closer. "I love it. This has to be the best gift I've ever received."

I left out all the things I was thinking; that in all the years I was with Max he never took the time to get me something this personal. He didn't like art and couldn't understand my interest in it. Xander didn't spend too much money on the tickets, but the idea of him taking so many steps—looking up the artist's name, finding her on the Internet, and finding an upcoming show—the thought and planning that went into it made me wistful.

I leaned forward pressing myself against him. My hands ran through his hair, I kissed him without abandon, eagerly chasing away all my doubts. He grabbed my waist; his fingers were tender against my skin as he rolled on top of me. Our kisses were fevered, and my hands pulled him closer, wanting more.

Guiltily, I accepted his touches, taking in his adoration. I knew I'd regret it if this fell apart, but I craved his embrace, his kisses, his lips in my hair, the way he held me so tight. I felt as if we were falling together, down into a frightening abyss.

We made love and I laid my head on his bare chest as he stroked my hair. I ran a finger over a large scar below his left rib. The second time was even better than the first. We fit together perfectly. He knew how to touch me, how to kiss my skin, when to pull away and when to delve deeper. I'd only been with one other person in comparison. I was pretty sure life couldn't get better than these moments of passion we shared.

I pulled away to look up at him. His hand was behind his head, and he was watching my hand move along his scar.

"I fell off a longboard and scraped up my whole left side. Max dared me to go down Route 203," he explained.

"Where did you get a longboard?"

He furrowed his brows in thought. "I think Max stole it from Damon Porter's house during a party." He glanced at my face before looking away quickly. "I didn't really ask him. I know he didn't buy it though." He chuckled low.

"How old were you?" I asked softly.

"Fifteen, or so. I think. Something like that," he mused.

I sucked in my breath. I knew Max did things like that, I would've been completely blind not to see it, but it still came as a shock finding out these secrets years later.

"He didn't go down on it?" I asked.

Xander shook his head. "No. After I crashed, we chucked the longboard in the woods and went home. I probably should've gone to the hospital, but we didn't want to explain how I got hurt. The board would've been discovered, and Max and I would've been in big trouble. Plus, my dad didn't have the money for medical bills."

I struggled to find the right words. A sense of loyalty to Max feuded with outrage over the situation. "But Max was the one who stole it."

He shrugged, "That's how it worked out. You knew how it was, Ana." His eyes caught mine, so much never needed to be explained between us. I was right to tell my mom that Xander understood. That kind of magnetism was undeniable. When I was in the center of Max's life, it was a level of happiness nothing could compare to. But Xander understood the price of that loyalty. Max hurt me, repeatedly, but he hurt Xander too.

"I do," I murmured.

He leaned down, grabbed his sweatpants off the floor and pulled them on. He kept his back to me, clutching the side of the bed with tight fists.

"Look, I hope I can say this to you without it sounding like some crazy sob story. The thing is, all my life, I've played second fiddle to my best friend. Even with him gone, having to fight with both the memory of him and the guilt for wanting what was his." His back was tense, his head hung down. "More than anything I want my best friend to be alive and I didn't want to want you this way. I feel guilty, because I realize that without Max around, I might finally get a chance to show you how happy I could make you. It's enough to break me."

"So, you felt guilty?" I asked softly.

He turned to me, frowning. "Of course, I felt guilty. That I should be the one who lives when he was such a... big person. The world is a darker place without him around. People loved Max. You loved Max." He chuckled under his breath, shaking his head. "Do you remember that day we all met?"

I nodded, remembering the way I'd seen them getting chased by that awful boyfriend of Dana's. I'd never seen an adult act that way in public. On TV I'd see clips of two men fighting before my mother would quickly change the channel. But I'd never seen that level of anger in person, and certainly never seen it focused on kids. "Of course. It's a hard day to forget."

He bent his knee and leaned toward me. "The thing is no one had ever tried to defend us like that before." He shook his head, a wistful smile on his face. "And certainly not someone like you. You wore lacy socks, for God's sake. Your little hair clippy things always matched your dresses. I can remember it all. You were so different from us. You had a brand-new bike, with wheels so shiny you could see yourself in them. You owned two pairs of rollerblades; your parents threw you pool parties at the private country club. No one like that had ever spent any time with kids like us, let alone risked their pretty white tights to try and protect us from Max's abusive stepdad."

"I never saw it that way," I argued.

"But we did. We knew from the moment we saw you standing in the road, something in all three of our lives irrevocably changed."

I agreed with him, nodding softly, and gripping his hand. He sighed loudly, looking away from me. "It was my idea to come back for you. Did you know that?"

I stilled, the memory of that day changing before my eyes.

He kept talking, his voice wavering. I knew we were on the edge of something we could never come back from.

"We thought you were right behind us, but when I saw you weren't I told max we had to go back to check on you. You came toward us and though it was me who wanted to look for you, it was Max who hugged you. It was Max you cried to. In that moment I knew that's how it was going to be. I knew it'd be Max's arm around your shoulder as you cried, while I stood there looking like a fool, watching you two and knowing that if anyone deserved a hug, it was me."

"I never knew," I whispered.

"It doesn't matter now. The thing is, I shouldn't have been surprised. Max was always picked before me in sports. He was the one who made people laugh. The teachers let him get away with turning in assignments late. He had something about him that made things a little easier." He shook his head at me. "He had you and I never would. For so long I told myself I would not be jealous of a single thing Max had, if only I could have a chance with you."

I was speechless. How could I argue with this? I wasn't sure if I wanted to be upset with Xander or happy about his confession.

"Falling in love with your best friend's girl breaks all sorts of rules. I knew better than to act on it. I was used to Max getting his way and stepping aside so he could get everything he wanted. I lived on his scraps, profiting from the boost in popularity, from the friends he attracted, with the alcohol he scored and the girls who always swarmed around him. I'd tell myself it was enough."

"But it wasn't?" I whispered.

"Not without you." He pushed his hair out of his eyes, looking dejected. His voice was soft. "I will always feel guilty because I've always wanted you. I feel guilty because I wanted us to happen for the right reason. I didn't want you to want me because of Max, or despite Max. I wanted you to want me for *me*."

He sighed loudly and roughly scrubbed his face, his facial hair scraping against his calloused hands. "But most of all, I feel guilty because I'm finally getting everything I wanted. I get a chance to try to be with you. I'm guilty because all my waiting around, being second string in Max's life, was the price I had to pay to be with you. I feel awful, but that doesn't make me want you any less."

"If you feel so guilty, why did you pursue me?"

A wistful smile crossed his face. "Max, honestly. I thought about how upset he was when I wanted to date you. He did everything he could to stop it. I wondered if he'd still be upset. But then I thought about what he did when the situation was reversed. Max knew he wanted you and he got you. So, I decided to honor him and take a page out of his playbook. For once, I was going to do what he'd do. I'd go after what I wanted and let everything else be damned."

I hesitated before admitting. "Even if Max was exactly like that, I doubt he'd be happy with us being together."

Xander laughed, shaking his head. "I know he wouldn't. But it's the truth. Sometimes we don't see ourselves clearly. To be honest, I understood Max better than he understood himself." He paused, tilted his head to the side slightly, his face growing more serious. "You, too. I understand exactly who you are, better than you realize."

I scoffed loudly. I didn't want him to see how much those words rocked me. "And what about me, Xan? If we're going down the road, then who do I know best?"

"Me," he said plainly, his face open. "You know me, Ana. You may have spent a long time trying to fight it. But we get each other, more than you want to admit."

I bit my lip; his earnest tone made my chest hurt. I understood everything he wasn't saying. He was right, we did get each other. Max never really knew me. He never wanted to, and I never wanted to know the real him either. Our relationship was built on the falsehoods of what we both thought the other wanted us to be.

Xander did know me. He understood me at my core, and I understood him. It'd always been that way. I may have been infatuated with Max, but Xander was the one I needed. He was the first one I wanted to confide in, the first one I wanted to tell about my day.

I closed my eyes and took a deep breath, the cold air ached through my ribs. I knew I should be horrified by his revelations about his guilt, but I couldn't be. He was showing me the darkest parts of himself. He was telling me that he understood the gruesome, dark place inside me, that he felt it too. If we were going to hell for what was happening between us, we'd go together. I crawled across the bed and climbed on top of Xander. I had no words to give him. The only thing I could offer was my embrace. I hoped he understood.

# Chapter Twenty-Five

I N THE WAKE OF New Year's, Xander and I found ourselves spending every free moment together. After that first night, I invited him to stay in my room with me. After that, his bed became extraneous. When we weren't in bed together, we were watching TV, my feet tucked under his legs, his hand on my knee. We shopped and made all of our food together. In a way nothing had changed. It was amazing how little of our routine had shifted, yet everything felt headier and more intense. While cooking, he'd sneak behind me, his hands on my hips and kiss my neck, as he pinned me to the counter, and I'd melt into his body. In the middle of the night, his leg would wedge between mine, and he'd throw his slack arm across my waist. We'd find ourselves sleepily turning to each other to make love.

Soon though, I learned that the glow of my newfound happiness couldn't take away the sting of a truly bad day. Everything seemed to go wrong. I forgot my lunch at home, forcing me to get the soggy, sodium-ridden cafeteria food. I spilled coffee on my scrubs and had no replacement pants in my locker. I was stuck with Dr. Larson, the most patronizing doctor on the floor. I kept walking away from my desk only to forget a crucial item: the clipboard, the medication, my coffee mug. And final insult to injury, I dropped my phone in the toilet, completely ruining a new smartphone.

By the time I got home from work I was completely done with humanity. All I wanted was to go home, shower, and watch a corny comedy on TV in my pajamas.

I'd barely walked through the door when Xander greeted me, wearing a light blue button-down and a pair of khakis. My jacket was dangling off my shoulder as I stopped to stare at him.

"Hey," I said carefully. He never dressed up like this. It was weird.

He looked a little embarrassed. "I was thinking maybe I could take you out to dinner?"

"Oh, well… I've had a long day and…" I groaned loudly, rubbing my forehead with my stubby nails. I paused, trying to find the words. I knew he was only trying to be sweet by taking me out. There was no way he could've known what a hard day I had and how I'd be feeling. If I was a less anxious person something like that would be wonderful to come home to. But I was me. I couldn't help feeling the way I did. "I'm not feeling it tonight."

He wrapped his arms around me, and I ducked my head into his chest, taking a deep breath of the sweet smell of soap and sunshine always lingering on his skin. His fingers drew little circles on my back, and I pulled away to press a kiss to his lips. This was new too—kissing when we came home. We hadn't ventured out of the home yet. We hadn't had the conversation about what we'd be to each other outside our apartment walls.

He rubbed my cheek with his thumb, smiling big. "I made reservations at that Thai place you like."

I pulled away from him. I hated to be a spoilsport, but I was so tired and the idea of a restaurant with other people exhausted me further.

"Well, let me shower and see how I…"

Walking into the kitchen to grab a drink of water, I turned the corner and stopped short at the sight before me. "What happened?" I gasped. In addition to all the dishes in the sink I'd asked him to wash, there were several food-encrusted pans sitting on the stove. An opened jar of peanut butter sat on the cutting board next to a dirty knife. Coffee creamer sat next to the coffee maker, its lid still gaping wide.

Xander stood behind me and I could feel him tense. "Oh, right. The dishes…" he trailed off.

"Well, I'm not going anywhere now," I muttered, irritated. I stomped over to the counter picking up all the dirty dishes and tossing them into the sink, the slam of the glasses and silverware against each other reverberating through the small kitchen.

"I can do those. I'll clean everything up when we get back," Xander interrupted, taking a plate from my hand and setting it on the counter behind me. I picked up the plate, and placed it on top of the other dishes, turning the water on and adding soap. I began to furiously wash the dishes. I didn't trust myself to look at him and betray how annoyed I was.

"No, they need to be done now." I knew it was petty to be upset about dishes in the sink, but he knew I liked things clean. It was more than that. I couldn't relax when things were like this left around the house.

He bumped me lightly on the hip, pushing me away from the sink. "Why don't you take a shower? You'll feel better."

"Are you going to clean up this kitchen?" I asked with a raised eyebrow.

He looked around, frowning. "I could start, I guess."

"I'll do it." I huffed loudly turning back to the dirty dishes. I scrubbed the dried egg off the pan, pushing hard on the bristled sponge, trying to release my frustration onto the baked-on food.

I didn't want Xander to see me this way. I didn't want to feel this way. I wished he'd leave so I could fume in peace.

I could feel his eyes on me as I scrubbed the pans. He cleared his throat, a tone of surprise in his voice. "Is this our first fight as a couple?"

I didn't correct him referring to us as a couple. It was hardly the time for semantics. That was a completely different fight, and I could barely stand this argument over dirty pans.

"I know it may not matter to you, but after the kind of day I had, all I wanted was to come home and not worry about more work."

"I know how you are about keeping the place clean. You asked me to do the dishes and I didn't do it. It's my fault."

The foreign words rippled over me. I wondered what it would've taken for Max to apologize for something. So much more than dishes, I knew that.

I knew the reason Max wouldn't say sorry for anything. Apologizing for something meant taking responsibility for the effect his actions had on other people, and that kind of weight was never something Max could bear. I didn't trust Xander's apology. I was waiting for the follow-up of why it was my fault too.

When I didn't say anything, he kept talking, his words tumbling over each other in a rush. "Look, I'm not perfect. I make mistakes too. I know I should've done the dishes like you asked me to, but I forgot and then I got excited about the idea of taking you out on a date and I forgot again. It's an innocent mistake." He paused, cocking his head to the side. "But just so you know, I'm going to make this mistake again. It's unavoidable. We're going to have this fight again."

"Whatever," I muttered, turning away from him. I didn't want to watch him leave the way I knew he would, the way Max would. At any minute I expected him to stomp off in a huff. "Why don't you go then?"

"Go where?" he asked, his voice incredulous. I pulled the drain plug out and watched the water go down. "Do you want me to go?"

"No," I mumbled. I hated this feeling—the anger inside me, the doubt of how valid my feelings were, this shame in the reaction I was causing in Xander. The way I was making him leave me. This was surely it. He had to realize if I was going to go off over a few dirty dishes, I was hardly worth sticking around for.

"Then, why would I go?"

Slowly I turned my body toward him. I couldn't look at him. I couldn't handle seeing the rejection on his face.

"Because we're fighting, and that's what people do. We fight, then someone leaves. That's how it works."

I expected him to storm off but instead he leaned against the counter, crossing his feet at the ankles. "That's not at all how it works."

I glanced up at him. Did he not understand how fights between couples went? I was a master of this kind of thing. "Uh, yeah, it is. That's what..." I bit my lips before I finished my sentence.

He tensed his jaw as my words trailed off. His words were low between clenched teeth. "I don't know how many times I need to say this to you, but I'm not Max."

"Yeah, I know," I scoffed. "I am well aware of that."

He narrowed his eyes at me. I prepared for whatever barb he was going to sling my way. He stood straight, took the two strides across the room to stand in front of me. He grabbed my arms, not roughly, but hard enough to pull me closer to him.

"However you think relationships work, what worked or didn't work with you and Max, that is not me. That will not be us."

I stared up at him, perplexed. How could he think I didn't know how relationships worked? I was in one for years. I knew exactly how these things worked.

"We're going to have problems. Everyone has problems. You and I are going to fight. I'm going to forget to do the dishes and that'll piss you off. You'll do things that make me mad. I'm not saying this is going to be perfect between us. But whatever issues we have, will be *ours*. Do you understand?"

Dumbstruck, I nodded.

He let go of my arms, stepping back. "Good. That's good."

I wrapped my arms around myself, looking down at the floor. My face felt hot, confusion pulsed through me. "I don't know what we're doing, Xander," I whispered. "I don't know how to do this with you."

His face softened and he wrapped his arms around me, pulling me close to him. "Well for one, don't tell me to leave unless you want me to leave."

Slowly, I wrapped my arms around his waist, taking in the scent of soap on his skin. Without my shoes I barely came up to his shoulder. I closed my eyes and felt the soft fabric of his shirt against my cheek. "I don't want you to leave."

He rested his chin on top of my head, sighing loudly. "Look, I'm not going to act like I have all the answers about how to do this. But you need to know that you can talk to me. You don't have to be ashamed of getting mad at me." His fingers traced little circles on my back.

"I'm sorry I got mad," I whispered.

"Don't be." He pulled away, looking down at me. "Why don't you shower, and I'll get us some takeout instead. Sound good?"

I nodded against his shoulder, taking one last breath of him before pulling away. "You're too good to me."

He smiled at me, tucking a piece of hair behind my ear. "No. I'm trying to be enough for you."

That night, as Xander fell asleep next to me, I turned to look at him in the low light of the hallway. His mouth was slightly open, his hair was in desperate need of a trim, the erratic curls falling across the pillow. His words echoed through me.

*However you think relationships work... that will not be us...*

I thought about how his eyes lit up as I came into the room, and the way his light blue shirt contrasted so well with his blond hair. He held my arms as if he was trying to anchor me to him—to that moment. My heart ached at the hurt that cracked across his face as I nearly said Max's name.

*I'm trying to be enough for you...*

I flung back the covers of the bed, scrambling for something to wear. I found Xander's discarded shirt on the floor and pulled it over my head. The shirt smelled of him, a unique mix of fresh earth, soap, and clean air. I glanced back at Xander sleeping in the bed. Seeing him now, it was bewildering to think I never noticed how beautiful he really was. The way his hair curled over his forehead, his full lips, the scars, and rough edges only served to add to his appeal. I had never in my life touched something so inherently good, so pure. He only wanted to take care of me and to love me. If I were any other girl, if I weren't so fractured deep inside, what he offered would be a dream come true. I couldn't help how broken I was. I wanted to think Xander's love for me could transcend every wrong, but I knew it was only wishful thinking. I laid a hand on his cheek. It was so selfish for me to want him the way I did. He stirred in his sleep, and I pulled away, not wanting to wake him.

I padded to the living room and settled on the couch. I could hear the highway noises, the high-speed cars, and the hiss of the rain against tires. I tucked my legs up and settled my chin down on my knees. It wasn't long after Xander left to get the takeout that I realized he meant to take me out on a date—a real date in public. He might've reached for my hand across the table. He might've put his arms around me in the waiting area. Someone could've seen us; word could've gotten out about what we were doing. I still wasn't sure I was ready to go public with whatever was between us. I hadn't even told Scarlett.

I knew we couldn't keep on with this behind closed doors. He wanted more. He wanted something public. As much as I wanted to be with him, I had a hard reconciling how I felt for him and the impression it would give people. What would everyone think of me? How callous would I be, giving myself to Max's best friend in this way?

That wasn't even touching on how he'd feel if I told him about how Max died. If he knew all the things I left out of the story, I doubted he'd want me.

A loud pounding on the door, ripped me from my stupor. I huffed over to the door, flinging it open to see a wobbling Eloise standing on my doorstep. She leaned against the door frame and gave me a sloppy smile.

"Hey, sister," she slurred.

"Eloise?" I stepped back as she stumbled through the doorway, bumping into me. "What... Why... huh?"

"I know, right?" She laughed for a moment before narrowing her eyes at me. "Are you wearing Xander's shirt?"

I looked down at my chest, realizing that not only was the shirt obviously too large for me, but had *Eberhardt Landscaping and Gardening* printed across the left breast. I blanched, darting my eyes back up to Eloise's confused face.

I scrambled for words. "Oh, yeah, I guess..."

"Hey, is someone here?" Xander called from down the hallway, his voice soft with sleep. I couldn't take my eyes away from Eloise as the sounds of Xander coming down the hall got louder. He rounded the corner and stopped short at the sight of me and Eloise. He blinked several times, before his eyes widened. "Oh, shit. Hi Wheezy."

"Uh, Xan." I pointed at his bare chest. Since I was wearing his shirt, he was only in his boxers. I could feel Eloise tensing next to me.

Xander looked down to blush at his near nakedness. "Right." He turned away to retreat into his room.

Eloise turned to me with her mouth open. "Whoa." Her eyebrows raised she shook her head. "I can't believe..."

I tried to think of the best excuse I could use to explain what she was seeing; I didn't want to hurt her. While there'd been a seismic shift in my relationship with Xander, I still wasn't ready to talk to anyone about it, especially not Max's younger sister.

Eloise laughed. "Dude, Xander got hot. When did that happen?"

I let out a strangled laugh, feigning nonchalance. "Yeah, I don't know." I hoped my answer was cryptic enough not to get any more questions.

Xander came back wearing a T-shirt and sweatpants, his hair sticking up worse than before. I could tell he was nervously running his hands through his blond curls. He avoided my eyes, knowing that if we looked at each other, what we'd been doing would be plain on our faces. He cleared his throat as he sat down on the couch, throwing an arm over the back. "So, what are you doing at two a.m. to show up on our doorstep?"

"I got in a fight with Dana. My friends and I were at a party, but it got broken up. I couldn't go home so I asked my friends to drop me here." She explained as she collapsed on the couch. Her eyes drooped shut and she wrinkled her face.

"The person who drove you here wasn't drinking, right?" I asked, biting my lip.

She glanced at me then quickly away. "No, of course not. Geez, lighten up, Ana."

"It's a valid question, Eloise. You know we worry about you," Xander backed me up.

With her eyes closed she flapped a limp wrist at me. "You're being ridiculous. If I wanted a fight, I would've gone home. At least at home, Dana doesn't guilt trip me for having a little fun."

"Eloise…" I hesitated.

Somehow, Eloise looked like she was drunker than when she arrived. She opened one eye to glare at us. "I have a better question for you two. Why did you come out of Ana's bedroom and not your own, Xander?"

I glanced at him, my face tight. This was not the time to have this conversation.

"You're shit-faced," Xander murmured as he shook his head. Eloise coughed and I felt a jolt of fear for my new area rug. I ran to the kitchen to grab a large mixing bowl.

"Whatever, *Alexander*. I'm not that drunk," Eloise groaned.

"Yes, you are." He grabbed a blanket off the chair and draped it over her body.

"You didn't answer my question," she retorted.

"I don't need to." He threw back at her. "You're too drunk to stand right now, let alone ask those kinds of questions."

"Why do you care?" she sneered, her temper flaring up. It seemed defensiveness was something that ran through Dana's side of the family. Eloise was being the same as Max used to be when confronted. She was looking every bit the child she still was. "You're not my family. You're not my brother, Xander. You can't swoop in here with Ana and act like my brother. You're not Max. No matter what you do, you'll never measure up to Max."

Xander leaned back, pain crossing his face. "I know. I'm not…"

"He's not trying to, Eloise." I scowled at her. I glanced up at him. "Xander, she didn't mean that."

"Yes, I did!" she slurred, her eyes closing. "I see you Alexander Eberhardt, I see both of you. Don't think I don't know you're hooking up. I know."

"I wouldn't call it…" I started.

"Oh, bullshit, Ana. I see the way you look at each other."

Xander stood up, shaking his head at us. "No. No, I'm not doing this."

He paced in front of us, scrubbing his face with his hand. Beside me Eloise's head swayed, her hair hanging down like a curtain around her face.

"Eloise, you're drunk. You're saying things I know you're going to regret. Stop now and we'll all be fine in the morning, okay?" I pleaded.

"I know what I'm talking about Ana. How could you? Both of you?"

Tears flooded my eyes as her words sliced into me. They were the same questions I had been asking myself, not for the reason Eloise was thinking, but I had been thinking the same.

Before I could respond Xander sunk down next to the couch, in front of Eloise. His voice low and firm. "You need to knock this off. I love you, but you sound too much like Max right now."

"Good," Eloise spat.

"No, you listen to me. I loved your brother—he was my best friend. Don't think you were the only one who lost him, Eloise. We all lost him. We all have a chunk missing because of what happened. Your pain isn't special, Eloise. We all have it. Instead of trying to hurt Ana and I, why don't you stop talking and get some rest. Whether you like it or not, I'm your brother too. We're family. You, me, Ana. And I know Max would want me to look after you. So, knock this shit off now, and go to bed."

Eloise narrowed her eyes, opening her mouth to give him a retort before sneering at him. "Whatever."

Suddenly she lurched forward, her hand over her mouth. I quickly placed the bowl under her mouth where she retched into it. The smell was awful, though not something I was unfamiliar with. After a minute she sat up, wiping her mouth with the bottom of her shirt.

She moaned as she closed her eyes and leaned back against the couch. I sat next to her for a moment before bringing her from a sitting position to prone, where

I covered her with a blanket. I crouched down next to her and placed a hand on her back, feeling her breathing.

As I stood up, I glanced at Xander who'd stood back watching us, the streetlight through the window illuminated his face. His arms crossed against his chest as he looked down at Eloise.

"Is she okay?"

"Yeah, she should be fine. She's already thrown up, so I'm not worried about her aspirating. She should feel like crud in the morning, but she'll be fine on the couch."

He stepped closer, brushing a lock of hair off Eloise's face in a move so tender I felt my heart break.

*We all lost him. We all have a chunk missing because of what happened.*

Xander's words rippled through me.

*We are family. You, me, Ana.*

"Did you mean it?" I asked.

Xander straightened, looking over at me. "What I said to Eloise? Of course. You know I don't say things I don't mean."

I thought back to when he told me he loved me, and the fervency in his gaze. The way he insisted I let him take care of me.

"I do," I whispered.

In the dark of the living room, I stepped closer to him. The only sound was the dull roar of cars on the street outside our window. We stared at each other, and the silence stretched out into a palpable form. He was first to look away as he rubbed a hand over his face.

"I should probably…" he trailed off, motioning to his room. I nodded at him. It was a good idea for us to sleep separately for the rest of the night. We might be able to fool a drunk Eloise but, in the morning, she'd see right through our lies.

At his doorway I grasped his arm and waved my hand in the direction of the living room behind us. "Is she right? Do you think what we're doing is wrong?" I asked softly.

"No. We can't think that way." He hesitated, looking away from me. "Though, I got to say Eloise's words hurt. I mean, I know I'm never going to be Max…"

"I don't want you to be Max," I murmured, leaning forward. I laid a hand on his neck and lowered my voice, the words coming out before I could catch them. "That girl who fell in love with Max hasn't been me for a long time."

He looked down at me, surprise coloring his face. Our eyes locked as he cupped my cheek, his thumb slowly ran over my cheekbone.

"For over fifteen years I didn't let myself admit the truth. You were everything I wanted but I could never have you. I couldn't let myself think of you that way," Xander whispered.

I stood on my tiptoes and rested my cheek against his jaw, my lips inches from his ear. "I'm here now."

He wrapped his arms around my waist and lifted me up off the ground. "You are, aren't you?"

I pulled his face down to mine, pressing a quick kiss to his lips. "I'll miss you in my bed tonight."

# Chapter Twenty-Six

Eloise was gone the next morning. The couch cushions were askew, and the blanket was balled up in the basket under the side table. I'd hoped we could talk, but she sent each of my calls to voice mail and wouldn't return any of my texts.

I wanted desperately to explain what was going on. I needed to tell her I still missed her brother every day and that I loved her as a sister.

I wanted to tell her that for the first time since Max died, I had flickers of hope that maybe I could get back some of the happiness I had when he was alive. She needed to know that the emotion I felt was different. It was a calmer sensation. Being with Max held an edge of fear. When he and I were together, I knew I was in constant danger of being cut down.

Xander wasn't any less intense and I had a deep desire to be with him and touch him. But there was a reverence to what Xander and I had, that I never felt with Max. I wanted to tell Eloise how I felt safe with Xander. No matter how much I loved Max, he never made me feel safe that way.

For so long I thought I didn't need something safe. I thought safe meant boring, that practicality was the enemy of passion. Xander stirred something in me.

I wanted to tell her so many things, but I knew I couldn't. Eloise would see me and Xander together as a monumental betrayal of her brother. I think she could've handled it better if I was dating some random guy, but Xander was different. I knew she felt it too. By being with Xander wasn't I betraying her as well?

If things kept going under the cloak of secrecy, it wouldn't be long before everything imploded. Neither Xander nor I were capable of any true deception. Though somehow, I'd managed to hold on to the last vestige of my guilt over Max. I had good reason to.

What Xander and I had was a dream. But the moment he found out what I was capable of, he'd leave. I'd have to face the world without Max and without Xander.

The night before it seemed like a good idea to sleep separately from Xander with Eloise in the apartment. I hadn't factored in how large a bed can feel when the other side is empty. In the past month I'd gotten used to having him next to me—the weight of his arm around my waist and the warmth of his body against mine. Without him there I couldn't get comfortable. I didn't realize how used to having him next to me I was, until he was no longer there.

I sat on the edge of the couch, pulling the balled-up blanket from the basket to shake it out. As I was laying the blanket across my lap to refold it, Xander walked into the living room wearing a pair of basketball shorts. He scratched his bare chest sleepily, his eyes still bleary. I watched him silently as I smoothed the fabric under my fingers. The moment he walked into the room my heart started beating faster and blood rushed to my cheeks.

"Where's Eloise?" he asked as he grabbed an apple off the breakfast bar.

I focused on making smooth creases on the blanket as I spoke. "She took off, I guess. She was already gone when I woke up. I tried texting but she hasn't answered me."

"Good. So, I can do this now." He walked over and bent down to give me a soft kiss. His lips felt so good against mine. In the hours we spent apart I'd missed him. I wanted so badly to pull him down on me and to feel his skin against mine.

With my mind a flurry of conflicts I pulled away ducking my head. "She didn't even leave a note."

He didn't seem to notice my reluctance. "She must've needed to be somewhere."

"I doubt it," I mumbled into the blanket. I frowned at the uneven corners and shook the blanket out to try folding it again.

"What do you mean?" He sat back on the couch; his long legs stretched out in front of him.

"I think she suspects," I said into the blanket as I lined up the corners to fit together exactly.

"Suspects? Like you and me?" he asked, smiling. I nodded at him. "Would that be such a bad thing? I'm telling you, the sooner we tell people about us, the better."

"I don't want to tell Eloise. It's too soon to say what's going on."

"Nope." He argued. "Not at all. I'm disputing that, right here, right now."

For the first time since he walked in, I looked him in the eyes. He'd finished his apple, setting the core on the side table next to him. His expression was serious. I leaned a little closer to him. "I mean it. Telling her would hurt her. You heard her last night."

"She was drunk," he countered.

"She hates the idea of us together. You heard her. *How could you? Both of you?*" I mimicked her.

"Yeah, but she was drunk. She got into a fight with Dana. She was already pissed off. I'm sure we weren't the only ones who got to see that side of her last night."

"We deserved it," I mumbled. "At least, I deserved it."

"What?" he asked incredulous. "What are you talking about? We didn't deserve any of that stuff Eloise said last night."

"I do." I ran my hands over the top of the perfectly folded blanket before setting it in the basket carefully. "I deserve worse than anything Eloise could say."

He scoffed loudly. "You're being dramatic. We're not doing anything wrong." He paused, his face clouding over. "Unless you don't want to tell her because you don't want to be with me? You don't want to be seen with me?"

"No, that's not how I would say it..."

"So how would you say it? What do you think we're doing here?" He crossed his arms against his chest and waited me out as I tried to get the words together.

"I don't know, okay? I want to be with you, but I also know I'm no good for you," I blurted out, shocking myself with my candor.

He rolled his eyes at me. "I'm an adult, Ana. Let me make my own choices," he scolded.

I sighed, the pain in my chest bursting through, my eyes running over. I stood up to put some distance between me and Xander. "You don't realize, do you? You think I'm this sweet girl. You say you love me, but how can you love me when you don't know the real me? You have no idea what I'm capable of. If you knew, you wouldn't say you loved me."

He stood up to grip my face between his hands, his gaze fierce. "Nothing you could tell me could change my mind about you."

I pulled away from him, stepping back. "You don't know what you're saying. If I told you the truth..." I covered my face, shaking my head. "It'll destroy you. It'll destroy us."

He stepped closer to me, not allowing me space. His eyes were bright and bore into me. "You can't know that. Try me."

I shook my head and tears leaked through my fingers. Even though he wasn't talking anymore, I kept shaking my head, trying to shake the words from my head and figure out how I could've ruined such a beautiful moment between us.

"Just tell me," he pleaded. "It can't be as bad as you think."

A wave of exhaustion set into me. The burden of keeping this to myself in the face of Xander pleading for answers was too much. I wasn't by nature a secretive person. I cupped my cheeks and refused to look up at him as I confessed.

"It's my fault he died."

"No, it isn't. There's a difference between killing him—physically killing him—and not seeing the signs for what they were, Ana."

"I know that. I'm trying to explain this to you..."

"You remember what I told you after Max died?" He interrupted softly, his long fingers tapping a rhythm. "We sat on the edge of his bed, and you cried into my chest. You kept talking about how you should've been able to save him. Do you remember?"

I shook my head at him. "No. I don't remember."

"You asked me who can you blame. I told you I didn't know. But I did. The only person who's responsible for Max's overdose was Max. The only person who could've saved Max was Max."

"You're wrong. I killed him—it's my fault he died."

And I told him about finding the pills. How I ignored the warning signs and the sleepiness when he shouldn't be tired. I told Xander everything—how Max got fired from all his jobs and money and jewelry went missing. My mother's sapphire earrings went missing two Christmases before; forty bucks went missing from my wallet and the powdery film I'd find in the bathroom.

The way I kept it inside for weeks until I found him dead. I had so many moments where I could've confronted him, and I didn't; I couldn't face his wrath I knew would come. The way I never mustered the backbone it'd take to tell him I loved him, and I needed him to get clean because the road he was going down was a dangerous one.

These are the things I never told anyone. Max wasn't the only one keeping secrets. I knew what he was doing, I knew the danger he was in, and I didn't say a word. I could have saved him. Instead, because of my cowardice I let him die.

Xander sat back, his eyes narrowed. His jaw tensed as he swallowed. Inside my chest was a flood of shame and relief. I understood why they tell people not to admit affairs. There was a catharsis in telling the truth, but in relieving yourself you've thrown the pain onto the ones you're closest to.

"So, this is the big secret you've been keeping from me?" he asked slowly, his face blank. I wished he would show his anger. I didn't know what to do with this impenetrable wall he'd put up. "This is the reason you keep pushing me away?"

"Yes," I whispered, glancing up from my hands to his face. His face didn't betray a single emotion. "Do you hate me?"

He leaned forward, scrubbing his face with his hand, the familiar scrape of his hands against the bristle of his unshaven cheeks. "Of course not."

He wouldn't look up at me and I felt the reticence in his shoulders. "I think I should…" he sighed, standing up to grab his jacket where he'd flung it onto the stool the night before. Soundless, I watched as he shrugged it on his bare shoulders. "I need a minute."

I pulled my knees up to my chest, watching him as he paced. I didn't trust myself to talk; nothing I could say would take back what I did. His silence sent rejection coursing through me. He might not hate me, but he wasn't going to love me again. I'd ruined it. I'd destroyed the first good thing I had in my life in years.

I wanted so many things. I wanted to rush to him and beg him to forget everything I'd said. I wanted him to touch me the way I needed to be touched.

"Look, if you want to end it…us…just do it," I whispered. My voice couldn't get any louder, as if the words were soft enough, he wouldn't let me go. "I know you're mad at me."

"You're damn right I'm mad at you." He sank into the couch next to me, tilting his body toward mine. He looked down and took a deep breath as if he was trying to muster the courage to say something.

Tears stung my eyes as they threatened to overflow. "So do it."

"I'm not doing anything," he said firmly.

"You're not?" I asked softly, not understanding. "So why did you act like you were going to leave?"

"I was pissed," he replied. "I had to cool down for a bit."

"Good. You should be pissed," I mumbled more to myself than anything.

He squeezed my hand and set it down on my lap. I stared down at my hands, the pink places where his hands had touched mine. He got to his feet to look down at me. "This was your big secret? This was the big thing you were using as an excuse not to be with me?"

"Yes," I replied.

"All that time we could've been together. Years that we could've had together. You held on to this bullshit for years and let it drag you down."

"It's not bullshit. I really sat back and did nothing."

"I know. And I don't care."

"What?" I sputtered. "But I—"

"I love you, Ana. I don't know how many times I need to say that. I don't get how you can be so oblivious. How could doubt my feelings? How could you think I'm going to stop caring for you?"

"Because why would you stay? After what I told you, you should leave me. This is more than you bargained for."

He took my hands in his. "I told you I know you. I might not have known what was going on, but I'm not surprised. And I'm not surprised you'd react that way. You're not going to scare me away with this confession, Ana. You cannot keep doubting how deep my feeling are for you."

"But I—" I stammered.

"You think I don't have the same regrets?" he interrupted me. "There were so many times when I should've spoken up. There were nights when I let him get behind the wheel after he'd been drinking because I didn't have the fight in me anymore. There were nights I'd watch him drive off, with you in the passenger seat. I stand there and think I'd be the one at fault if both of you died."

"But it wasn't your fault. It was—"

He interrupted me. "It was Max's fault. It's always been Max's fault. I don't care if you found the pills, I wouldn't have cared if you *gave* him the pills. He was an addict; he was an alcoholic; there's nothing you could've done that would get him clean. He didn't want to be sober. He might have cared for you, but you trying to make him stop wouldn't have changed a single thing. He always felt guilty about letting you down. If you'd told him you knew about the pills, it would've made him feel worse."

"You can't know that..." I murmured. I wanted to believe what he was saying. I wanted to let go of what happened to Max. "You can't possibly know..."

"I do know. Max and I may not be similar, but I know this—both he and I have spent our lives trying to deserve you and failing every step of the way."

"But you more than deserve me. You deserve more than me! You're the only thing I can count on." The words hit me in the chest with a force that took my breath away. I knew I shouldn't touch him; I knew I should give him up, but I couldn't do it. I brought my hand up to cup his cheek, pulling his face closer to mine. "You are the one thing that has never failed me."

I leaned forward to kiss him. His lips were soft and warm against mine. He wrapped his arms around my waist and pulled me closer to him. I climbed on his lap, deepening our kiss. His hands roamed under my shirt over my ribs and across my back. His lips moved from my lips, over my chin and down my throat. He gripped my shirt tight in his fists to bunch around my waist. His mouth was on my throat, his hands felt like fire trailing along my skin.

He leaned forward to lower me onto the couch. My shirt came off followed by his. His hands were everywhere. All I could feel was him above me, his kisses, his touch, and his love. I threaded my hands through his hair, pulling on his curls to bring his mouth to mine. We fumbled together, the rest of our clothes ending up on the floor.

A sense of urgency burned through me. I needed him closer to me. I needed him on top of me. I needed to know that, for that moment, I could have him, and I hadn't ruined everything.

I needed to trust in him, to trust in how he made me feel. For the briefest moment I needed to allow myself to be adored and not worry it could crumble away.

His face was between my breasts, brushing the lightest of kisses against my skin. Words traced across my body. "Love me," he pleaded against my skin as his kisses moved farther down my body.

"Love me, love me, love me."

I flung my head back, drinking in the sensations. I savored it all in that moment I whispered the words into the night.

*I'm trying... I want to... I do... Is it enough... will I ever be enough...?*

# CHAPTER TWENTY-SEVEN

I T'D BEEN OVER TWO weeks with no contact from Eloise. She wouldn't return my texts and all my calls shot straight to voice mail.

I tried to distract myself with work. I'd started helping Barbara with the new grads, not so affectionally called "baby nurses," who showed up in the emergency room fresh-faced and idealistic. Over the past few years there was a gradual thaw toward me as I had apparently proved my worth to Barbara and I was no longer placed in the same category as the other "ninnies from nursing school." After treating a man who'd been shot in the foot by a friend while celebrating, a new nurse commented, "This is so exciting! It's not every day someone gets shot." I had to inform her in the emergency room, it was in fact, every day.

Spring brought an increase in work for Xander as he was called out to clear out flower beds, clean up the various landscapes, and do other general things I didn't understand. If we were lucky enough to be home at the same time, we were both so exhausted we didn't venture outside the confines of our four walls.

The night of St. Patrick's Day I was working a double, with more charcoal and IV drips than I cared to see in a single night. I even had the pleasure of treating Tracy Penrose's boyfriend who was brought in crying. I had to fight my urge to smirk at the turn of events when I brought her a towel because he threw up all over her Frye boots.

When I got home, I collapsed onto the bed still wearing my scrubs. Xander wasn't getting home for hours, having left only an hour before I got off work. I barely remembered closing my eyes before my phone dinging woke me up. Bleary-eyed, I grabbed my phone off the nightstand. I glanced at the message and bolted upright in my bed. It was Eloise asking me if she could stop by. Quickly I replied I'd be home along with a smiley face emoji. The clock on my nightstand said it was nearly three in the afternoon. I'd slept more than seven hours.

I peeled off my scrubs; grimacing at how smelly they were. I didn't have time to take a shower but at least a pair of clothes would mask the funk of running around the ER for twenty-four hours straight. By the time I heard the knock on my door I was pulling my greasy hair back into a stubby ponytail.

She stood on the doorstep, rocking back on her heels. Her face was scrubbed clean from makeup, and she looked so much younger than her eighteen years.

"Hey," she said quietly. She glanced at me and then away quickly. I realized I had grown so used to how she looked with her thick black eyeliner, I'd almost forgotten what she looked like without it. "You want to take a walk?"

The sky was a blank sheet of marbled clouds that looked light enough that we wouldn't be risking too much rain. "Sure, let me grab my jacket and we can go."

I followed her down the road to the small park at the end of the street. When I was a child Scarlett and I used to play down here. We played princesses and pirates (She was the princess; I was the pirate). When we got older, I'd come with Max and his friends, ignoring them smoking pot on the merry-go-round while I'd do a paranoid watch on the road for cops.

Eloise settled into a swing, and I took the one next to her. The whole walk over she was quiet, as I tried to ask her about how she's been. I found myself babbling like a lovesick schoolgirl trying to impress a crush. I deftly avoided any mention of Xander, hoping that somehow, she wouldn't ask about us.

"Have you heard from any colleges yet?"

She frowned across the playground, narrowing her eyes at a little girl who was running up the stairs. "Yeah, I got into WSU, San Diego State, and Southeastern."

I reached over and squeezed her arm with my hand. "That's great! I'm so proud of you."

She sighed loudly, shaking her hair out of her eyes. "Not that it matters. If I don't get a full ride, there's no way I can afford it. I don't think college is in the cards for me. I kind of want to go to LA."

"Los Angeles?"

Eloise nodded at me. "I need to get out of here."

I nodded at her. "I know you do. I'll help you. College, LA, whatever you choose. You know that right?"

She frowned at the ground but nodded at me. "I didn't want to see you just to talk about LA or college," Eloise admitted. She kicked the bark under her sandal. I worried for a moment about her toes getting cold, but I didn't say anything.

"No?" I asked, looking at her. Once again, she was wearing my old sweatshirt. I vowed to let her go through my closet and pick out a few things. If she was going away, she couldn't leave town with her meager wardrobe. I knew most of the nicer stuff she wore were outfits she borrowed from friends.

"No. I was going through some stuff the other day and I found this." She pulled a crinkled envelope out of her sweatshirt pocket.

Eloise slowly handed me an envelope; the seal ripped open. I looked at the front and was surprised by the familiar messy scrawl I never thought I'd see again. Tentatively, I pulled the letter out. Written on lined notebook paper, the scrappy border was still attached. I fought the urge to pull the perforated edge off.

*Dear Ana,*

*I know you're a sucker for that epic love story bullshit. I suppose this is my form of a fucked-up love letter. Just this once, I'll tell you the truth.*

*I'm a shitty person. I don't know if you know that about me. You never seem to realize it. You should've stayed away, back when we were kids. I think about how different both our lives would've been if we hadn't kissed that day in the field. I don't know how different my life would've been, honestly. I was never going anywhere. Even if I'd wanted to, I wouldn't have been able to get out of Ridgewood. I'm pretty sure every choice I've made would've led me right back here. Back to this shitty town with my shitty friends.*

*But you, my Ana-Sweet, you really could've been something. All the places you could've gone without me. All the things you could've been. A bigger man would have seen that and let you go. But we both know what kind of man I am.*

*I love you. I hope you never doubt that I do love you. I love you more than anything else in my life.*

*In any drug and alcohol addiction program there are steps you're supposed to take toward recovery. You start at the beginning, admitting you're powerless against the substance and the drugs have become more crucial to you than anything in your life. Powerless. Shit, if that's not the story of my life.*

*You're supposed to make amends to those that you've wronged. Some of this is easy. Apologizing to my old boss for all those times I left him hanging with no one to open the shop. To the friends who had to bail me out of jail. My sister for that time I forgot to pick her up from school, or finally having your best friend pick her up from the police station when no one could get a hold of a family member.*

*But the stipulation to making amends is that you don't cause further harm to those you love. So, this is my letter to you, my Liliana. What good can ever come of having you see this? How could anything I say make up for the shit I put you through? A letter I'll never send. I have to do this to recover but I pray you'll never see this. Because what kind of amends will I make, making you hate me forever? I'm getting off track here.*

*You never saw the real me. I'm not big on reminiscing. All this shit you always try to get me into.*

*"Max, did you like me right away?"*

*"Oh, of course. I thought you were so brave."*

*"Max, did you know we'd end up together?"*

*I'd hug you and give you that smile I know looked the sincerest, and you'd settle into me.*

*I hate to think back, but that's what this step is all about right? So here we are, this is what you never understood about me.*

*There were times when I knew I should've left you alone. Turning points, you might call them. Maybe if I'd stayed in Boise, maybe if I hadn't kissed you that day in the field. Maybe if I hadn't been the one you hugged that first day on the road when my stepdad was trying to beat us up.*

*Would your life have been better? I don't know. Like I said before, I'm a selfish prick when it comes to you. Your life may not have been better with me in it, but you were always the best thing I'd ever had. Take what you will from that.*

*You were always a big believer in all that destiny shit. Signs and fate and all that crazy mysticism. I never believed in any of it. Bad stuff happens, and then good stuff, and worse.*

*I don't know where I fall in your life.*

*I don't know if I'll ever be able to tell you how sorry I am for all the things I've done. For kissing Carrie, for the other girls, for all the times I fucked up and you were there to help me. When it comes down to it, I don't think I'm capable of even saying sorry. One apology could lead to more, and I don't think I could handle you knowing all the awful things about me. I want to be so much more for you. I know I fail at that, but it's the truth.*

*Hopefully, I'll be able to prove that I can be better, that I can make it up to you. We'll have that epic love story and all that bullshit, I don't know. All I do know is I want to be with you. I want you. And hopefully you want me.*

*And isn't that enough?*

*~Max*

I wiped a tear from my eye. "When did he write this?"

Eloise pursed her lips. "When he was in jail, I think. I found it in a box of stuff he left at my mom's. When he was in jail was the only time, that I knew of, when he was trying to get sober."

I stared at the letter in my hand. "He was sober for about six months. He did good for a while."

Eloise sighed loudly, she let her hands drop down from the chains on the swings, she held her hand out and I put the letter in it. "I found one for me too. It doesn't really apply though. He wrote it when I was twelve. It's about not protecting me from my mom. There's not much Max could have done about that."

She looked over the letter again. "You know, I thought what you guys had was so romantic. I thought, *when I grow up, I want to have a relationship like that. I want to love someone the way Max loves Ana.*"

"You will," I told her.

"There's always a price though isn't there? That was something mom taught us. Nothing is free, we all have to pay our price and some people pay more."

I wasn't sure who she was saying paid more, me or Max. She handed the letter back to me. "Sorry I read it. I couldn't help myself. I was too excited to see his handwriting again."

"It's okay, I get it." I told her, putting my hand on top of hers.

"Are you really dating Xander?"

I paused as I considered lying to her, not wanting to hurt her further, but she wasn't the baby I helped feed anymore. She was eighteen now, practically an adult. I thought about Scarlett's words to me outside the funeral home so many years before.

*Eloise is tougher than you think, and you were not her mother, Ana. Max was not her father. It's not your responsibility to take care of her.*

I nodded. "Kind of, yeah. I don't really know, but there's something there."

"He's a good guy. You deserve a good guy." She looked away, "Judging from the letter, maybe my brother wasn't such a good guy."

"Max was a good guy, too. He made some bad choices and unfortunately, they cost him his life. I always felt that he was a good guy, though. I hope you know that. People don't fall into good and bad categories like that. Life isn't black and white. He made mistakes, I made mistakes. He wasn't any worse or any better than either of us. No one is."

"Aren't you angry with him?"

"Honestly, some days I am. But most days no, I'm not."

"I'm mad at him. For leaving me alone to help my mom. For not being here when I graduated high school. For not seeing me finish growing up. That he only knew me up to seventeen. It hurts."

"No matter what happens with me and Xander. I don't think I'll ever stop loving your brother."

"I know that. Never for a second did I doubt that." She tilted her head to the side. "You know Xander was like a brother to me too. So, if there is anyone who'd be a replacement for Max, I guess it'd be him."

"Oh, Eloise, I'm not trying to replace Max. I would never do that."

She nodded her head at me, her eyes wet with tears. "He was special, wasn't he?"

"Max was everything to me."

She put her hand out between us and I took it in mine. We sat there on the swings together, all the words on the letter between us.

Barbara slapped the chart down on the counter in front of me with a loud thwack, making me jump. I shoved Max's letter down under a file as quickly as I could. She stared me down in that long cold stare that made me want to confess things I'd never done.

"You're on room seven. I'm done with stupid girls today," she barked.

I fought to keep my face blank, ignoring the barb I was sure she'd aimed at me. I grabbed the clipboard and walked to the room, glancing at the intake paperwork.

The second I walked in I could see why Barbara gave me this patient. The young woman sat on the edge of the bed, a pair of oversized sunglasses still on her head.

Her swollen ankle was propped up on several pillows, her uninjured foot was still clad in a large wedge heel.

"Fucking finally!" she huffed. "My ankle hurts like a bitch! Can I get something for the pain?"

I walked to her side as I continued looking at her chart. "I'm sure we can, let me ask a few questions before the doctor is in."

We went through her chart, height, weight, medication allergies, current medication, any drugs or alcohol in her system, last menstrual period.

"Why do you guys always need to know my period?" she snapped.

I turned away from her, directing my answer at her ankle. "Among other things, if you need to get X-rays, we need to make sure you're not pregnant as it could be harmful to a fetus."

"I'm not." Her voice softened slightly at the admonishment. "I'm on my period now."

I turned back to her and gave her my best professional smile. "Great. The doctor will be in to see you in a few minutes."

I briefed the doctor on the patient and retreated to the desk to write in her chart. I paused at the part about her period. I glanced at the calendar on the chart, counting the days a few times.

*When was my last period?*

I knew I had one in early February, and it ended right before Valentine's Day. Xander was less embarrassed than I expected he'd be when I told him the reason that we'd need to hold off on sex for a few days. I counted the days, weeks really, since. A chill worked its way through me. I was over a week late. I'd stopped taking my pill a year before. There was no point when I wasn't having sex with anyone.

I kept meaning to go to my OBGYN, but things kept coming up to distract me from making the appointment.

*Stupid! How could I be so stupid?*

Xander and I used condoms most of the time, but there were a few times we didn't have any.

*Shit.*

I vowed to run into the drug store, buy the test, and go straight home to take it after work. I wouldn't tell Xander unless there was something to tell him.

An arm wrapped around my waist, squeezing me from behind. I twirled around to see Scarlett standing in front of me with a matching basket on her arm.

Scarlett glanced down at the basket, reaching in before I could stop her. "Isn't this that blush that's supposed to be the hack for NARS Orgasm?"

She pulled the blush out, shifting the contents of my basket. The test sat in the center, perfectly visible in the space where the blush was before. She stared down at the test for a moment, confusion lacing her face. "What..."

I pushed the bag of cotton balls on top of it quickly. Scarlett's hand darted down and pulled the test out and held it up closer to her face. "Is this..." she glanced at me; her face still confused. "A pregnancy test?"

I sighed. "Obviously."

Her brows furrowed. "Why would you..." she scoffed under her breath. "Girlie, what that fuck is going on here? Who are you hooking up with? And why didn't you tell me you have some new guy in your life?"

"I don't." She raised an eyebrow at me, and I stammered. "I mean, it's nothing, it was a one-time thing. A mistake."

The lie scorched my mouth. The words felt so wrong to say. I wanted to tell Scarlett that it was the opposite. That what Xander and I had was permanent, that in the span of months he had become everything to me. But a busy drug store wasn't the right place to have this conversation at all.

Scarlett laughed, "You little minx! I can't believe you didn't tell me that you had a one-night stand."

I struggled to come up with a response, blubbering nothings to her.

She put a hand up to silence me as she threw the test back into my basket. "Say no more, I get it. You were embarrassed. You've never had one before and it sucked and were too embarrassed to tell me."

Her phone beeped in her purse, and she pulled it out to glance at it. "Shit." She opened her purse and started shoveling the contents out, dumping them in my basket. With a jingle she pulled out a set of keys and narrowed her eyes at them. "I guess I took Emma's keys and mine when I left. Shit, that's the third time I've done that this month."

I let out the strained breath I had been holding, relieved that I was being released from this line of questioning. I handed her the items she dumped into my basket. "Well, you'd better go rescue your damsel in distress. We'll catch up soon."

"Yes, we will." She tossed her phone back in her purse and leaned forward kissing my cheek, "You still need to pick up your maid of honor dress from the shop."

I nodded at her, glad for the change of subject. "I'll be down on Tuesday, it's my day off."

"Good, you know what to do if it doesn't fit, right?"

"It'll fit, Scar. Plus, the wedding is two months away. I can figure something out in that time."

She looked agog at my statement. Shaking her head at me. "I'm not even going to start in on how wrong that statement is." She made a pointed look at my basket. "Let me know if you need anything, okay." She raised her eyebrows. "Day or night."

"Of course, now get out here." I pushed her away playfully.

I watched her walk away from me, the smile slipping from my face and the weight of my basket on my arm.

# Chapter Twenty-Eight

WHEN I GOT HOME, I dumped the contents of the plastic bag on the counter and studied them. I picked up the test, turning the box over in my hands to read the instructions. I'd taken a few of these before. I knew that while the description said the results would take five minutes if you took the test correctly it was a matter of seconds before you had your answer. I ran a finger over the edge of the flap, teasing it open.

I could feel the foil wrapper under my shaking fingers. I set the box down on the counter and studied myself in the mirror. I had taken the lie too far. I was lying to Scarlett, to my mother... Holding the test in my hand, I pictured how seeing a positive result would feel.

So many times, with Max I'd pictured our child together—the olive skin, the blue eyes, the thick dark hair. I could close my eyes and conjure up exactly what our baby would look like, but never once could I imagine Max as a father, as a responsible parent, a caregiver, and a provider.

Every time we had a scare, I'd be terrified of the idea of being pregnant. The timing was never right for us. I wasn't sure if there'd have ever been a time when it could have been right.

I loved Max, but the farther from his death I got, the more I realized how different we were. We never wanted the same things; we never had the same aspirations. The kind of love we had was never sustainable through real struggles. It wouldn't have withstood the vigor of a child.

It was different with Xander. Because we'd only been together for a few months, I expected fear but the idea that I might be pregnant with Xander's baby didn't scare me. He'd be a great father, he loved me, and he would love a child. I could imagine it. Coming home to him, falling asleep in our bed with a child wedged sideways between us. I could picture the soft curls under my fingers and the spray of freckles across his nose.

I was ready. If the test was positive, I was ready for a future with Xander. It took this for me to realize everything I'd been holding back. I loved him. I've loved him for years. I loved him that day on Scarlett's couch while we watched the movie, and I loved him that night in his car after prom. In my own way I even loved him that day on the curb where I pressed my lips to his, trying to destroy the jealousy that'd haunt me for years to come. All those nights we spent together before Max had died. I never allowed myself to see past what I thought Max and I had to feel what I'd always known was there with him. I was meant to be with Xander. Every misstep I had taken on this journey to find myself led me here to this moment. I loved him fiercely. I loved him beyond all my reasoning. I craved him, I needed him. I loved him.

*I was in love with him.*

*I loved Alexander Eberhardt.*

Suddenly the box felt too heavy in my hand. I set it down at the counter. I didn't have to take it yet. The moment I took that test I knew I was facing the chance that my entire life was going to be turned upside down. I had the impulse to have one last day with Xander without all these serious concerns. I wanted one day when I could love him without sharing myself again.

I would tell him when he got home from work. It didn't matter what the test said, I loved him either way. I didn't need a pregnancy test to determine how I felt about Xander. It was simply the push I needed to realize my feelings.

As much as I wanted to tell him my revelation when he walked in the door, I wanted to wait until we ate the lasagna, I'd specially prepared for us. I knew that every time I looked over my plate at him, I would want to scream, "*I realized that I'm crazy in love with you!*" but it would be worth it once the perfect moment presented itself.

All through dinner Xander was quiet, answering my question with one-word answers and avoiding my eyes. I kept telling myself that he must have had a hard day at work and was in a bit of a funk. I went to wash the dishes, a job that he'd normally do since I was the one who cooked. I told him to relax on the couch. I could hear the TV turn on; some show about diners on Route 66.

I practiced what I was going to say in my head as I loaded the dishwasher. First, we would have sex and then when we were in the moment, I would say the words. Simple and straightforward.

He'd told me that he loved me enough that I wasn't nervous about him saying it back. I knew he would. I could already see the new direction we'd go from here. I would tell Scarlett as soon as I could. I'd ask my parents to have him over for dinner to get to know him in this new capacity.

Once I was done with the dishes I settled into him, resting my head on his shoulder. His arm was stiff on the top of the couch above me.

I placed my hand on the front of his pants, leaning in to deepen our kiss. He barely kissed me back, his body was tense. I had a sinking feeling in my stomach as he took my hand in his to pull it away from him and dropped it between us.

"I don't want to," he said stiffly.

"You don't want to?" I sat back, scoffing at him, "Are your serious right now?"

He looked away from me, grimacing. "Yeah, I am."

"What the hell is going on Alexander?" I asked perplexed. "You were moody all through dinner and now you don't want sex. What happened to you today?"

Xander muted the TV and turned to me, his face serious. "Do you not want to be seen in public with me?"

I glanced at him with my cheeks burning red. "What? No, I mean, yes... I mean..." I huffed loudly, screwing up my face. "I don't mind being seen in public with you."

"But you don't want me to act like your boyfriend," he stated.

"Where is this coming from?" I asked. I racked my brain trying to think of what could have possibly changed in the hours since I was at work.

"Are you going to answer the question?" He strung out each word slowly. "Am I your boyfriend?"

"In so many ways yeah, but boyfriend seems like such a funny word..." I sighed, shaking my head. I never like the sound of the word. How I felt about him transcended all those silly names. I couldn't trivialize what we had with a label like that. "I don't know... I feel like what we have is more than..."

"I don't get you," he interrupted. "When we're home it's like we can be together, everything is so wonderful here, and then I try to take you out on a date, or hold your hand at the store and you pull away like I'm poison?"

"That's not true." I asserted. "That time at the store, I had to get something in a different aisle. You know how I feel about you."

"You are a terrible liar," he leaned forward pressing his hands together and setting them on his lips. "I don't get it. Why do you keep pushing me away?" he demanded. "What do I need to do to prove to you that what we have is real?"

"I know it's real. You don't need to convince me of that."

*Tell him, tell him you love him, say the words and this can be over.*

"You don't get it both ways. I told you as much that night Sherie was over."

"I thought this is what you wanted. I thought you wanted to be with me. I'm giving you everything I have."

"No, you're not. You can give me more. You have so much more. You don't want to admit it. You don't want to go there. You don't want to take the chance that I'll hurt you the way Max did."

"You couldn't possibly hurt me the way Max did." I retorted. It wasn't possible for anyone to hurt me the way Max did. Xander wasn't capable of inflicting that level of pain on someone. Never had I known that Xander was the opposite of Max more. "That's impossible."

"I know that." He closed his eyes, and I could see him working through the words. Fear sliced through me, chilling me. "You know why I can't hurt you like Max did? Because you won't let me."

"What? Why would you..."

"You want to know why I was so pissed off? I bumped into Scarlett earlier. She asked me if I knew who it was that you were seeing? She said she had it on good authority that you were seeing a new guy. At first, I thought she was trying to tease me, but then I realized she didn't know about us. I kept asking myself why she would be asking me about who you're seeing if she knew about us. And then I realized she can't tease me about something she has no clue about."

I sat back, scoffing. "I was in the middle of the drug store. I'm not going to tell her in the middle of the aisle between the tampons and the shampoo."

He sat back on the couch with his hand in his hair. "You shouldn't have to tell her there. She should already know. You tell Scarlett everything. So why are you keeping us a secret from her, from your parents?"

"There wasn't a good time to talk to her and honestly before, I wasn't sure what I'd say to her about us."

He pulled his hand out of his hair leaving it a crazy mess sticking up everywhere. "How about the truth? How about we've been sleeping together for months. Literally sleeping in the same bed after we have sex. How about that I told you I love you and you didn't say anything back?"

*Now is the time. Say it and this fight can be over. Promise him that you'll tell Scarlett. Say the words and it will be fixed.*

"I have been patient; I know I said I would wait for you. I kept thinking that if I gave you the time, you'd come to care for me. But I'm out of time now. I can't keep doing this with you. I won't be your dirty little secret, Ana."

"You aren't, that isn't at all how I feel."

*Tell him...*

"No, tell me how you feel then?" He countered, looking me right in my eyes, a dead stare fixing me in place.

"I..." I stammered. I had this vision of how I'd say the words. How it'd be so romantic. This was the last way I wanted to say them. I didn't want them to be a final plea to diffuse a situation.

"Just like I thought. I know I can't hurt you like Max did, because you'll never love me the way you loved Max," he chuckled to himself as he shook his head. So softly I could barely hear him he whispered, "I was an idiot to think you could."

"Xan, don't say that," I mumbled. "You're putting words in my mouth. How I feel about you... about us..."

He stepped back from me, his eyes hardening. "You don't love me enough to hurt you. But goddamn it..." he grimaced. "I always knew I'd be the one who loved you more than you loved me. But I thought, eventually, I'd get back a fraction of what I gave."

"I do though," I pleaded. "For so long I thought if you knew what I did to Max you wouldn't..."

"I already told you, you're not allowed to use that excuse. Not anymore. You held on to that, so you didn't have to take a chance and care about me. You needed an excuse to use me the way you did." His words hissed through his teeth. I'd rarely seen him this angry. I was used to Max's loud outbursts—the yelling, the punching. This low cold voice put a whole other level of fear into me.

"This isn't going how I wanted it to. You're misunderstanding me. You know how hard this is for me. I'm trying here, I really am."

"No, you're not," he retorted. "All I've ever wanted from you was for you to love me. I guess I wanted too much from you."

"But I do love you. I do." The words burst forth with thick tears.

I watched his face as the words came. I expected him to soften, but instead his jaw clenched and before he looked away, I saw something pass before his eyes, a resignation, a pain. "No, you don't. I've been so stupid not to see it. All this time I wasted on us, on you."

I cried into my hands. "I do though, I really do love you."

"No. You don't want to lose me."

I reached forward to grab his hands in mine. "Of course, I don't want to lose you. I don't want to lose you because I love you. I love you, Alexander."

"It's too late. You think I can't tell when you're lying, Ana? I told you—*I know you.*"

"I love you. *I love you!* Why aren't you hearing me? I love you," I pleaded.

"Stop saying that. Stop lying to me. Just stop!" he yelled.

This kind of anger I knew. It felt all too familiar. "You wanted this. You kissed me, you pursued me. Don't act like I was the one in charge here. As if I was the one who controlled how you felt. You started it."

"Maybe I did." He stepped away. "If I started it, then I guess I can end it."

I stood, frozen, as his words echoed through me. He stomped to his room, and I could hear drawers slamming and hangers rattling. When he emerged several minutes later, I was in the same spot.

"I'll crash on someone's couch. But I don't think you should be here anymore when I get back. My name is on the lease."

"Don't go, please," I pleaded.

"I can't do this with you anymore. I can't love you like this anymore."

"But I need you—" I cried. I knew how selfish I sounded. I couldn't form the right words. "I love you! I love you, please Alexander. Don't leave me. I love you, so, so much."

He closed his eyes and I hoped he was reconsidering leaving. "I waited so long to hear you tell me that."

"So, stay! We can figure this out. You said we'd be different. You promised me..."

"I never promised you I wouldn't leave," his words held an icy edge.

Looking down at the ground, I summoned the courage to lash out. I had nothing left but to hit him back where I knew it'd hurt. "How are you any different from Max right now? Leaving me all alone. You said we'd talk, and we'd work things out. But just like Max, you yell at me, and now you're leaving me. You promised me things you had no intention of giving. You make me think I could be happy, and then you destroy me. You think I don't know how that feels? I spent years in this misery. So go ahead. Leave me ruined, just like Max did."

His voice softer now. He stepped closer to me. His hand was on my arm. I stood frozen in my anguish. "I'm tired of talking about this, Ana. I can't be your crutch. I can't be this pillar for you to lean on. I'm tired of waiting. I've been waiting for years for you. I can't keep having you tear me to pieces."

"And what do you think you're doing to me right now?" I cried.

"You'll be fine. We both know I was only a distraction for you, anyway." He stepped forward and pressed a kiss to my forehead. I grasped at his shirt, trying to pull him closer to me. He slowly pulled away, peeling my fingers off his shirt. I kept my eyes closed as he walked away. When the door closed, I sank to my knees, the carpet cushioning my fall. It all felt too familiar, the way my legs felt against the ground, the stifling silence around me. The feeling came upon me, a relentless wave crashing into my chest. I loved him. I loved him. I loved him, but it wasn't enough.

Eventually I was able to get myself together enough to find my way to my room. I pulled on my nightgown and retreated to the bathroom to wash my tear-stained face. My eyes were red and puffy, my hair was a lanky copper mess around my head. I looked like how I felt. How could I so quickly ruin everything? I bent down to splash water on my face. Out of the corner of my eye I saw the box on the ground, resting on its side. I dried my face carefully before bending down to retrieve the box. I read the instructions twice before pulling the stick out. I took a deep breath as I ripped the foil aside to pull the test out.

How quickly everything changed for me. I thought this test was going to be the beginning of something for us. Now no matter what the test said, it was the end of me and Xander.

I picked up my phone and texted the only other person I could rely on.

*I need you.*

Scarlett replied in seconds.

*I'll be right over.*

I sat down on the edge of the bathtub and waited for Scarlett. I know how much I had to lose soon enough.

I picked up my phone and sent one more message to Scarlett.

*I screwed everything up.*

Scarlett set to work the moment she walked in, making me a cup of chamomile tea. *I would have preferred wine,* I joked. She responded with a pointed glance at the pregnancy test.

Finally sitting on my bed, the unused test sitting between us, Scarlett took my hand. "It wasn't some random one-night stand, was it?"

"No." I wiped a tear from my cheek.

"Did you tell Xander?" she asked softly.

"How do you know it was Xander?" I whimpered.

"I suspected at the store, but Xander's reaction told me everything. I shouldn't have opened my big mouth the way I did."

"It's not your fault, it's mine. I should have told you." I rubbed my hands against the side of my face, willing the tears to subsist.

"And I should have known. That boy has been in love with you for years. And I've suspected you felt the same way. Honestly, it was the reasons I knew I'd never get into him when we dated in high school. I saw you guys together. It felt inevitable that you two would hook up. I always hoped you'd figure it out. Though I was hoping it was going to be a few years ago, not after this shit."

"It doesn't matter now. He's gone," I whispered.

"Does he know about the test? That you think you might be..." she trailed off, looking glumly at the bedspread.

"I didn't have time. We got in this big fight, and he left."

"I'm sure he'll come back," she consoled.

"No, I really screwed things up, Scarlett. He was so mad I was keeping what we have together a secret." I glanced up at her. "When you said I had some mystery guy he flipped out."

"You fought because of what I said?" she frowned at me, pulling her brows together.

"Kind of," I shook my head. "Not really. I told him I'd tell you. But I kept chickening out. I was so scared, and I kept putting it off. I think he got tired of waiting for me."

"That doesn't sound fair," she mumbled.

"He was right. I was using him. When he was trying to leave, I kept telling him he had to stay because I needed him. How selfish is that?"

She reached over and rubbed the top of my hand with her thumb. "He was mad because you didn't tell me? Here's your chance. Give me the story. I'll let you know if you're as selfish as you think you are."

I wrapped my hands around my mug, staring down at the half-moon imprint my lip balm made on the rim of the mug. All my energy behind hiding this from Scarlett faded away. I couldn't lie to her face, if anyone would understand, it would be Scarlett. I wanted desperately to talk to someone.

I glanced up at her, before looking out the window, my voice a low whisper. "I was so clueless. I had no idea what I was doing, Scar."

She reached her hand across the bed taking mine. "Tell me everything."

I sighed, leaning closer to her. "I'm not even sure where the beginning was."

"I'm here all night. As long as you need me."

So, I tell her. Hearing the words out loud makes the choices I made feel worse. Why couldn't I have seen how I felt sooner? Why did I waste so much time on worrying about Max? How could I have been so blind?

Two more cups of herbal tea, a shared package of cookies and a bathroom break for each of us later Scarlett sat across from me, leaning back on her hands, and studied me with a perfect cat-eye lined look.

"So, you've been sleeping together for a few months now?" she asked.

I nodded at her glumly.

"But you think it was going on for a few months before that even?"

"Yes," I replied, my cheeks burning red. "Honestly, closer to a year if I'm being honest." I sunk my head into my arms on the table. "Ugh, I'm a horrible person."

"Why? Because you're moving on? It was going to happen, eventually."

"Because I moved on to Max's best friend."

"You can't worry about Max. I think Max would…"

I raised a hand to her. "Don't say he'd want me to be happy."

She pursed her lips together, raising her eyebrows. "I wasn't. I'm sure Max would be pissed. Honestly, Max was a selfish ass when it came to you. I think if he was alive and you guys broke up, he'd flip out if you hooked up with Xander, and who knows, maybe he's turning in his grave every time you two make out…"

"Scarlett! You are not helping me," I admonished.

"But he loved you. He might have been an asshole. He might have had his issues, but you were one of the few good things he had in his miserably short life. He loved you more than anything. So yeah, Max would be pissed. But he would be pissed about anyone. The only other person he came close to trusting was Xander."

"So, you're saying you think I'd get his blessing?"

She smirked at me. "I doubt even in the afterlife, Max is that evolved. But I think begrudging acceptance would be attainable."

"What about you? What do you think?" I asked, my voice wavering.

"Baby girl!" She threw her head back and laughed. "What do you think I'm going to say?" Still laughing, she shook her head incredulously at me.

"So yes? No? I don't know…"

"I *love* Xander. He has been in love with you for years. I can't imagine a better guy for you." Smiling she grabbed my hand in hers. "If you care about him half as much as he cares about you, it could really be something."

"If I hadn't screwed it up." I reminded her my voice choked with tears. I break down again, the sobs wracking my chest.

I cry and she rubs my back. Once my cries quieted, she retreated to the bathroom to change into her pajamas. I can hear the water turning on and off. In the wake of my confrontation, Scarlett's non-reaction is bewildering. When she comes out of the bathroom, she holds the test in her hand.

"You have to take it."

I stare at the test, willing it and the question it poses to go away.

"I mean it, Ana. I know tonight has been rough. But you need to know," Scarlett chided.

I look up at her and grimace. "It's been more than rough."

"Take the test." She thrusts it in my hands and pushes me toward the bathroom. I scowl at her but follow directions.

I watch as the test began to change, the window showing the thick blue control line deepened in color. I sit on the toilet, waiting for the other line to show up but after five minutes there was still a single blue line.

Negative.

All that stress, the fight, the heartache. I didn't need to get the test. I didn't need to tell Scarlett. This whole thing could've been avoided because the test was negative.

I walked out of the bathroom and past Scarlett who was waiting on the edge of the bed. I returned a minute later with a bottle of wine, swigging it straight from the bottle as I walked back into the room.

"I guess that answers my next question," Scarlett remarked.

I handed her the bottle, and she drank, her eyes never leaving mine.

"Are you happy or sad it was negative?" she asked softly.

I took the bottle back from her and ran a finger over the label. "I don't know. Both, probably. With Xander dumping me it's for the best but I think in a way, I was ready for this."

"You really love him, don't you?"

"I do," I replied softly.

"Well, shit." She cursed under her breath as she laid back on the bed.

I laid next to her, looking up at the ceiling. "I know."

# Chapter Twenty-Nine

WHEN I LOST MAX, I counted every minute going by. I kept track of the days, the weeks, the months, where all I had was my grief to keep me rooted to the ground. There was a solace in that level of pain. I had every reason to sink into the blue, I had every excuse to leave my world.

Losing Max taught me how much pain I could endure. It taught me that no matter how much heartbreak I had, the world still turned around me. It seemed that, after years of resisting, years of telling myself I was only friends with Xander, I learned too late that I was wrong on every count.

In a nasty twist of timing, I got my period the day I moved out of the condo. It was two days after Xander left. My parents didn't ask questions when I came home, mismatched suitcases in hand, asking if I could stay. My father hired a moving company for everything else. Normally, the idea of strangers touching my belongings would've set me on edge, but I couldn't dredge up enough energy to fight it.

Inexplicably, my parents kept my room perfectly preserved. Coming back to that room, all I could think about was how Xander and I made out on my bed as the New Year's party was going on without us only a few months before. I thought about how we'd gone home that night and forged ahead down the perilous path to our mutual heartbreak.

My mother subdued her curiosity when she left me alone for weeks. Sure, she was always asking if I wanted to talk, but when I refused, she'd quickly change the subject. I never loved her more. I think she knew my heartache was different from all the other times before it when Max hurt my feelings.

She never liked Max; she never liked the way Max treated me. I knew she was right to feel that way. If I had a daughter, I'd feel the same way.

I was lazing around in bed when she sauntered into my room, a basket of clothes under her arm. With a creased brow she set the basket down on the bed beside me.

"I'm sure it's all terribly old fashioned for you, but I was getting rid of some clothes and figured, since we wear the same size, you might want to look through them before I donate them."

I reached into the basket, answering in the affirmative. She sat down on the other side of the basket and began pulling out items she thought I'd like. While some of the clothes weren't my style, she had an eye for classics I could certainly wear. Her clothes were all name brands, expensively made and therefore well-constructed.

"So, I know I'm not supposed to ask," she paused to smooth out the front of a white button-down shirt she had laying across her lap. "But I'm guessing your moving out of the apartment has something to do with Alexander."

I fought back the sting at hearing his name out loud. "You could say that."

"Did he or did you two…" she trailed off. I glanced over and saw that her cheeks had pinkened at the unfinished question.

A long, tense silence settled over us. I opened my mouth several times before I was able to will the words to appear. "We were involved… romantically."

"I see." She pursed her lips. "And he did something to hurt you. Like Maximilian did?"

"No. The opposite, actually." I shook my head. Despite all the hurt I'd suffered from Xander, I couldn't bring myself to disparage him. "He's not like Max. I know they grew up in the same neighborhood, but Xander is inherently good. I didn't expect he'd begin to have feelings for me. I didn't expect that."

I gulped the words down. "He was good for me. How I felt," I grimaced knowing words would never be enough. "How I feel, it's different than it was with Max. It feels more..." I struggled to find the right word to describe the difference and came up short. All I knew was I felt safe with Xander. I knew that would matter to my mother. "Substantial."

"Substantial?" She frowned at me. "I never thought I'd hear you use that word as a positive."

"Things change. I changed. When I lost Max, I was so broken up about losing him and the life I thought I'd have with him. Things changed in me. I found some stuff out about Max, and I grew up. I had to."

"If I could've done something to help you, or to help him..."

"Xander helped me. He saved me really, and I think that I saved him. We helped each other get through the grief. Once the dust settled, it felt like I could see him. For the first time I really saw Xander. He's such a good person, and for so long he wanted to protect me."

"He's in love with you," she replied softly, taking my hand in hers. My mother had spent so much time trying to talk me out of the relationship when I was with Max. I assumed she couldn't understand what Max and I had. At that moment, I looked down at our entwined hands. Her perfect half-moon nails were polished with a tasteful sheer shade. An unusually small diamond solitaire ring graced her left ring finger. I remembered years before, when I asked her why they'd never upgraded her wedding ring, she'd laughed and said something about sentimentality. Suddenly, I was overcome by the sight of it. My mother could never be called a modest woman, but that token of love given to her by my father in their earlier days was the only piece of jewelry she was never without.

"He *was* in love with me. I doubt he still is. I messed everything up," I whimpered. Tears welled in my eyes, and I couldn't fight them back any longer. I'd ruined my shot at happiness. I had a chance at love, the silent and tender kind that endured through the years. The kind I now knew I'd never have with Max. I'd had a real chance at that with Xander and I ruined it.

"I keep thinking about what you used to tell me when I was younger. *No man who is worth your tears will make you cry and no man who makes you cry is ever worth your tears.*"

I was surprised when she scoffed loudly. "That's a dumb saying. It may have been true when you were fifteen, but not anymore. Anything worth having is worth a few tears. No relationship is ever perfect. You think your father hasn't made me cry? That I haven't done things that hurt him equally bad? It happens. Loving someone is choosing to believe the good in them every day. But that doesn't mean we always make good choices handling each other."

"Isn't believing in Max's good the very thing that got me hurt?" I asked softly. "If I'd only been a little more realistic about him, maybe I could've spared myself the heartache."

"Maybe," she demurred. She leaned forward and tucked a stray hair behind my ear. "But if you want my opinion, it wasn't you wanting to see the good in Max that got you in that mess. It was not seeing the good in yourself."

"You're supposed to say that. You're my mom," I remarked.

"I know, but that doesn't mean it's not true. There's nothing wrong with wanting to see the good in another person, as long as you hold yourself to the same standard."

"I don't feel like such a good person right now," I whispered.

"Because of Alexander?" Her face softened. "Do you love him?"

"I do," I whispered.

"Well then." She frowned at me. "When you two figure things out, you bring him around for dinner, okay?"

"There's nothing to figure out, mom. It's over," I mumbled.

She patted my hand softly. "Don't be so sure, sweetie. If you care for each other the way I think you do, it'll work out. When it's meant to be, it will happen."

I laughed through my tears, "I never took you for such a hopeless romantic, Mom."

She reached forward, wiping the tears off my cheeks with her thumbs. "Of course, I am sweetie. That's probably why I was always so hard on Max. I knew what you deserved. I wanted the fairytale for you, and Max could never give you that."

I wrapped my hands around hers, holding them tight. "If this is a fairytale, I'm pretty sure I'm the villain."

She laughed softly. "Now *you're* being melodramatic. It's going to work out."

I wanted to believe my mother, but in the weeks that followed, Xander wouldn't return my phone calls or my texts. I wrote him a letter, but he sent it back to my parents' house unopened. Scarlett offered to talk to him, but I told her I wouldn't risk any more friendships over what happened.

This heartbreak was different from anything I'd experienced before. When fighting with Max it felt as if the ground opened beneath me and I was falling, it was all encompassing and suffocating. With Max it was the kind of pain that warranted wailing, breakdowns in the store, getting drunk and making bad decisions. It was a child's pain and my reaction to it was childish.

The moment Xander walked out the door, I felt a physical ripping down my chest. The pain was so intense, I lost my breath from it all. The mere memory of his words cut through me anew. I couldn't fully heal from it. It was a quiet torture that followed me around, drowning me. I couldn't share my pain; I couldn't talk about it. I was far into the waves, and I alone had taken myself in so deep.

On the eve of Scarlett and Emma's wedding, Scarlett surprised me by asking me to come to her mother's house before we traveled to Emma's family home for the rehearsal. When I arrived, she pulled me into her room, asking for my opinion about several dresses before I stopped her.

"What's this about? You know I can't help you with fashion. That's your department."

She sank down on the papasan chair across from me. "I know. I was trying to ease into telling you..."

When she didn't finish, I quirked an eyebrow. "Tell me what?"

"I was hoping you'd be okay walking with Xander tomorrow, or tonight. I mean you'll practice tonight and then do it again tomorrow."

My face grew hot, "Oh." I'd known that Scarlett asked Xander to be in the wedding.

"I thought I was going to walk with Troy?" Scarlett was having Xander and I on her side of the altar and Emma had her cousin and Troy on her side.

"I guess Emma's mom and the wedding planner already printed the program books. They're insistent we stick to what's written." She paused, her brow creasing. "If it's going to be too hard for you, let me know now. I can fight it. I didn't mention it at first because I thought you guys..."

"That we'd be back together?" I finished.

She sighed and glanced away. "Well, yeah. I mean you guys are meant to be. I know it. How can the both of you be so stubborn right now?"

"Me? I'm stubborn? I've been trying to talk to him. I sent him messages. I called him. I even sent him an actual pen and paper letter with a stamp and everything. It's been almost a month and I haven't heard a single thing from him."

"Yeah, but you did all that the first week, when he was still mad. Then you hid out at your parents' house and have someone else box up all your things. Someone else move everything. You left and you haven't been back."

I put a hand up. "I don't need to be reminded how badly I screwed everything up, Scarlett. I am aware."

She frowned at me. "I don't think you screwed it up by yourself..."

I started to interject but she shot me a quieting look. "Could you have been more forthcoming? Maybe. But you have to realize how insecure Xander is."

"He's not insecure. He's the one who pursued me! He's the one who..."

She shook her head. "Think about it. He gets upset because he wants you guys to go public. He's been waiting years to be with you. Then you want to wait. You won't even tell your beautiful, smart, totally understanding best friend about it. I think after a while anyone would get insecure about how much you were invested. And this is Xander we're talking about. He's been in love with you for years."

"I know all this, Scar," I reminded her. "We already talked about this. What's your point?"

"Apologize again. If you still want to be with him, tell him again. Figure out a way to get the point across."

"What? Like some grand gesture at the wedding? That sounds humiliating for everyone," I scoffed.

Her eyes widened in horror. "Don't you dare. No one is allowed to upstage my beautiful bride and I at our wedding." She paused. "Talk to him. You love each other and both of you have had enough heartbreak to last a lifetime."

I sighed and grabbed a dress sitting on the bed beside me. "Put this on. We'll be late for your rehearsal if we keep dissecting my love life."

She caught the dress in midair and frowned at me. "We're not done with this."

I chuckled. "Wouldn't expect anything less from you."

The Navarro-Vega home was a sprawling beachfront log cabin boasting five bedrooms and as many bathrooms. Set on two acres overlooking Oyster Bay it had to be one of the nicest houses in Illahee. I'd been there once for a backyard barbecue and was surprised with the expanse of the property. I felt like a snob for thinking it, but Illahee was considered a lower income area compared to Ridgewood.

Scarlett led me into a large bedroom at the back of the house. She explained we'd be getting ready in there, while Emma and her cousin are on the other side of the house. They were insistent that they kept things as traditional as possible and not see each other until the ceremony.

The wedding planner, Pam, gave us a quick run through of what we'd be doing before the ceremony. I kept looking for Xander, but after not seeing him for thirty minutes I began to relax. I accepted a mimosa that Emma's mother, Miriam, thrust in my hand as the wedding planner brought us out into the backyard to begin the rehearsal.

Out in the backyard, we retreated to the beachfront area where we'd be doing the ceremony. Emma was standing under the driftwood archway, managing a few young men who were decorating it with cedar boughs. A woman had her arm wrapped around Emma's shoulder and was interrupting to add her opinion about how it should look. Still there was no sign of Xander. I turned to Scarlett to ask her if she knew where he was. Was he going to ditch rehearsal because he knew I'd be here? Did Scarlett give him the same heads up she gave me?

Emma and the other woman broke away and walked over to us. "Dulcie Navarro, I'm Emma's cousin." She gave me a big smile as I tried to hide my surprise hearing this was her cousin. They looked nothing alike. Emma was a tiny blonde thing, whereas this woman was a whole head over my five-foot-two stature. She shook her thick, wavy black hair out of her face. "And her maid of honor."

"Ana Pryce, Scarlett's BFF." I nodded my head at Troy who was helping carry a large wooden bench with Emma's father. "So, I heard you're walking with Troy. Did you meet him yet?" I asked.

Her eyes focused on him, and a familiar light lit up in her eyes as she looked him over. "I did. Who is it you're walking with?"

I bit my lip, "Xander. He's supposed to be here now. But I haven't seen him yet."

"Wait," she leaned closer. "That's right. I met him earlier. Scarlett's friend. He was here earlier. He was helping fix something or another. He left to get more of those leafy things for the seats. He should be back soon."

So, he wasn't a no show because of me. He was doing what he did best, helping others and working. I was simultaneously relieved and disappointed. Maybe he wasn't missing me the way I was missing him. Did he not feel like it would be hard to be around me?

"Oh, good." I mumbled, as Pam instructed us to get into our positions to rehearse the processional. I watched as Troy's face lit up as he walked toward us. He gave me a quick, platonic hello before offering his arm to Dulcie. Despite my fears about seeing Xander, I smirked at the obvious chemistry between them. Just because seeing Xander at this wedding was going to be painful for me, didn't mean that someone else couldn't find a little happiness this weekend.

I stood where Pam told me to stand, trying not to worry that I still hadn't seen Xander. She muttered something about people being late and turned to berate Scarlett for not telling him what time he needed to be back. But then I heard familiar footfalls. I'd know them anywhere.

"I'm here." Xander called out as he ran to stand next to Scarlett. He stopped, placing his hands on his knees, and panting from exertion. "Sorry, there was," he gasped to regain his breath, "an issue with the... uh" he waved his hand around in the air, "you know, the lumber for the benches. But I'm here."

Pam gave him a pinched assessment, eying his dirty work shirt. "Perhaps you'd like to change before we get on with the rehearsal?"

He glanced at his shirt, where little wood chips were clinging to the front. "Oh, yeah, okay. I'll be right back."

He turned to Scarlett, giving her arm a quick squeeze. I thought of his hand on my arm, his fingers on my skin, his mouth against mine. I looked away, swallowing hard. As I watched his retreating form, a lump formed in my throat. In the two minutes he was here he'd avoided looking at me.

Scarlett stood next to me, lacing her arm through mine.

"He hates me," I grumbled.

"He could never hate you." Scarlett chided. She glanced back over our shoulders at the house a small smile playing on her lips. "Just give him a little time to work up the courage again."

When Xander joined us a few minutes later, he wore a new, green button-down shirt I was sure Scarlett had made him wear. I noticed how the green brought out the gold flecks in his eyes. He'd gotten a haircut recently and his curls were much shorter than they were before I left. I looked for any signs that he wasn't sleeping well, that he was as heartbroken as I was, but I couldn't see any. He looked amazing.

When Pam instructed him to offer me his arm, he put his arm out, but avoided my eyes. With a pit in my stomach, I took his arm and drew myself close to his side. We both looked forward, awkwardly waiting for more instructions. I could feel his warmth through the shirt and the smell his soap. I closed my eyes, taking in the feeling of having him so near to me and yet knowing I couldn't get any closer.

Our footsteps were in perfect sync as we walked down the makeshift aisle lined with cedar boughs and ivy. Pam had us run through the procession several times. The whole time, I had to stand next to him with my arm laced in his. It was the perfect torture.

After our fourth run-through we were sent to the benches as they discussed the verbiage used in the vows. I was sure Xander would flee again or look for another errand he could run to get away from me. I was surprised when he sank into the spot next to me on the bench. He wasn't close enough to touch, but I could feel him all the same. He was looking away from me, staring at Scarlett and Emma with a forced concentration that led me to believe he may sense me the same way I sensed him. From the corner of my eye, I studied him thoughtfully.

"You cut your hair," I remarked, the words escaping before I thought about how silly they sounded. The first thing I said to him after so long was about his hair—good job, Ana.

He raised a hand to his head, rubbing his scalp. "Uh, yeah. Scarlett asked me to clean myself up for the wedding."

I wanted to say that I liked his hair longer, that I liked the way the curly blond tendrils would fall across his forehead as he slept, or the way they felt against my fingers when he'd kiss me. I rubbed my fingers together in my fists, trying not to think about touching him. "It looks good."

We sat there, looking around the yard for something else to talk about and falling short. The urge to touch him, to say all the words I wanted to say, was pressing through me. I studied the waves as they rolled onto the beach bringing a line of seaweed against the shore. I concentrated on the assurance that Pam would try her best to rid the shoreline of the invasive plant before the ceremony tomorrow.

We were saved by Pam's call to resume practicing. He was silent for the remainder of the rehearsal and disappeared into the house for a while, only returning later to sit at the opposite side of the long table when dinner was about to start. I watched him engage in a long conversation with Emma's father. Once he glanced over at me and caught me looking at him. I could see him blushing red when he saw me. Though not nearly as red as I was for getting caught. Scarlett tried to get me into the conversation but after a few failed attempts she left me to wallow in my puddle of self-pity and anxiety.

Afterward, I walked alone to my car, my maid of honor dress slung over my arm. I fumbled with my bag, trying to fish my keys out of my purse while simultaneously not allowing the dress to touch the ground. I stiffened when I heard footsteps behind me. I glanced up and noticed Xander's truck parked in the only spot that was left—directly behind my car.

I debated getting into my car without acknowledging him, but he was too close to pull off that kind of evasiveness without looking like a complete weirdo. I held my key fob in my hand, clicking the unlock button three times before opening my door. I could hear Xander's footsteps slowing as he must've realized that I was standing there. I threw my purse and sweater on the passenger seat before turning to face him. Xander stopped in front of me with a pinched expression.

"Hey," he mumbled.

"Hey," I replied.

We stared at each other for a long moment. As he shoved his hands in his front pockets, a breeze whipped through the street, blowing the cherry blossoms off the trees to drift down the road. A single petal fell into his hair, balancing on top of the one section of curls that was lighter than the rest of his hair. I fought the urge to move forward and pluck it out of his hair. That was an intimate gesture, and I no longer had the right to do that.

I opened my mouth to say something, but I wasn't sure how to form the words. All the things I wanted to say lingered between us.

"Tomorrow should be fun," I offered, hating the stilted way the air settled between us. I dragged the tip of my keys against my palm, scoring the skin in three lines before lacing my finger through the ring and letting them fall in a jangle.

"Yeah. I'll be kind of glad when it's over, though. It's a lot of work and Scar's got me running around all over the place, like I'm an errand boy."

If we were on better terms, I would have teased him that he liked being her errand boy. But I couldn't do that now. I glanced away from him, rubbing my key fob in my hand. "I know what you mean. I love my dress but it's not the most comfortable thing to wear. I hope I don't pop out of it."

"I'm sure you'll look great."

I let out an awkward laugh, trying to mask my reaction to such nice words from him. I couldn't allow myself to hope. "Yeah, we'll see."

"Ana, I mean it." Xander leaned forward, his hand came up to pinch a tendril of hair that fell across my forehead. I held my breath as he tucked it behind my ear. His eyes watched his fingers, still avoiding my eyes. "You looked really nice today."

My breath caught in my throat, and I watched his face as he steadied his hand and drew away from me, stepping back. He shoved his hands back in his pockets and glanced at his truck.

"Thanks," I replied, my voice throatier than I wanted it to be. "You, too."

Finally, mercifully he looked me in the eye. We stared at each other, locked together in a moment of longing. He opened his mouth as if to say something then closed it, stepping away from me. "I should head home. We got a big day tomorrow."

He ran a hand through his hair, trying to muss curls that weren't there any longer.

I knew I should look away. I knew I should keep it casual, but I could still feel the static of his hand on my hair. I could still smell the scent of wood on his skin. "It was good seeing you, Xan." I stepped forward and touched his right arm lightly. "Great, in fact."

He looked down at my hand and I saw his jaw flex. His left hand came up and for a moment I thought he was going to take my hand in his. Instead, it moved to cup the back of his neck. He stepped back and my hand fell from his arm, dropping between us. "Yeah, I'll see you tomorrow."

The rejection stung, burning cold in my chest. I turned away, throwing the dress across my passenger seat, not even caring if it got wrinkled at that point. I slammed the door shut and rushed past Xander, not able to look at him again. I could feel his eyes on me as I climbed into my car. In the rear-view mirror, I saw him disappear into his truck. There was a moment when I thought he was staring at my car. For a second, I thought our eyes had locked, but when I adjusted the mirror to get a better look, his truck turned on and he drove away.

# CHAPTER THIRTY

WHILE I WAS THE only woman standing up with Scarlett, she invited a few girlfriends to get ready with us. We had a great time, reminiscing, drinking, and helping each other with makeup. By the time the wedding was about to start, I'd been primped and preened over, my hair pinned and sprayed. My nails were painted a soft lilac, all the while drinking mimosas with little flower garnishes. In all the revelry I almost forgot about how cold Xander had been the night before or how nervous I should be at seeing him again.

I slid my dress over my body. I was unsure about the style when Scarlett picked it out, but sure enough, the deep purple Grecian style dress fit like a glove. The top was a little tight. I probably should've gone on the diet I kept saying I'd go on. But I was happy with my reflection. For a moment, I wondered if Xander would think I looked pretty, then I chided myself for the thought. He made his opinion clear the night before.

I helped Scarlett into her lace and satin column dress, the ivory color complimenting her skin perfectly. I buttoned the small pearl buttons along her back, taking care not to snag the lace. She turned toward me with tears in her eyes.

"It's really happening," she choked out.

I grasped her hands in mine, my eyes filled with tears. "I know. I'm so happy for you. Emma is so lucky to have you." I grabbed a tissue from the bedside table and dabbed beneath her eyes. "Now stop crying. You'll smear the masterpiece that is your face."

She laughed. "If I'm already crying now, I'm going to be a mess during the ceremony." She took the tissue from my hand and stuffed it into her bra. "I'm going to need this later."

"A beautiful mess, the both of you." I handed the birdcage veil to her mom who had Scarlett duck to secure it in her hair with small pearl-adorned pins. Scarlett and Emma's dresses were opposites in style but they got the same veil to wear during the ceremony.

Scarlett stood up slowly and faced us. "How do I look?" she whispered.

Scarlett's mom and I glanced at each other both our hands over our faces. "Oh darling, you are so beautiful..." she sobbed out the last word.

I stood back as they embraced. I wondered if I'd ever have this moment with my own mom. If I'd ever find someone who I could be this happy with.

I couldn't help but remember how many times I thought I'd have this with Max. In my fledgling dreams, I imagined the dress, the ceremony, the way I'd cry so prettily. I imagined the sappy county song we'd dance to—and everything would be perfect. I could imagine the perfection of the night and then I could picture exactly how the perfection would fade. As much as I could imagine the wedding, I could never fathom a *marriage* to Max.

In the days before our breakup, there was one perfect afternoon. Xander had brought home my favorite ice cream from the store. We sat on the couch, and he let me watch the teenage fantasy series I'd become obsessed with. I could still feel his hand on my ankle, the way his fingers vanished into his hair as he rested his head on his hand while watching the show. I could still taste the mint and chocolate on my tongue.

I closed my eyes as tears threatened to appear. I willed them away as I scored my thumbnail up the side of my pointer finger. By the third scrape I could open my eyes. Scarlett was looking over at me, her brows furrowed.

"You doing, okay?" she asked softly.

I tensed my jaw in the best smile I could muster. "Of course. It's your big day, I'm great." I glanced out the window overlooking the beach. I could see the event planning crew moving things around, placing flowers, chairs, and various tables around the area. Pam was marching after people with her clipboard in hand, pointing at different things with force.

"You sure? We can still switch the walking order if you..."

"We probably need to get down there. We don't want Pam looking for us." I turned away from her, grabbing my shawl off the bed and draping it over my shoulders as I hurried down the stairs.

I got to the back door before Xander. Dulcie and Troy were already standing together, her arm laced through his and their heads tilted toward each other in new familiarity. I wondered what they got up to last night. Dulcie wore the same dress as me, but on her, it draped over her lithe frame like she was a mannequin. Suddenly, my dress felt too tight around the hips and too long around my ankles. Her long curly hair was pinned up in a style that looked intricate. I touched my own hair and worried my curls were falling out.

I felt him stand behind me before I heard him. Having him near felt like being near a live electric current. I didn't turn to face him right away. I was still embarrassed and unsure after last night. Standing still, I stared out the back door and fiddled with my lush bouquet of lilies of the valley, violets, and multicolored roses. I pulled the small pin out of the ribbon wrapped around the flower stems, pulling it up and down, up and down, up and down. The last time I pushed it down I felt the tip poke out of the bottom of the ribbon, jabbing me in the finger. I jumped at the pain and dropped my bouquet. A hand flew out to catch the flowers as they hit the ground. I glanced up at Xander next to me, the bouquet in his hand. "Thanks," I mumbled, taking it from him.

He nodded at me. I didn't want to look at him, but I couldn't help it. The last time I saw him in a suit was the night of our senior prom. Back then he was still gangly, his face dotted with acne, and his facial hair came in patchy. He wasn't the same person today as he was then. He filled out his suit beautifully, with broad shoulders and muscular arms. As much as I missed his long curls, he looked older with his newly shorn hair. He was a man now.

How different would our lives have been if I'd leaned in that night in his truck? I knew what that kiss would've meant. If only I'd waited one minute longer if I had turned to him and really looked at him. Staring at him now, I was struck by the heartache I could've been spared if only I let myself see what had always been there. If I'd let myself see and feel the love I had for Xander in that moment when his lips brushed against mine.

Pam came rushing up to us, clapping her hands like a schoolmarm on too much coffee. Xander put out his arm and I laced mine through his. I took a deep breath and fought to ignore the hard thud of my heart and the pain knowing I may never be this close to him again.

I barely heard the ceremony. I did all the right things. I handed the ring over when I was supposed to. I took Scarlett's calla lilies when they clasped their hands to recite their vows. I teared up when Scarlett did, but I wasn't sure if it was happiness for her or my own heartache.

Holding both the bouquets in my hands, I tried to wipe the tears from my eyes. A stem from my bouquet got caught in my hair and pulled a curl out of my updo.

I shook the hair out of my face and tried to ignore the welling tears. At the end of the ceremony, I felt Xander touching my elbow and I realized I was supposed to put my arm through his. I considered not doing it. It was acutely painful to touch him and know this was all I'd ever get from him. But formalities must be maintained. I laced my arm through the crook of his elbow but tried to keep my distance as best I could. The aisle felt impossibly long with him next to me. When we got to the end, I stepped aside to allow for Dulcie and Troy to come in behind us.

I could feel Xander's eyes on me, and the heat of his presence flowing through me. I worked to ignore it. His hand reached up and grasped the lock of hair the bouquet pulled from my updo and tucked it behind my ear. It was such a familiar gesture and so like what he did the night before when he rejected me. I brushed his hand away, tucking the hair behind my ear myself. "Don't."

His hand dropped between us as if I'd burned him. He stepped back and his face was grim.

Dulcie and Troy stepped beside us, laughing at some inside joke they'd created in the short time they'd walked down the aisle. They didn't drop their embrace as they stepped to the side but when they saw me and Xander their smiles wavered. But it wasn't long before they were standing close together again, speaking in hushed voices and laughing.

I avoided Xander's eyes until I counted to thirty, and he stalked away toward the party.

Emma and Scarlett twirled around the dance floor to a love song. I grasped my champagne glass and watched from the side next to my parents. My father had deserted me and my mother in search of canapes. At the next table over, I could see the price tag stuck on the bottom of Emma's aunt's jeweled sandal. I turned my head to try to read it. Fifty percent off 34.99 from TJ Maxx. I laughed wondering what Scarlett would think about marrying into a family that purchased shoes from a bargain basement store.

"Scarlett looks lovely." My mother's comment ripped me away from my musings on sandal prices.

I nodded at my mother. "She does."

"She looks happy. I'm sure Miriam is pleased, even if she might not have grandchildren."

"Mom!" I glanced around trying to ascertain if anyone overheard her.

She gave me a half-hearted shrug. "What? It's true."

"That is not true at all, and you know it. Just because she married a woman doesn't mean that she can't have children."

She took a long sip of her diet soda and shot me a disdainful look as if I was the one to make the comment. "Scarlett marrying a woman has nothing to do with becoming a parent. I'm saying that she never seemed like the type who wanted to have children and now there's no way she'll accidentally get pregnant, so—problem solved."

"You're ridiculous."

"It's true though, she won't have a pregnancy scare like you did."

My mouth dropped wide open in shock. "How did you know that I had a pregnancy scare?"

She glanced over at me. Even in her heels, she was barely eye level with me. "Miriam told me. Did you know that Scarlett tells her mother everything?"

I cursed under my breath. "If it wasn't her wedding, I'd kill her."

"No need to murder anyone tonight. Now, I'm going to find your father and remind him he was supposed to bring me those crab cakes I love." She glanced over my shoulder, a small smile creeping up on her face. "And I get a feeling that you're going to be a little busy in a minute."

I turned to find Xander approaching me, frowning. I crossed my arms against my chest staring down at his open hand. "We're supposed to dance now. Pam's orders." I looked behind him to see Dulcie and Troy already together, his hand covering hers and their eyes locked. Scarlett and Emma stood together in the center of the dance floor, performing a beautifully choreographed number.

"I don't want to dance with you right now," I said, not meeting his eyes.

He stepped closer, pulling my hand out of the crook of my elbow. "You don't have a choice. We have to." When I tried to pull my hand away from him his mouth set in a grim line. "For Scarlett and Emma, An."

I considered walking away, but over his shoulder I saw Scarlett giving me a quick shake of her head, warning me against refusing him.

I took his hand and he led me out on the dance floor. We stood in front of each other awkwardly before he stepped forward, resting a hand on my hip, and drawing me closer to him. My skin seared under his touch, and I closed my eyes at the sensation, reveling in the pain of it all. I hated how quickly his touch affected me. His mouth was at my ear, his breath warm. "I would have thought you'd bring a date to this." Xander said as he looked around. "Matt was looking at you."

I glanced over my shoulder at Matt Hansen who stood at the outskirts of the party, eyeing one of Emma's cousins who couldn't be older than nineteen.

"That is disgusting."

Xander laughed softly and I thrilled at the sound of it. "Yeah, he never really grew out of the sleazeball stage, did he?"

"What about you? You didn't want to bring a date? I bet Sherie would have come with you if you'd asked."

Xander tripped a little over his feet at my words. "No, I wouldn't do that to you."

I let the words wash over me, trying to decipher the meaning. Was he seeing someone and didn't want me to be upset or because he still cared for me? I fought to keep the venom in my tone. "Why not?"

Xander's jaw tightened. "I just didn't." He glanced away from me and over my shoulder at Troy. "You know I had to get ready with your boyfriend."

I frowned at him. "He was never my boyfriend. We only went out on a few dates."

Xander smirked at me. "So, you admit the last one was a date?"

"No, I won't. You're being ridiculous." I looked up at him and he smiled down at me. "You're pretty jovial all of a sudden."

"Troy and I had a couple of shots after the ceremony."

I pulled back a little, surprised. "Really? That's not like you."

He shrugged. "I think we were both a little nervous."

"About what?" I asked. "You don't have to make any speeches or anything. The ceremony was the hard part, now it's a party."

"No, not that." He looked down at me and I was stuck in his intense gaze. We continued the awkward back-and-forth dancing that was the height of our dancing abilities. Max was the good dancer; he knew how to lead me into looking capable and even talented after a few beers. I realized it didn't bother me how terrible of a dancer Xander was. Being in his arms would be enough if it was where he truly wanted to be. I stared down at our feet. My bare toe narrowly missed being stomped on by Xander's wing tip.

"Troy's over you, by the way. If you were worried about that. You've been replaced."

I glanced over at Dulcie and Troy standing on the edge of the dance floor, their arms locked around each other. He whispered something in her ear, and she ducked her head into his shoulder to laugh.

"I wasn't worried. I'm happy for him. Dulcie seems nice. She's gorgeous, smart, and all that."

"Yeah, she does. He's not such a bad guy either, I guess," he conceded.

"So, you like him now?" I asked, smirking.

"Well, yeah, once he stopped being into you, I liked him plenty." He frowned at the admission. "I don't think I could've handled being here if you two were still into each other."

I was struck by the honesty in his response, the way his words offered me a hope I didn't want to take. I pulled away slightly. "I should go sit down."

I stepped back and Xander grabbed my wrist softly. "Wait, I'm sorry. I shouldn't have said that. That was creepy."

"What am I supposed to do with that comment?" I shook my head and tried to pull my wrist out of his grip. "You can't say that to me. Not anymore. You made the choice to leave and with that you lose the right to comment on my love life. Now let me go, Alexander."

He dropped his hand and I turned to stalk away from him, toward the beach, kicking my heels off once I got to the sand. Picking up the hem of my dress I walked until I hit the edge of the water where the sand was cool. The thin waxing crescent moon hung brightly in the dark sky, casting light onto the water. I realized I'd left my shawl sitting on the back of my chair and rubbed my arms to warm myself against the wind picking up over the bay. It was much warmer back under the reception tent where heating lamps were strategically placed to warm the late spring night.

I willed myself not to cry. I'd gotten through most of the night without completely ruining my makeup and ruining Scarlett and Emma's big day. I only had to get through the next hour and then I could leave. I could go back to my childhood room and stare at the old pictures taped to my mirror. I contemplated finding my parents and asking them to take me home early. My mom would if I asked her.

"You're right. I shouldn't have said that," Xander said from behind me. I startled at his voice, glancing over my shoulder at him. "It's the shots, loosening my tongue, I guess."

I turned to face him. The lights from the party illuminated the space around him so his face was only a shadow—yellow rays filtered through his light curls in a corona. "I don't believe that. And I know you don't believe that. Alcohol doesn't put fake words in your mouth, they only twist them, but in the end, when you strip it down, it's the truth." I stepped toward him, stopping a few feet away. "You told me once that I couldn't have it both ways. I can't want you—I can't ask you to want me and not commit to us. So why are you doing it to me?"

"You're right. I did say that," he whispered.

"You're the one who left me. You're the one who pushed me away. I told you that I needed time. I know I made mistakes, but in the end, it was you who ended things. It was you who broke us." My voice cracked. "Broke me."

"I know I ended things. I know that, but it was only because..." He raised his hand to rub his hair in that familiar gesture I loved. "I don't know what I'm doing. I'm scared shitless. I built up this idea of what we'd be in my head, and I had these plans of how it was going to go. About how I'd handle myself once I finally got the chance to try with you."

"I didn't want to come tonight, I didn't want to do any of this," he continued. "Without you, knowing that I'd see you and you might not want to talk to me, knowing I'd lost you. I was miserable." He glanced back over his shoulder at the party. "You know, yesterday, at the rehearsal, I got back earlier than I said. I saw you guys walking out to the beach and I couldn't bring myself to go out there yet. I hung back and watched you."

"What?" I scoffed. "But you wouldn't even look at me. Why would you..."

"I couldn't. Not right away. I knew if I looked at you, you'd see how broken up I was. I didn't want to look as pathetic as I was feeling. So, I stood back and watched you until Pam started yelling for me. You looked so beautiful. I thought maybe you'd look as miserable as I felt, but you didn't."

"Xander... why can't you see?" I bit back a small cry. "I am miserable."

He scoffed loudly. "Yeah, right."

I shook my head. "I thought you said you knew me. What happened to your big talk? How can you not see how utterly devastated your leaving made me?" I stepped closer, dropping my dress in the water. I could feel the wet sand sticking to the hem, dragging heavily against my ankles. I reached out, laying a hand on his arm. His skin felt warm and familiar. When he didn't pull away, I rubbed my thumb against his downy hair. "Being without you, I am bereft."

Slowly he brought his eyes up to meet mine. He was so incredibly sad, it made me let out a small sigh. The sound of laughter and late seventies disco music carried over the beach to us. He stepped closer to me, wrapping his arms around my waist. He pulled me tight against his body, my chest crushed to him. His hand spread across my lower back, and he set his chin on the top of my head. I could see the party in full swing, a clump of guests muddling through the cha-cha slide. I could hear a hoot of revelry and felt so far from it. Xander's hand burned through my dress.

"Can I take you home? Just to talk, I promise." He asked, his voice so soft I could barely hear it against the waves and the party.

The word 'home' rang in my ears I nodded against his chest. He pulled away, looking down at me. I wondered if he was going to kiss me but instead, his hand slid down my arm to take my palm. With damp, sandy hems, we took the long way around the house, bypassing the party.

# Chapter Thirty-One

THE ENTIRE TEN MINUTES in the truck we didn't speak. He held my hand, and my favorite radio station was on. When we parked at his condo, he hesitated, turning to me. I could hold his hand, but I couldn't face him, I couldn't lean into him. Not yet. I pulled away and walked to the front door, pulling out the key I never gave back. Silently, he followed me into the foyer.

Without me living at the condo for two months I expected a huge mess, dirty dishes littering the floor and garbage on the counters. Instead, the place was clean, with fresh vacuum marks along the hallway. The hook where I always hung my purse was empty, the bowl we kept our keys in had a new flattened penny in it. Xander stood behind me, sliding my sweater off my shoulders, his fingers brushing against my bare skin to rest on my elbows. I knew I could lean back into him and feel his lips against that spot between my neck and shoulder. His hands would be on my hips, and I'd sink against him.

I pulled away, not ready to have his hands on me. I knew if I turned to him in this place where we were always safe to be together that I'd lose my resolve to speak.

I walked into the living room and stopped short. When I moved out, I only asked for my essentials to be packed up. I left the furniture, the dishes, the plants. I didn't want to look at the things that Xander and I shared, even if it was only a spoon.

The painting hung at an odd angle on the wall, the left side inches lower than the right. I walked up and set my hand against the canvas feeling the rough paint under my fingertips. I could feel Xander behind me, even without looking at him I knew how he would be standing. His hands would be pushed into his pockets, his head ducked down, an errant curl falling against his forehead.

"You kept it up," I whispered.

"I took it down, actually. After you left, when I wasn't sure what I was going to do, I took all your things and packed them away. There's still a pile in your old room. But a few weeks ago, I woke up in the middle of the night and I had this urge..." he sighed, and I heard his feet on the carpet as he moved closer to me. "I hung it back up. I couldn't stand the thought of something you loved so much being kept in that back room."

"It's just a painting."

"Not to you. I don't really understand it or honestly even like it all that much aside from her being half naked, but I knew you love it."

I shifted the bottom of the frame until it was centered. "Thank you. That means a lot to me."

"If I couldn't have you, I thought this would be something. Like you hadn't left."

I still couldn't turn around. "I didn't leave because I wanted to. I left because you told me to."

"I know," he whispered. "I think about that night all the time. All the things I said to you, the words I shouldn't have said. I regret so much about that night. I told you that you wouldn't regret me, and you do, anyway."

"I don't regret you, Xan." I whispered, shaking my head at him. "You're making it hard for me to stay mad at you. And I really want to stay mad at you."

"I know you do. I'm mad at you too." He ducked his head, glancing up at me. "But I love you more."

I took a deep breath and let my eyes meet his.

"Ana, I meant what I said. I can't keep doing this. I know I said I could handle whatever you wanted from me. But I can't. I want all of you. I want to be with you every day, I want to kiss you whenever I want. I can't be here with you unless this is for real."

"It is real, though." My voice soft, I stepped closer to him. "I love you. I mean that, I know that now. I was too blind to see it before, the depth of it."

He took my hand in his wrapping his fingers around them tight. His voice was a low whisper. "You know I love you. I've always loved you. Loving you was never our problem."

I had known I loved him. How do I explain that loving him was so easy I could scarcely believe it was true? I thought love was supposed to be a pendulous fever running through you, yanking you around all the time. But since the night he kissed me, holding my face in his hands, it had known I always belonged to him.

"Falling in love with you was so effortless it couldn't be real. But when you hold me, all I can think is: *This is what I've been waiting for; now it all makes sense.*"

"So, I don't understand, I never understood why..." he gently shook his head.

I closed my eyes as I spoke. "Before, I wanted to believe in what Max and I had so badly. When I found out that all my trust in him had been in vain, I figured I couldn't rely on my feelings or my judgment anymore. I'd been wrong about Max, who's to say I wouldn't be wrong about you too? That I could be wrong about how I was feeling? It was never that I didn't trust you, Xan. I didn't trust myself."

"He hurt me too, Ana." Xander brought his hand up to cup my cheek. I could feel his thumb wiping away a wayward tear.

"I wish I hadn't put you through that." How could I explain the difference to him? "I wish it wasn't the case—that I could have come to you with this clean slate. I wish I could be the kind of girl who trusted right away. But I couldn't be that girl. I was too broken then."

"You know I can't fix what happened with Max. I can't fix the way we handled things. I can't fix how you feel about him or about me."

"Xander. I've had a lot of time to think about you, about us. But mostly about me. I let myself be stuck in the past. I know that. Not anymore." I laid a hand on his cheek, willing him to stop talking. "I never needed you to fix me. I only needed you to love me."

"I do love you," he said, both his hands were on my cheeks, and he was pulling me to him. I let him kiss me, the feel of his lips against mine igniting something, a hunger but a bereavement as well. He needed to hear my truth, he needed to understand. I pulled away.

"You were right when you said that you couldn't hurt me like Max." I watched the hurt pass over his face, but I held onto his arms not letting him move. "Because the way Max hurt me, the kind of person who could be caught off guard by that kind of betrayal, isn't me anymore. I realize now that you could never hurt me the way Max hurt me, because I'm not that girl anymore. I'm more than her now. I'm stronger. I can bear more. I'll understand if you don't want to see me anymore, Xander. But I needed you to know that this woman..." I tapped my chest with my finger. "She is stronger, and she can endure if she needs to. This is the woman who loves you. I'm not that scared little girl on Queenie Hill Road. This is the woman who loves you. So, if this is the woman you want to be with, then I'm ready."

In one fluid motion he stepped forward, pulling me into his arms. When his lips possessed mine, I became irrevocably his. How could I think love should anything but this?

# Epilogue



I LEARNED SEVERAL THINGS in the days following our kiss on the beach and the nights we spent together after. I learned that my parents were either perceptive or completely negligent because they never came looking for me that night or any night following. I learned that the horn in his truck was sensitive to the slightest touch and will sound if bumped by a bare back in the throes of passion. I learned that Xander moved into the bigger bedroom. He led me back there, skipping his old bedroom, his hand on my hips and his mouth on the back of my neck. I learned of the honesty in his kiss, a thunder and calm all the same with every embrace.

But most importantly, I learned that I had a four-day maximum before spending my time in his old T-shirts and boxers made me crazy. In the end I had to choose between leaving the condo wearing my floor length maid of honor dress or Xander's oversized clothes. Both items declared a walk of shame. After a single phone call, my mother arranged for my stuff to be returned to the condo.

A week after I moved back in with Xander, Eloise came to live with us to finish out her senior year. As I promised her, we got her to Los Angeles where she found a job as a personal assistant to a musician. I wasn't a fan of the man, but Eloise seemed happier than she ever did living in Ridgewood.

At the Lisandre art show in Seattle, Xander stopped me in front of my favorite painting, fell to one knee and asked me to marry him. We were married on New Year's Day in a small ceremony with only twenty guests. Neither of us wanted a big event. All we wanted was to begin our life together.

After we married, I got off birth control and we stopped using condoms. We thought having a baby together would be an easy process, but it turns out conception is more complicated than we knew. Conditions have to be exactly right for a pregnancy to occur. I was diagnosed with luteal phase defect. After years of medications, monthly blood draws and ultrasounds. Xander and I gave up on trying. We hadn't had the extra money for the fancier medical treatments.

When we struggled to get pregnant, I couldn't help but wonder if this was the universe telling me that I hadn't deserved happiness with Xander. That God, or whoever was punishing us for being together while Max wasn't here. After we got married, Xander suggested I see a therapist. Working with Dr. Ang, I was able to talk through my relationship with Max. I could see all the places I'd let myself down.

The greatest lie I ever told, was that I held no value without Max. I let everyone, myself included, believe that he was everything to me. Through therapy I could admit how angry I was with him. How I hated the person he'd turned me into. That I hated that I let myself be lost in him. And through that I could truly heal. It was hard work. I'd been lying to myself for years, and no matter how much Xander loved me, I needed to discover my truth myself.

Four years after we married, I stood in the bathroom of our small bungalow, staring down at the little stick in my hand, not believing what I was seeing. A plus sign. For weeks I'd been feeling run down and food tasted weird. I tried to drink a beer and it tasted off. I heard the slam of the door and Xander's heavy work boots as they made their way down the hall. He called out to me, and I let him know I was in the bathroom, not trusting that if I moved, the stick might say something different.

Popping his head into the bathroom he frowned at me. "Sweet, what's going on?"

With a shaky hand, I held up the stick. He took it out of my hand. "Is this? Are you? Am I? Are we?" He stumbled over his words.

I nodded, my throat thick with emotion. He dropped the stick on the ground, picking me up around my middle and bringing my lips to his. He kissed me with abandon. His touch hungry for me. Pulling away I saw wetness in his eyes. I brought my hand up to his cheek. "You're crying."

He smiled, wiping my cheek with his thumb. "So are you."

He kissed me again with cheeks wet with our joy and our growing future between us.

# Acknowledgments

While this story is deeply personal to me, the journey I traveled to get here was not.

To my editor, Heather E. Andrews thank you for taking the time and love on this story. Your fangirling over Xander brightened my life. All my writing friends I have made during the journey, so much love.  Shayna and Heather, for reading it in it's rough form. Cassidy for being my number one cheerleader. To the Raveonettes for writing, <u>Last Dance</u> which served as the catalyst for the prologue.

Heidi for being my go-to person with all nursing and hospital-related questions. Thank you to everyone who helped with the research, Bryan and Chrissy for not batting an eye when I asked, *when can a person be declared dead?* Any inaccuracies are my creative liberties.

Thank you to my family; I love you all beyond measure. To Liz for letting me take creative liberties with *that* story. Now I know you love me.

My sons; Jackson, and Bennett, thank you for being such fans even when I won't let you read my books.

Most of all, to Rusty. These are my dreams because of you. Thank you for being my first reader and biggest fan. I'll always be yours.

# Also By Linnea March

**Faultless Notion**

*They didn't mean to get married.*

Eloise Dunning ran far from her small town in the Pacific Northwest to Los Angeles with little more than the clothes on her back and a dream of being a singer-songwriter. Now she is a personal assistant to the rock band, Prevalent Notion, and leaving her songbook in the bottom of her bag.

Keller Grant is everything a rock star should be. Sinfully attractive, an enigmatic artist with a dark past, and an immensely talented drummer. He loves the revolving door of women in each city, creating music with his bandmates in Prevalent Notion, and teasing an uptight Eloise.

The night before the band kicks off their American Tour, Eloise and Keller wake up in each other's arms with wedding bands on their fingers. Forced by the record label to maintain the marriage for the public, they face a hungry press, rabid fans, and jealousy from all sides.

As they get the world to believe in their facade, they find that, maybe, this marriage doesn't feel like a performance.

For fans of music, bungee jumping, steamy moments behind closed doors, and heartfelt moments on the wings of the stage. Here is your new favorite rock star romance.

Faultless Notion is a full-length contemporary standalone romance. It is book one in the Prevalent Notion Series

**The One You Chose: A Holiday Novella**

A chance meeting

A steamy one-night stand

A whirlwind holiday season

When Lina McConnell headed to her hometown bar the night before Thanksgiving she wasn't expecting to find a connection with a mysterious newcomer. New to town, Fitz Dier wants to keep his head down and settle into his new job. Fate has other plans as they are pulled together for a single steamy night.

In the light of day, they are separated from one another. As they go through the holiday season they can't help but think of the other. Can fate bring them together again?

Who will they kiss when the clock strikes twelve?

# Afterword

Thank you for joining me on this journey with Ana and Xander.

I hope you enjoyed their story as much as I enjoyed writing it. This novel was a long time coming. I started it in 2016 and wrote ninety-five percent of it before it sat in a lonely file on my laptop. It was only when I started writing Faultless Notion that I pulled Ana and Xander's story out, giving it a real ending and some fresh eyes. This isn't the last time you'll see Ana and Xander. Eloise's story as a singer-songwriter in Los Angeles is available now as Faultless Notion. Expect a few familiar faces.

If you enjoyed this story, I hope you'll consider leaving a quick review or rating. Your feedback helps my story reach readers.

This book took on a deeply personal turn only a few months before publishing. In March of 2022, I lost my own dear friend. It was a struggle for me to come back to the story after hearing of her passing. It was only after she was gone that I found a Facebook post she made supporting my first book. I knew that she would give me such a hard time if I never published this story. She'd tell me to be the badass bitch she knew I was. I was lucky to call her my friend and I'm not alone in that. She was loved. Many people who are gone too soon are loved beyond measure. That is why I wrote this book. If you or someone you love is struggling with drug or alcohol addiction, know that you are not alone. According to the National Institute of Health, over 23 million Americans have struggled with problematic drug or alcohol abuse in their lifetime with only ten percent seeking professional treatment.

Resources that may help:

SAMHSA's National Helpline, 1-800-662-HELP or at www.samhsa.gov
The National Alliance for Mental Illness at 1-800-950-NAMI or at www.nami.org

# About Author

Linnea March is a contemporary romance author who writes steamy stories about self-confident women and the rugged men who love them. She lives somewhere in the wilds of the Pacific Northwest with her husband, their two boys, and a plump dog. After fifteen years of teaching early childhood education, she put down the googly eyes and picked up a pen. When not writing, she can be found reading her way through an ever-growing pile of books while drinking copious amounts of coffee. She proudly refuses to use umbrellas.